MAGIC
IN THE
WOODS

EVI JAMES

ISBN: 979-8-9911988-5-1 (Paperback)

ISBN: 979-8-9911988-4-4 (e-book)

Library of Congress Control Number: 2025920390

Cover Art by Miblart

Editing by Mandi Andrejka, Inky Pen Editorial Services

Visit evijamesauthor.com for more information.

AUTHOR'S NOTE

Magic in the Woods contains adult themes that may be difficult for some readers.

Please read the content warnings on this website for more information.

www.evijamesauthor.com

To those with rage bubbling deep inside.

PART 1

CHAPTER ONE

July
Dafni

"My kindness is *also* fleeting," I said, taking a step toward Wilder. "The next time I see you, I'll end you."

We stood in the damaged home of Elise's parents, where practically everything had been destroyed from a mix of my air magic and my mother's attempts at ending all our lives. I exhaled out of my nose, keeping my eyes on Wilder's sniveling face. Out of my periphery, I could see everyone behind him standing frozen in silence.

What could they be thinking, seeing me, a kitten transformed into a woman spitting threats at one of their pack members? Well, Wilder used to be one of them, a member of the Cedar Moon Pack, but if his face was any indication, Everett's words revoking his pack membership had fully destroyed him, his knees buckling and a gasp leaving his lips.

Only after he'd stumbled backward into Everett did I see the woods beyond the doorway. The trees were green and inviting, their leaves rippling lightly in the wind. It wasn't long ago that I'd spent days in the woods after I'd escaped Wilder, but this time was different. I didn't need to hide. I'd defeated my mother, the witch who'd wanted her daughter dead. I could walk through these woods freely, with my chin held high. Now there was nothing to stop me.

I took in a breath through my nose.

Freedom smelled good.

My freedom—no, my vengeance lay just beyond the door. This was my chance. My mother was inside the pail I was holding, in her cat form, frozen in ice. Her orange fur looked blurry beneath the frozen surface. I'd never had a chance like this—my mother had always bested me—but now, where I stood, she was at *my* mercy.

Wilder, my former captor, stumbled outside the house, disappearing into the woods. I no longer feared him—I was a powerful witch. I'd just bested the Prime.

That made me smile, the muscles in my cheeks instantly burning with the unfamiliar movement. When was the last time I'd smiled? I couldn't remember. But then again, nothing had ever felt as good as having my mother confined.

The pail swung from the handle as I stepped down the stairs and walked toward the woods. Elise sighed behind me, and I stopped, using my water magic to gather ice crystals from the pail. I sent them fluttering down over the top of her as a gesture of thanks, a reminder of when she'd found me in the woods weeks ago. Even though I wanted to say goodbye, I didn't know how. How did you say goodbye to someone who'd saved you, who'd nursed you back to health and now was letting you go so you could pursue your destiny?

The flurries raining down on her would have to be enough.

It only took a moment of walking before Elise and her parent's house disappeared as the woods enveloped me.

With my mother trapped, I no longer needed Elise and Everett to protect me. They'd been kind, taking care of me when I'd been at my most vulnerable. I'd miss them, the pack-house—and Kleio. I'd probably miss her the most. We'd gotten as close as a kitten and a wolf shifter could—and I hadn't had the chance to say goodbye to her either. I'd have to get a message to her, to let her know I was okay. Maybe once I got settled...once I'd found the Coven and taken it over, I could reach out. Maybe all these goodbyes weren't necessary. Everyone could come and visit— No...I was getting ahead of myself. One thing at a time.

Find the Coven.

Study the Coven.

Take over the Coven.

The threat of my mother finding me had loomed over me in the last weeks, but now that the *Matilda* cloud had lifted, I felt lighter, though technically I was heavier in my human form. I wouldn't miss being a kitten. It was a constant reminder that I didn't have poison and therefore couldn't transform into a full-grown cat. *That* I'd have to hide from the Coven.

But I'd figure that all out later. *One thing at a time.*

This, right here and now, was my time—my opportunity.

The Coven, which my grandmother had raised me to lead, was mine for the taking. I just needed to get there.

When I arrived, my name, Dafni Sarracenia, would get me through the doors, though I couldn't expect them to welcome me with open arms. No, I'd have to prove myself to them some-how. Looking down at my mother inside the pail hanging along-side me, I was yet again reminded that I was a powerful witch—I'd trapped her in this frozen prison. Maybe all I had to do was show her furry body, encased in ice—show that I'd bested their

Prime and therefore was the next rightful leader. Then I could take my place as Prime.

Running a Coven couldn't be too terribly hard...my mother had done it for years. After all those years, it was entirely possible that the witches hated her as much as I did.

After taking my place as Prime, the first thing I'd do would be to rid the Coven of whatever horrifying policies my mother had put in place. If I knew my mother, there had to be a long list. I'd start with something big—something that would improve the lives of the witches who lived there. Maybe then they'd come to trust me.

The dirt beneath my feet crunched as I walked, a steady metronome as my mind rolled through all the terrible things I'd heard my mother talk about over the years. I couldn't imagine the witches were happy with the mandatory procreation my mother had instituted. I'd heard snippets of conversations between her and my grandmother. Constantly bent over her cauldron, my grandmother had always been busy making anti-nausea and fertility potions for my mother to bring back to the Coven. Mother had been obsessive about growing the Coven and creating new witches to take over more of the woods. She'd even taken the lifestone from the ground so that the woods would die and the shifters would leave. My mother didn't care about the woods; she just wanted more—more power, more land, more control over the shifters.

After living with the shifters of the Cedar Moon Pack, I didn't see the point. The shifters weren't bad or evil. I knew Everett. He had no intention of taking over more of the woods —he had his hands full with his pack lands as it was. We could coexist and share the woods.

That was what I'd do. First I'd find the Coven. Then I'd present my frozen mother as proof of my strong powers. Finally I'd rid the Coven of her terrible policies that forced witches to reproduce and challenged the shifters who shared the woods. Maybe I could be a witch-shifter liaison of sorts...

I could do this.

The first miles into the woods were promising. My feet felt light. The handle to the pail holding my mother's frozen body was firmly in my grip. An air of confidence surrounded me. I was on my own. Master—no, mistress of my destiny.

The cloud cover that'd made the entire morning overcast had cleared, revealing the sun was now past its tallest point in the sky. Its rays were hot. The leaves above me provided some coverage, but I already knew more freckles would be sprinkled across my nose and cheeks by day's end.

Inside my chest there was a pull, an ache that drew me forward. It had started as I'd walked away from Elise and only had gotten stronger as I hiked.

I looked down at the pail. Was I being pulled toward the Coven because I was now Prime? Had my mother once felt this pull? I let the feeling guide me as I walked, and a sense of peace came over me. I was going in the right direction; I just knew it. The feeling was deep down in my gut—I would find the Coven.

———

The adrenaline I'd been floating on wore off slowly in the hours I walked, and I let that ache in my chest pull me in whatever direction it chose. That direction apparently was full of rocks and sticks—rotted logs that were hidden beneath the tree's fall shed from last year. I had to keep a close eye on my feet, though it was hard when the breeze rustled the high branches of the trees, the sun light dancing through the gaps, periodically blinding me.

The Coven couldn't be far away.

The brush and plants beneath my feet tickled my ankles as

I walked through them. I should've taken my shoes into account when I'd walked away from Elise. They were the same shoes I'd been wearing when my mother had pulled me from the cottage right after she'd...

I shook my head. I couldn't think about that right now.

My feet stopped moving as I heard barking in the distance. Some sort of dogs...or coyotes. What else was in these woods? Bears? Bobcats?

The sun was already beginning its descent toward the horizon, lowering in the sky too rapidly for my liking. Soon I'd either have to find a place to rest or decide to continue walking through the night.

The coyotes got louder, their barks turning into yips as they got more and more excited. They must've caught something for dinner. There was no way I'd feel comfortable enough to sleep out here on my own—that could mean becoming someone's midnight snack.

Decision made. I'd be walking through the night.

The barking ceased, and I continued through the woods.

The drive to Elise's parents had been along highways. I was here...on foot, without a car, and without a path. I couldn't push my body to move any faster, especially not when every rock threatened to twist my ankle and every pile of brush hid a tripping hazard that'd easily send me and my frozen mother flying.

I stopped again. This time I took a moment and looked around. There were no markers, no way to measure how far I'd gone, or even know if I was going in a consistent direction. I could've been walking in circles for all I knew.

I had nothing. There was no food in my pockets. I only had the clothes on my back and my mother frozen inside a pail. There was no map—my only direction was the ache in my chest. It pulled me, guided me. My gut told me to trust it, that it was leading me in the right direction, but there were still so many unknowns.

I wiggled my toes in my too-thin shoes. I really needed boots or something sturdier for the terrain.

Could I do this? Walk miles and miles through these woods?

Walking along a road wasn't an option. I had a frozen cat in the pail that hung beside me. Anyone I'd run into would ask too many questions—questions I wouldn't be able to answer.

I couldn't stop. Not only because I didn't feel safe resting, but because my mother would thaw if I didn't pay attention, if I didn't refreeze her at appropriate intervals.

I closed my eyes, taking a deep breath in through my nose.

I could do this. I had to.

I could push myself for my future. For the Coven.

CHAPTER TWO

Dafni

I LET THE ACHE IN MY CHEST PULL ME FOR THE REST OF the evening and into the night. It wasn't long before I could barely see in front of me. Every sound in the woods made my heart beat quicker—made my feet move faster. I had nothing for protection against what I could come across in the woods. Yes, I had my magic, but there were predators out here who would take advantage of my lack of night vision and attack before I even knew they were there. The only thing I could do was move. I feared if I stayed in place for too long, something would scent me.

My ankles ached from slipping on rocks all night. The woods hadn't been kind. Tree branches had scraped against my face for hours now, and the heels of my hands were raw from catching myself from landing face-first into the dirt. Blinking didn't help my dry eyes, and closing my lids only made me wish I didn't have to open them again.

The grumbling of my stomach was loud enough that I glanced around to make sure nothing had heard it. I'd gotten used to eating well with the shifters; I wasn't used to missing a meal. Burning calories from walking and the amount of adrenaline still pumping through my veins had me feeling practically ravenous.

There were plants all around me, but I didn't know what was edible and what wasn't. I'd walked by several bushes with red and purple berries, and it had taken a strong amount of willpower not to pluck off the fruit and eat it. But I couldn't risk it. Becoming sick in the woods would be a disaster. I'd be stuck in one place without the energy to refreeze my mother.

Changing into my kitten form to forage for bugs along the ground would produce the same outcome. By the time I'd transformed and eaten, the summer weather would've melted the ice in the pail.

I just had to keep moving.

My dress stuck to my skin as I sweated out what little liquid I had left in my body. Through the dense trees, there was little breeze, and the air grew warm and thick. I kept a close eye on the pail, using my magic to continually refreeze the ice. It was melting quickly. Too fast for me to become complacent for even a moment. If even a single paw thawed, my mother could use her magic. *That* would be a problem. I had no doubt she would conjure some magic to end me right here in these woods for what I'd done to her.

Refreezing her took energy I didn't have. Energy I couldn't replace.

It became harder to pick up my feet. I let out a yelp as my toe crashed into a root that stuck up from the ground.

"Who's there?" a voice called out ahead of me.

I instantly froze, the pail squeaking as it swung back and forth on the handle I held steady.

"I can hear your breathing..."

I pressed my lips together tightly, trying to contain my ragged, adrenaline-fueled breaths. "Come out with your hands where I can see them!"

A string of giggles followed the man's command. "Dad, you sound like Judy Hopps from *Zootopia*."

There was a *click*.

"I'm...I'm gonna shoot!"

"Wait!" I pushed through the branches that separated us, stumbling over more roots and branches on the ground. *Does he have a gun?* Three gasps met my ears before I balanced myself and raised my eyes.

There was a *man*. I immediately flinched. He had a silver gun in his hand pointed right at me. His black hair, turning gray along the temples, was in stark contrast to the tan camouflaged shirt he was wearing. Two little girls with matching curly blonde pigtails stood next to him. I glanced around, looking for more threats. A green tent stood pitched behind them, and a small campfire crackled inside a nearby ring of large rocks.

"I'm not going to hurt you," I said as I raised my hands in the air. I kept the handle of the pail hooked on my thumb. The tendons in my hand trembled, holding its weight. My nostrils flared as the scent of grilled meat hit my nose. Patties of meat cooked on a grate over the campfire. I missed the chicken and burger meat from the packhouse. Maybe they'd share...

One girl took a step closer to me, standing on her tiptoes, trying to get tall enough to sneak a look inside my pail.

I pulled the pail to my chest, the icy cold metal burning my skin.

The man grabbed ahold of his daughter by her elbow,

pulling her back behind him. "We don't have anything for you here."

"I'm sorry. I didn't mean to scare you," I said, looking down at the faded green sundress I was wearing, my shins scratched up from stray branches in the woods. I probably looked like something out of a horror story.

My stomach rumbled again. The smell of the cooking food consumed me. Saliva flooded my mouth.

The man followed my eyeline to the campfire and the food cooking over it. "We only packed enough food for ourselves." He pulled his daughters in a little closer—like there was something wrong with me. Like *I* was something they needed protection from. All three of them stared at me, waiting for a response.

My mouth opened, willing words, but none came. I slammed my mouth shut, my cheeks feeling warm. I hadn't expected him to ask me to join them for dinner—but just flat-out refusing someone food that obviously needed some...that was rude, right? They could've thrown me a patty or something, anything.

"*Get!*" he yelled.

I flinched.

"Leave us alone!"

I staggered back as my nostrils flared, unfortunately inhaling the scent of the food on the grill. With my lips pressed together, repressing a hiss, I ran around their campsite, giving them a wide berth so they couldn't sneak a peek inside my pail.

I heard the girls' voices as I ran back into the woods. They were surely talking about me...asking their dad questions about the dirty, scratched-up woman with a growling stomach who had approached their campsite. Maybe he'd make up a story about me to make them feel better about shooing me away, one that would make me the villain.

Why had I expected anything else from a *man?*

What was I doing? The people out here were prepared. They had camping supplies. I should've asked Elise for supplies before I'd left, or at least some food to take with me. My stomach rumbled again.

I'd never walked this far before. My muscles ached, and my head hurt from the mental thrashing I was giving myself. I hadn't prepared for this—I'd been too excited, too impulsive. I was Dafni Sarracenia, a powerful witch. I should be able to take care of myself in these woods.

I continued walking, the pail becoming heavier with every step.

Who was I kidding? I was tired, hungry, and a complete mess. The woods had bested me in a matter of hours. If I couldn't provide for myself out here, what right did I have to march into the Coven and take it over? What would I do? Hold up my mother's frozen body as proof of her defeat? Then expect all the witches to follow me?

This is all your fault, Mother.

I lowered the pail from my chest as soon as I was far enough away from the campsite and gave it a kick.

I winced. That only hurt my already stubbed toe, and meanwhile, my mother probably hadn't even noticed.

CHAPTER THREE

Dafni

At first I noticed the twinkle of lights, a few glimmers I thought might've been a mirage. The woods thinned as I walked, and after a few more flickers, I realized the lights were not a hallucination. I was walking toward *something*.

It was dark when my feet hit the gravel road that ran right up to a building with the words *No Bars* lit up in blue neon lights. The parking lot was full of cars, and several women stood smoking in front of the door.

I kept to the shadows, setting the pail next to me as I watched them. They were laughing together—they must've been *friends*.

I'd never had friends. Kleio and Elise had been kind, but they'd thought I was a kitten the entire time I'd been with them. They weren't truly my friends.

The women outside the bar looked happy together, like

they enjoyed each other's company. One even untwisted a strap on her friend's shirt. Another one laughed at something a woman was saying while animatedly gesturing with her hands.

That would be nice...having friends.

A group of large men exited the bar. All the women went quiet as they stopped their conversations and turned to stare in their direction.

It was shocking how fast the men's attention immediately went to the group of women. Whistles and low mutterings erupted from the group of men, and I watched as the women squeezed close together, moving as a group back into No Bars, away from the men. A few of the men laughed once the door closed behind them.

There was no way I was going to walk through those men to get to the front door.

I tucked myself back into the woods and snuck around to the back of the building.

A door was propped open, the smell of food wafting out from inside. It smelled so good—the spice of the meat they were cooking made my mouth water. My stomach no longer rumbled. Instead, it hurt, cramping from the lack of food.

I couldn't focus on anything but that smell. I needed food. Maybe if I just looked inside, I could find something that was within arm's reach. I could stick my hand inside the door and grab it quick—before anyone noticed. It'd been too long since I'd eaten. I'd been walking and burning through my magic. I didn't know how far I had left to go or if there would be another restaurant along the way. There might not be another opportunity like this.

I didn't have money to pay for a meal. This was stealing—it was against the rules, but I was desperate and hungry. I needed food if I was going to keep walking. If I could just grab something, anything, I'd be on my way.

Climbing the wooden steps up to the door, I let my eyes adjust to the light as I leaned in, assessing my surroundings. It was a kitchen, an empty kitchen. Food sizzled on the grill on the far side of the room and a large silver refrigerator hummed on the other side, but there were no people in sight. Perfect. A plastic bag of buns sat on the counter in the center of the room. It was farther than arm's length, but that was all I'd need. It was perfect. I could just grab the bread bag and go.

I pushed the door open a little wider, just enough to where I could slide in sideways. I got my torso through the opening—

Thunk.

The pail wouldn't fit.

Gently, I set it on the top step outside the kitchen, my fingers stiff from being wrapped around the handle. I slid the rest of the way through the door, looking in either direction before I raced over to the counter, my hands wrapping around the bag and pulling the bread to my chest.

Food. I could smell the yeasty bread through the bag.

I turned, ready to leave as fast as I'd arrived.

"*Damnit*, Bill! Ice goes in the ice machine!"

The door that I'd just slipped through flew open, and a woman with the name *Dorothy* stitched onto her shirt stood in the doorway. She was holding my pail in her hand.

"*What in the world?*" she yelled.

I turned away, looking for an escape.

The door on the side of the kitchen near the grill opened, and a large man strode through.

I squeezed my eyes closed and the buns tightly to my chest —as if the bread would offer some sort of protection. "I'm sorry!" I yelled.

"What are you doing in my kitchen?" The woman's voice met my ears.

"What are you doing here?" The man's voice echoed hers.

"Let me handle this, Bill."

He paused, his nostrils flaring for a moment before he deeply inhaled. "You aren't from around here…"

I cracked open one eye, squeezing the buns even tighter against me. I knew that gesture. He was a shifter…he could smell me.

Dorothy stood with her legs apart and her arms crossed in front of her, my pail swinging from her hand.

"I'm sorry, okay?" My voice came out as a whimper. "I just needed food."

Dorothy didn't even flinch. "And you don't want to pay like everyone else?" She glanced down at the ice pail. "Wait…what *is* this—"

There was no time to think.

Dropping the buns to the floor, I pointed my index and middle fingers at the pail, taking precious ice from my mother's tomb, and threw it in liquid form at her. Dorothy screamed, dropping the pail and jumping away from the door.

As fast as my feet could carry me, I grabbed ahold of the pail handle and leaped over the steps, my knees buckling as I landed on the ground.

"Get back here!" Dorothy called out.

"Hey, wait a minute!" Bill yelled. "Do you know—"

I ran away as fast as I could, their yells for me quieting the farther I got.

Using my hand, I swatted at the branches I could see as silhouettes in the dark in front of my face.

That had been way too close. What had I been thinking? I should've never began traveling through the woods by myself, without food. I only had my magic, and that was depleting as fast as my energy.

The crickets were loud tonight, their incessant chirping

making the inside of my head rattle. I kicked at a bush next to me, but of course, the crickets didn't stop.

No one would help me.

No one would give me a burger patty or a bun.

I was out here in the woods alone, apparently a burden to everyone I ran into.

CHAPTER FOUR

Dafni

I'd lost track of the number of days I'd walked. Whenever I came across the occasional stream I'd attempt to fill my stomach with water, only to heave it back up again moments later. My stomach was so empty that the momentary relief of the water filling it felt worth the agony of it all coming back up again.

The pail was getting heavier, and my feet began to feel like cinderblocks.

I started to forget to refreeze my mother—especially when the sun had come up and the air warmed. One time, the ice had melted down low enough to where her orange fur had stuck out like spikes from the ice, the block holding her body bobbing in melted water inside the pail. My heart had never beat so furiously in my chest. The pounding had still rung in my ears even after I'd refrozen the water.

Maybe that was when I'd realized I was slipping away.

I hadn't slept for days for fear of my mother thawing.

I wasn't eating.

My body was no longer absorbing water.

But still, I kept my feet moving, let the pull of the Coven guide me. The pull was getting stronger, and I had assumed that meant I was getting closer. I *had* to be getting closer. I couldn't last much longer.

No. I *would* last. I *had* to. If I didn't make it, my mother would thaw, and everything would resume as she'd planned it. With both me and my grandmother gone, she'd still be Prime.

Leaving no one else to challenge her.

I would keep going.

As I crested a steep hill, I spied a large silver rectangular box, its sides worn and weathered, in the distance. It had a door and a couple of windows.

I laughed.

I might've cackled. The way the sun glinted off the sides of the box made my eyes squint. This had to be some sort of joke—a mirage, perhaps. We were in the middle of the woods, with no signs of civilization in any direction. I really *was* losing it.

A silver house in the middle of the woods.

Good one, Dafni.

I just needed to rest for a bit, close my eyes for a second to clear my mind. When I opened them, the silver house wouldn't be there—maybe I wouldn't be here. Maybe this would all be some weird fever dream and I'd wake up with a cold washcloth on my forehead and my grandmother's homemade chicken broth being spooned into my mouth.

The woods were quiet. Or maybe my hearing was going. With my palm still on the handle of the pail, I leaned against a tree, its papery bark tickling the exposed skin on my upper back and shoulders. I tucked the skirt of my green sundress under my legs and closed my eyes—just for a minute.

———

"Are you okay?" I could hear a deep baritone voice. *A man.* My eyes, though, refused to open. They felt gritty, like a mix of sand and water had pasted them shut.

"Let's try to get you sitting up against this tree," I heard him say.

Aren't I already sitting? The thought came to me as I realized my head was currently pressed into the ground. I must've tipped over at some point after passing out.

"I'm going to have to touch you, okay?"

To my surprise, he waited for a response that I couldn't give him. Eventually, rough hands scooped under my arms, and my head fell to my chest as my body became more vertical.

"There." I felt his rough fingers beneath my chin, my ears ringing as he righted my head into the correct position atop my neck. His fingertips were warm against my cheeks. His thumb reached above my cheek bone, dipping into the hollow of my eye socket beneath my lower eyelid. Pulling down, he cracked the gritty paste holding my eye shut. Bright light I wasn't ready for flooded my pupil.

My reaction was less than perfect. I slapped his arm and attempted to headbutt him. He easily dodged my head, my movements comically slow as I tipped forward. I took a minute to catch my breath, bent over on all fours in the dirt. *What an embarrassing demonstration of strength.*

Tucking my feet beneath me, I slowly stood, making it about halfway up before I wobbled.

"Hey, careful." He reached out to steady me, his hand brushing against my arm.

I swatted at him again, an unintentional hiss leaving my lips.

He backed up with his hands raised in front of him. "I don't have time for this, okay? I've got to get to work."

He looked as though he might've been telling the truth. He wore tan leather work boots that went up over his ankles. Both his pants and shirt were a thick cargo material. His hands lowered, his eyes trying to focus on my own bobbing eyes. I didn't make it easy—there was too much to take in. The forest, my weak body failing me, the man standing in front of me.

The woods. I'd been in the woods and had seen that...silver house. I glanced behind him. The metal house was still there...

"Hey." His voice brought my eyes back to his. They were green, like mine. Shaggy blond hair fell across his forehead. He had it swept to the side like he was due for a haircut, but just like dealing with me, he didn't have the time. The lines across his forehead made me think he either worried too much or was several years older than me. Probably both. "Are you going to be okay?"

I tilted my chin in a nod. *I'll be okay...I think.* Pressing into my heels, I straightened my legs, trying to stand upright.

"Can I carry that for you?" He reached for the pail beside me, its handle stuck upright like a rainbow.

"*No!*" With one hand, I channeled my air magic, pushing the man away from me. Like a rag doll, he flew backward, landing on his butt ten feet away. With my other hand, I used my water magic to refreeze my mother. This was the closest she'd been to being thawed out completely. Bright-orange fur, although wet, had stuck out from the ice block. The tip of her tail had been flicking back and forth above the water.

That had been close.

Too close. How long had I been unconscious before he'd found me?

Catching my breath from the exertion of using my magic, I let myself lean back against the tree behind me. It caught me, the rough bark against my back giving me something to focus on instead of fixating on the way my body felt completely out of control. My chest pushed against the fabric of my dress, trying to take in enough oxygen to replenish my magic. I could sense that I'd used it all up. There was an emptiness in my gut that I'd always attributed to low magic, like I was missing an organ. I needed time to replenish. It took oxygen, rest, and food. All of which I was in short supply of.

My fingers brushed against the top of the ice block that held my mother. It looked frozen and opaque, but I needed to feel it. I needed to feel that she was still confined. Imprisoned. That the world was still safe from her wrath. I could tell that the pail had completely frozen solid from the dry surface of the ice. Relief flooded me.

Only then did I look in front of me at the man I'd pushed away. He was still sitting on the ground. I could see the green of his irises from ten feet away, his eyeballs almost popping out of their sockets.

"Uh..." His voice wavered as he produced several non-words before snapping his lips closed and reopening them, this time without sound.

"Don't touch my pail," I said. My knees locked straight beneath me. A breeze from behind me billowed my sundress between my legs, my hair blowing over my shoulders in front of me. The man's nostrils flared. Could he...smell me? Did I smell bad? I probably did. I'd been out here for who knew how long in the summer heat sweating.

"Got it. Message received. I will not touch your pail." He lifted one hand in the air in surrender as he used the other to lift himself to a standing position.

Now that he stood farther away, I could see how tall he was

—he'd tower over me if we stood side by side. He could easily overwhelm me if I didn't regain my magic.

"So, you're...a witch?" he asked with an equal amount of inquiry and observation.

I tilted my head to the side. He wasn't a witch. If he was, he would have surely retaliated with his own magic when I'd blasted him away. So, he was...human?

"You must be a witch."

Okay. A human, for sure. My tongue was dry. I kept my words to myself.

"Say, I work for the Coven." He motioned with his arm to the space beyond the silver house I'd been staring at behind him. "I can help you get back there."

My chin tucked into my chest as I tried to retreat, my heels only hitting the tree behind me.

If the last several days had shown me anything, it was that I wasn't ready. I was ill-prepared for this world—a world outside my grandmother's cottage, outside the protection of the Cedar Moon Pack. I could hardly talk to anyone...especially men. My body went into a panic when I was around them, my muscles tightening and my words vanishing. There would be men in the Coven, men that I was supposed to lead. Right now, I didn't have the strength or the experience to walk into the Coven and claim my birthright as Prime.

"All right, all right, I won't bring you to the Coven."

I lifted my chin, letting my eyes reach his once again.

"But I can't leave you out here. They'll...find you." He glanced around at the invisible threats around us.

I followed his eyes, my chest tightening.

"Just let me help you." He extended his arm, his fingers uncurling right in front of me, waiting for mine to land in his.

He was close. Too close. One step closer and he could grab me, overwhelm me in my weakened state.

I glanced down at my mother, still frozen in the pail by my feet. How much energy could I spare if I had to use my magic to defend myself from him again? Would it be enough to keep my mother frozen at the same time? Did I even have any to spare?

My wobbling knees doubted me. The sweat on my brow questioned me. Was I strong enough?

As if in answer, I felt a faint tingle deep inside of me—my magic growing.

His fingertips brushed my upper arm.

"No, wait"—he grabbed onto my arm—"stop..." I tried my best to scoot away.

He kept hold of my arm. "I'm just trying to help you—" he said as he attempted to pull me up to standing.

Struggling in his grasp, I looked down at his hand on my arm and flicked my wrist. Pointing at him with my index and middle fingers, I sent him flying away from me, his hands and feet trailing his torso in the air.

I'd overestimated my strength. I didn't get to hear the satisfying thump of his body landing on the ground—instead I heard the echo in my head of my body hitting the soil.

CHAPTER FIVE

Dafni

My eyelids wouldn't cooperate. I told them to open, and they flat-out refused. Though I felt weak, it was disorienting with my eyes closed—not knowing if it was day or night, not knowing who spoon-fed me broth and gently wiped the drips that fell down my chin with a cloth napkin. I could've been on a boat in the middle of the sea or deep underground.

But I knew I wasn't. I could hear birds chirping through the open window, letting in a warm breeze that tickled my nose.

Day.

I didn't have enough strength to scratch it with my fingers, so the itch festered.

The crickets were loud, playing in their own orchestra with their back legs.

Night.

There was a constant buzzing noise in my head, faint but

still loud enough that I knew I'd overdone it. I was lying in this state because I'd used too much of my magic.

I let myself relax a bit and my body replenish. No one was hurting me—in fact, they seemed to be taking care of me. I was somewhere quiet, maybe even pleasant. Somewhere that felt comforting, like my grandmother's cottage, once again hidden from the real world.

After the first few cycles of bird calls, followed by the chirping of crickets, my limbs stopped aching and my head cleared. My thoughts were no longer slow, like they were trudging through thick fog. They were quicker, my hearing clearer. I could understand what was going on around me. The scrape of a chair, the clink of silverware being set on a table. Quiet conversations and the occasional outburst of laughter. The stir of a wooden spoon in a pot.

Grandmother. A single tear fell out of the corner of my eye, making its way down my cheek and neck. I felt it pool along my collarbone.

"She still hasn't woken up," a male voice said—the first voice I'd heard clearly in days.

My mind snapped to attention.

"She's awake. She just isn't ready to open her eyes yet." This voice was female. Warm.

"Do you think she can hear us?" The third voice sounded honeyed. A young girl, perhaps.

"You know, I bet she can." The warm woman's voice drifted closer. A cool washcloth met my forehead, cooling my body. It was hot in here. I suddenly realized I didn't have any sheets draped over me, just the light draping of a nightgown perhaps.

Warm air brushed my ear. "You can open your eyes, you know. You're safe here," the young, honeyed voice whispered. She breathed softly again into my ear before she pulled away.

The breeze her body made as she retreated sent goose bumps along the side of my arm.

I tried. I really tried to open them for her.

"Give her more time, Emily. She'll come back to us soon." A hand brushed my cheek before I heard the shuffling of feet and the door closing.

I was alone. Safe.

Still, my eyelids wouldn't open. I needed more time.

"So fierce even without your poison—no one could ever tell that you didn't have it. But we all know that you lack it, don't we, Dafni? Lack what makes a witch a witch." My mother opened her mouth. Green liquid dripped from her gums and down her white teeth. "You may as well stay with the dogs; you no longer have a place among the Coven."

She threw her head back, cackling into the void. Every vibration of her laugh sent tremors through my body, making me shake uncontrollably.

I came to, gasping for air, my hands supporting my body behind me as I sat up in bed. A bad dream. It was just a bad dream. The sun was shining through the shades of a small window high near the bed. The pale yellow shades billowed in the breeze. As the curtains blew into the room, I caught a glance of the window that was propped open by a piece of wood. The glass was hazy, covered with grime.

Slowly, I took in my surroundings for the first time. It was a simple room. I was in a single bed with a pillow behind me and a quilt now covering me. The quilt was off-white, clean, but obviously aged. The walls were also a stark white with a few oily handprints and black scuffs. A wooden chair covered with scratches sat in the corner, and a bucket with a dry cloth draped over the side sat on the seat. A simple table sat next to my bed with an illuminated lamp on—just like the one back in our cottage.

There was still buzzing in my head. I reached over and pulled the chain that turned the lamp off. With a click, the room darkened slightly, still lit by the sun streaming through the curtained window. The buzzing sound continued in my ears. It was probably my body telling me I wasn't at full strength yet. Warning me to take the time to rebuild, regroup, and strengthen myself.

I couldn't take on the Coven, let alone a single witch, if I hadn't fully recovered. I needed more time.

The door handle jiggled, turning back and forth. A few muffled curse words met my ears before a man fell through the door, his eyes on the handle that had just wronged him. He twisted the knob back and forth with his wrist, testing the latch. Blond hair fell into his eyes as he leaned over. He shook his head, rearranging his hair away from his eyes. With a swift twist of the wrist, he let the door handle go, sighing deeply. My mind froze, though my arms moved, pulling the quilt on the bed tighter against my waist, as if it would afford me some sort of protection.

Without looking my way, he walked over to the chair, took the cloth that was draped over the side of the bucket, and dipped it in. He looked so large standing there, his back to me. He wore a cream-colored shirt that almost matched the quilt covering my legs. Sweat had soaked through the fabric covering his lower back, creating a line of circles along his spine. Tan baggy pants with lots of pockets covered his lower half, the right side sagging a bit with the weight of a large ring of keys clipped to his belt. *That's the man who found me—the one I pushed away with my magic,* I realized.

I figured I should lie back down, pretending once again I

was unconscious, void of the world. Instead I sat there watching him.

Water dripped from the cloth into the bucket as he squeezed it, taking his time folding it before turning around.

"*Ah!*" he yelled, dropping the washcloth. It landed on the floor with a *splat*.

I screamed. The sound leaving my throat before I could stop it. He stood there. I sat there. Our eyes locked, terror on both of our faces.

"What in the world..." A woman ran through the doorway, looking back and forth between the man and me. She wore an apron, the same discolored white as the quilt. Her hair, a light-red color, was tied up in a bun on top of her head, tendrils of hair that had escaped, framing her face.

"Luke, get out of here." Her voice was authoritative.

Luke, the young man with the washcloth, the one who'd found me in the woods, picked up the cloth from the floor and set it over the side of the bucket and walked out of the room, glancing back at me before turning the corner out of sight.

"You're safe," the woman said. "No one's going to hurt you here, especially not my son." She walked over to the chair and bucket, taking the discarded washcloth in her hands. "I promise you he's a kind man." After re-dipping it into the water, she squeezed out the excess liquid and walked over to the bed. "Lie back."

I lay down without a fight—I knew not to mess with a maternal woman. My grandmother had been the same way.

With the back of my head framed by the overly stuffed pillow, she pressed the cool washcloth against my forehead. My eyes reluctantly closed. The cool cloth felt amazing against my skin, which was covered in a thin layer of sweat. I might have moaned a bit.

"It's about time you opened your eyes," she said. "Your body's been ready for a while, but your mind just hasn't."

I opened my mouth to speak. A few incoherent sounds emerged. She put her index finger under my chin, closing my mouth. "Shush, now. You need your strength. We'll talk when you're ready."

"Can I come in?" That small, honeyed voice came through the doorway.

I turned to see a young girl, standing in the doorway with a steaming bowl in her hands.

"Come in, set it here." The woman motioned to the side table alongside the bed.

The girl set the bowl next to the lamp. She backed away several steps, her hands toying with the apron she was wearing over her cream dress. The girl had the same blonde hair as the man who'd found me—who the woman had just called Luke. They were probably siblings, although at least a decade apart in age.

"Now that you're awake, what would you like to do first? Eat?" The woman motioned to the steaming bowl of broth. "Bathe?" She looked toward the bowl of water on the dresser. "We have a shower, but I don't know if you feel strong enough to stand yet."

I sat under the quilt, frozen at their questions. They were asking *me* what *I* wanted to do? I scrunched my nose. Having choices had never been an option for me. I'd never gotten to decide anything—and now they were just going to let an inexperienced decider...decide? What if I made the wrong choice, did something that made them unhappy?

I sat in the foreign feeling. What *did* I want to do? I couldn't find the words.

Instead I reached over to the bowl of steaming broth and

shakily brought it to my lap, careful not to spill a drop on the quilt.

I looked up at the woman and girl for approval.

The woman nodded, and instantly, my shoulders relaxed. "We didn't want to change you while you were...sleeping." She looked over my green plaid dress I still had on. It looked wrinkled and stained. My skin suddenly felt dirty. "Emily, will you fetch some clean clothes?" She looked up and down at my form beneath the quilt. "A few items from your closet should work."

Emily nodded and disappeared for a few moments before she returned with a set of folded clothes, the same off-white shade that everyone in the house seemed to wear.

The woman nodded at me again. "We'll leave you to it," she said before they both left, shutting the door behind them, the latch clicking closed.

I took a minute, my breathing going from rapid to measured. The broth was warm in my lap, and the steam brought the scent to my nose.

My eyes darted around the empty room. There was no one here to tell me to eat. No one watching me to make sure I finished my food. I raised the spoon to my lips. It was the same broth I'd remembered tasting before, when I'd been in a semiconscious state and the family had dribbled the broth down my throat. My eyes closed involuntarily as I savored the rich soup. It was thick—full of fat bubbles and minerals I could taste on my tongue.

I gulped down several more spoonfuls before I set the bowl back on the side table, only half empty. Grandmother had always made me clean my plate, not wanting to be wasteful, and I hadn't dared to question any of the food the shifters had provided me with. This was the first time I'd chosen to be done simply because I felt full.

The green plaid dress suddenly felt repulsive to me, something I needed to remove so I could be clean, unburdened from what had followed me to this place.

I stood up on wobbly legs, letting the dress fall off my shoulders and down my slim frame to the floor. I stepped out of the dress, my footsteps surer, sturdier. I was naked, though suddenly stronger than I'd ever been. Leaving the dress on the floor felt like I was leaving my old life behind. I was free. Free of the life I'd been living for eighteen years. In a new world where I wasn't some innocent, sheltered child. I was a woman. Dafni Sarracenia.

I took the washcloth from the bucket of water—the clean water against my skin was soothing. I pressed the cloth harder against my skin, trying to scrub away not only the dirt but the film of my mother's wrath that never left my skin. The water turned gray, a color fitting for the filth that was my mother.

With each pass of the cloth, I felt more alive. I could do this, be on my own, take over the Coven.

CHAPTER SIX

Dafni

I SAT ON THE BED THE REST OF THE DAY AND INTO THE start of the night, my knees tucked into my chest. With my stomach full, there weren't any rumbling sounds to distract me from listening through the door to the people who lived here. There were three of them—a woman, a young girl named Emily, and a young man named Luke. I'd heard the female voices most often, along with the sound of pots being set on a stove and dishes being washed in a metal sink. There was no yelling, no chaos—just seemingly normal, everyday activities.

The home was quiet and dark at night. I found myself brave enough to turn off the lamp beside my bed and lie down on top of the mattress. The clothes Emily had left me were adequate and comfortable. Although she was younger than me, all the clothes she provided fit. I was naturally petite, and I'd lost weight from my walk through the woods as well as the time I spent here in bed.

There were black pants with a drawstring and a white shirt that was baggy, with sleeves long enough to cover my arms down to my wrists. Emily had even included an apron that matched hers, probably from her own collection. There had been two nightgowns included in the pile of clothes, sleeveless and the collars frilly with lace. I curled up my legs inside one of them as I laid there. I didn't want to cover myself with a blanket for fear I'd get tangled if I needed to flee quickly in the night.

My intuition told me that I wouldn't have to run or fight these people. Unlike anyone else I'd found in these woods, they'd been kind. They'd taken care of me when I'd been unconscious, but they didn't know who I was...

Still, my fatigue overtook my fear, and I found my eyes closed more than opened and soon drifted off into sleep.

———

I awoke to a high-pitched squeal and the sound of hissing—sizzling like a cauldron was boiling over.

"*Oh no—oh no, no, no!*" a voice whined.

I stood tentatively. After being immobile for so long it was hard to know how weak I'd still be. I pulled open the door, opening it just a crack, and looked out at the rest of the home. It was almost entirely a kitchen. With a refrigerator and freezer on one side and a stove and sink on the other, it left little room for a table with chairs, but somehow it worked. They fit a round table with four chairs alongside a window in the small space that was left. Where there weren't cabinets, there were shelves full of books, most of them with Latin titles.

I recognized the girl, whose name I remembered was Emily, hovering over the stove messing with the dials and waving a wooden spoon wildly in the air. She looked small standing next to the stove—probably five years younger than me.

"Oh gosh...oh no..." she continued.

Classical music played in the background, the sound coming from a small black radio with a long antenna perched on top of the refrigerator.

She hadn't noticed me yet. I tiptoed into the kitchen, craning my neck to see what she was cooking on the stove. White frothy bubbles poured over the rim of the pot cascading down the sides, hissing as they hit the flames of the burner below. Whatever she was cooking smelled good...it was some sort of food. Emily was still messing with the dial of the burner, now using her spoon to try to catch the white foam before it fell into the flames.

I walked up beside her, grabbing hold of a glass bottle of oil on the counter next to the stove and pouring a stream of it into the pot.

"Oh!" The girl squeaked, moving away from the stove once she'd seen me.

The bubbles instantly subsided—a trick from my grandmother.

Emily stood on her tiptoes, flipping on the light above the stove before she looked down into the pot. The water was now bubbling at a low simmer. She looked up at me, a smile on her face. "Thank you! If I'd burned those potatoes my mom would've been so mad—they're the last of our stores from last year. We'll have to wait until fall to harvest more."

I nodded, reaching across the stove and adjusting the dial before hunching over to check the flames below the pot. She'd had the flames too high for this size of pot. It would've continued to overflow until there was nothing left but dried starch on the stovetop.

"How do you know how to do that?" she asked.

I tilted my head to the side. "Do what? Adjust a flame?"

"No, how do you know how to cook?"

I looked down at the pot that now had white peeled potatoes rolling around in the bubbling water. I'd added oil to stop the overflow, just like my grandmother had taught me with potions. She'd also taught me about flame height and the heat it created. I knew how to make potions...cooking seemed similar.

I shrugged. "My grandmother taught me a little bit."

"Great!" Emily said, grabbing cloves of garlic and a few leeks from the counter near the stove and shoving them into my chest. I instinctively grabbed hold of the food. "Then you can help me. We have to make a soup base before my mom gets back from weeding the garden."

We?

She was asking me to help?

"There's a knife in the block near the fridge and a cutting board on the drying rack by the sink."

She was going to give me a knife?

Why did she trust me? She didn't even know me. No one in the woods had trusted me the entire time I'd been struggling to find my way. They'd all treated me like a *stranger*. Someone to be weary of.

Emily didn't know me, yet she was giving me a chance. Treating me like a person, not some alien creature that didn't belong. She was treating me like...a friend. That made the corners of my lips rise up a bit.

I got to work finding the knife and the cutting board and chopping the vegetables. The chopping motion was familiar and comforting. I'd helped my grandmother many times prepare ingredients for our meals and her potions.

Emily nodded after I'd presented my work and motioned for me to throw the chopping's into the pot. I let the vegetables tumble in the boiling water just as the door opened and the woman who had wiped my forehead yesterday appeared. She paused in the doorway, glancing between Emily and me.

Quickly, I backed away from the stove, moving across the kitchen to put some space between me and her daughter. Emily might've trusted me, but I wasn't sure her mother did just yet.

"Is everything okay?" her mother asked.

"Yes, it's great!" Emily chirped. She walked over to where I stood, grabbed the cutting board from my frozen hands, and set it on the counter. "The soup base is ready. Even *she*"—Emily motioned to me—"came out of her room to help."

The woman looked over at me, pausing at the knife I still held in my hand. *Oh no.* I slowly set it on the counter next to me. She kept her eyes on me as she walked over to Emily, continuing to stare at me as they spoke in whispers.

She noticeably exhaled, her shoulders moving up and then dropping down before she nodded and turned around to face me. The woman walked over to where I was standing and picked up the knife I'd just set on the counter. She backed away, placing it in the sink—out of my reach.

Okay, so she didn't trust me yet. That was fair.

"You look much better; some color in your cheeks," she said.

My hand went up to my face, trying to feel the warmth she saw.

"It'll take some time to feel like yourself again. You've been existing on only moose broth for the last week."

A week? I'd been in bed for a week? It hadn't felt like that long.

My heart started pounding, and my breath quickened. I'd wasted a week.

My magic tingled down my arm into my fingers. A week without using it.

Everything came rushing back to me.

Matilda. The pail.

My knees bent into a defensive stance, and my eyes glanced back and forth.

"I had a pail... When...I... When Luke..." My voice shook just as bad as my hands trembled. How could I have forgotten about that?

The woman put her hands in front of her, palms facing down, in a calming motion. "Your pail is in our freezer," she said. "It's still frozen."

She lowered her chin, motioning her head toward the room I'd been staying in for the last *week*. I left Emily to the soup base and followed her mother into the room. Standing by the bed, holding my still shaking hands, I watched as she turned around and closed the door behind her. I reflexively took a few steps back.

A moment passed between us before she spoke. "I know who's in the pail."

My stomach dropped. This was it. The moment where it all fell apart. This woman wouldn't let me keep my mother frozen in a pail—not if she knew who she was. She'd force me to release my mother, and then my mother would unleash her wrath onto me.

"I also think I know who you are," she said.

My heartbeat pounded in my ears.

"I'm not going to do anything about it," she continued. "And I have questions, but I'd prefer if you let me guide the conversation with my children. Emily is still young and naive to danger. Everyone here needs to be careful—if anyone at the Coven knew who's in the freezer, we'd all be in danger."

Breath slowly released from my nose. I nodded.

"Let's take this slow. We won't hurt you."

"I won't hurt anyone—I-I promise," I stammered. These

were the first kind people I'd met, out here all alone. If they turned me away, I'd have nowhere to go.

The woman nodded, continuing to stare at me. "Emily seems to like you. She's always been a good judge of character."

Then she reached behind her, grabbing a hold of the doorknob. "Can we trust you?"

Her body blocked the closed door as she stared at me. I understood what she was doing—she was protecting her family, as any good mother would. She'd just let an unknown woman into her home who'd brought a pail with a frozen cat; she only wanted my word. I could give her that.

"You can trust me," I said.

I watched as her shoulders dropped before she twisted the knob and opened the door, her body welcoming me past the doorway of my room into the rest of the house. "You've been bedridden for too long. Come help us make dinner."

She waved her hand, inadvertently wafting the smell of what Emily was stirring on the stove into the room. My nostrils flared. It smelled so good.

My knees buckled a bit. I wasn't used to standing for so long—not since I'd been bedridden.

"Emily!" the woman called out. "Can you help our guest to the table? I'm going to have her trim the fat while she sits."

Her daughter hurried over. "I've got you," she whispered, grabbing me, her arm reaching across my back under my arm. "We'll fill your stomach with more than moose broth tonight, okay? My mom's a great cook. We're having venison."

I let the scent and Emily lead me out of the room and back into the small kitchen. We passed the woman—Annabel, she told me—stirring the pot on the stove before Emily pulled out a chair, her support leaving me right before my body dropped into the seat. With strength I did not have, she pushed my chair close to the table, my stomach flush with the edge.

Annabel quietly spoke to Emily before she nodded, grabbing a bowl from the fridge, a clean cutting board, and a knife. She set the cutting board in front of me along with the knife and bowl of what I could now see was raw meat—the venison.

"Can you trim off the excess fat?" she asked right before she turned around and made her way to the sink where she began washing dishes.

I stared at the knife. They'd once again given me, a stranger, a knife in their own home. I wasn't going to use it for anything other than cutting meat like they'd asked, but that Emily's mother also trusted me with such a deadly weapon made me further relax.

They trusted me not to hurt them.

They weren't going to hurt me.

I was safe here.

Dumping the meat onto the cutting board, I got to work cutting off the fat. Annabel came over to the table, clucking her tongue in approval before gathering everything and bringing it over to the counter. I'd cut the meat thin and small enough that it would cook quickly in the broth Emily and I had made.

The exterior door next to the kitchen opened, revealing Luke, who walked in looking tired. I hadn't noticed the bags under his eyes or the dirt staining his off-white coveralls when we'd scared each other earlier. He paused for a moment; his eyes locked with mine before I looked down at the scratched tabletop in front of me.

I watched the three of them, Annabel, Emily and Luke, work in tandem to put together the meal. While their mother finished cooking the soup, Emily pulled out bowls from an upper cabinet and Luke gathered the utensils from a drawer. They both walked around me as they set the table for dinner.

When the soup was done, Annabel brought the pot from the stove to the table, placing a woven potholder on the tabletop before setting down the steaming pot of what was now a stew. She took a seat next to me, between Luke and myself.

Emily set a glass of something purple in front of her mother before taking a seat beside me, filling the last empty seat. Some kind of drink?

The place settings looked worn but obviously cared for. The glossy sheen of the bowl was scratched from the scrape of knives and forks. A spoon and fork sat on either side of the plate, the silverware tarnished. I kept my eyes on my bowl, my ankles crossed underneath me and my hands folded on top of my apron, trying to make myself small.

"Let's thank the higher powers for the food and for bringing this girl—" Annabel paused.

My face warmed from the eyes staring at me, waiting for me to say something.

"Dafni," I croaked, swallowing, trying to wet my throat.

"For bringing Dafni to us. May she continue to regain her strength to undertake whatever tasks await her." Her eyes bore directly into mine when I lifted my head. A shiver traveled down my spine to the end of my tailbone. "Let's eat!"

She stood, bending over the pot at the middle of the table, giving it a stir before reaching for each of our bowls and ladling heaping portions into them. The steam from the stew traveled up to my nose, my nostrils twitching at the scent. I waited until everyone had picked up their spoons before I picked up mine. My hand shook ever so slightly as I dipped into the stew and brought it to my lips. It was flavorful, with chunks of venison and spices. I swallowed, quickly bringing another spoonful to my mouth. My chest began warming as the food slid down into my stomach, and my hand became less shaky with every mouthful.

Spoonful after spoonful, I ate.

I put my hands around the warm bowl, lifting it to my lips

to drink the last of the broth. I closed my eyes as I swallowed, savoring the last drops.

My eyes opened as I put the bowl back on the table. Everyone was staring at me. Emily sat frozen, holding her steaming spoon between her mouth and her bowl. Luke looked at me, his bowl still full and his spoon resting on the side. Annabel stared at me from across the table with a smile on her face.

"Would you like more, Dafni?"

I almost said yes, opening my mouth to speak. Instead, a gas bubble I couldn't stop scaled my throat and exited my open lips. I slapped my hand over my mouth, eyes wide. Emily dropped her spoon into her bowl, the metal clattering against the ceramic, a laugh escaping her. Luke looked down at his stew, a smirk on his face.

"Now, now. There's nothing embarrassing about a full stomach." Annabel shushed her children before lifting a spoonful of stew into her mouth. She chewed, eyeing her children before she spoke again. "So, Dafni, Luke tells me you're a witch."

I froze. What had he told his mother? That I'd used my wind magic on him? Carried a frozen cat in a pail? But then I remembered she already knew about the cat. It was in her freezer. That hadn't prevented her from helping me.

My mind raced. Maybe they were just nursing me back to health to use me and my magic. Grandmother had told me stories about those without magic capturing a witch. The story she'd liked to tell me was about a witch the humans trapped and kept in a cage in their kitchen. I looked around—the surroundings looked so much like the story she'd told me. They'd prodded her with hot pokers until she did whatever magic they'd asked of her. The witch outlived her captors, still stuck in the cage as their bodies rotted around her. I'd always asked Grandmother to tell it again, even as my eyes were heavy and sleep took over my body.

Little did I know, the story would become so familiar.

No, those were stories. Nothing about fairy tales were real. What *was* real was that I didn't have anywhere to go. There wasn't a handsome prince coming to save me—there was *no one* coming to save me. I'd somehow ended up in a silver trailer with this family. Maybe I was lucky. They'd nursed me back to health for a week. They were feeding me and provided me with clean clothes. They'd given me a knife...*twice*. What would be the point of all that if they were just going to kill me?

"You don't have to share anything you don't want to, Dafni."

My eyes went back to Annabel. She knew who was in the freezer—it was understandable that she had questions and wanted answers.

"I'm a witch," I whispered.

Annabel took a moment to chew another spoonful of stew, all while staring at me, studying me. She took her time looking at my nose, my eyes, my mouth. I looked down at my empty bowl, not knowing where to look.

"Luke tells me you have two powers," she said.

Emily choked for a moment, coughing over her stew. Luke stared at me, awaiting my response.

"That's rare in a witch, you know."

I was rare? I'd only known two witches my entire life—my grandmother and my mother. Both women had more than one power. Like them, I had multiple: air and water.

"There was only one line known to produce witches with more than one power," Annabel said. My throat expanded as I gulped down more air. "Matilda's line."

I pulled my eyes away from the table and settled them on my hands—they were shaking in my lap.

"You're Matilda's daughter, aren't you?"

No one at the table breathed.

"I'm here to take her place in the Coven," I said.

Luke choked on his food. "You can't just show up and take over. There are too many customs...traditions... They're super stri—"

"Witches don't just walk into the Coven," Annabel cut off Luke. "There's a process. It's extremely controlled."

Luke cleared his throat. "To enter the Coven, you need to graduate from the Academy."

The Academy? I'd heard that word before...

"What do you know about this...Academy?" I asked, looking at each of their faces for answers.

Both Luke and Emily looked to their mother, their lips closed.

"You already know Luke works there," she began.

I nodded. That was what he'd told me when he'd found me.

"The Academy isn't far away...in fact, we're on their property now, above the soil instead of under it."

I looked down at my feet, to the linoleum floor of the trailer. *I'm already here?* I looked up, my mind simmering with even more questions. "So you are part of...it..." I waved my hand in the air trying to find the right word.

"No, no..." she tutted, waving her own hand at me. "We live here under the protection of the Coven; we aren't a part of it."

"But if you're under their prot—"

She clicked her tongue at me, the same way my grandmother had done to hush me. "That's all I'm going to say about that."

I bit my tongue between my teeth. I had so many questions, but I didn't want to push my luck. They were giving me food and shelter—I'd just have to take whatever information they were willing to divulge.

"There are two ways to enter the Academy: parent presentation or scouting," Luke began, glancing at his mother, who nodded at him to continue.

I let out a sigh of relief. It didn't matter if they didn't tell me about their situation; what I cared about was information about the Coven. I listened, ready to commit every word to memory.

"Witches can only enter the Academy once a year," Luke continued, "during the freshening."

"And since you don't have witch parents to present you..." I couldn't help but notice that Annabel's eyes darted to the freezer as she paused before looking back at me. "You'll have to wait for the scouts to gather this year's group of human-born witches."

"This year's freshening happened last month," Luke said. "They won't do it again until next year."

"That was only last month?" His mother grimaced as she took another sip of the purple liquid in her cup. "Time sure moves slowly around here." She glanced at Luke before looking back at me. "That's probably for the best. It'll give her time to prepare."

"Yeah," Luke said. "She needs time if she thinks she's going to enter the Academy..."

I watched them talk about me back and forth, trying to follow their conversation. I'd have to go to the Academy? But I needed to get to the Coven.

The Academy...I'd heard that before, only mentioned briefly in conversations between my mother and grandmother. It sounded like a school—maybe that was where I needed to be. Maybe that was where I could learn about this world I knew so little about. My grandmother had trained me the best she could, but if the few days I spent in the woods alone had taught me anything, it was that I knew nothing of the world outside the cottage or the shifters' packhouse. I needed to learn.

Annabel quieted, tilting her head, giving me a soft glance. "No one ever told you about the Academy?" It was like she could read my mind, like she knew me.

I shook my head. No one had ever told me anything directly.

"Witches have to go through the Academy to join the Coven. The process, as Luke said, is called freshening. When witches turn eighteen, their witch parents present them to the Academy for tutelage in their given magical ability." She looked at Luke, who bowed his head, looking at his lap.

"Also during this time, the Coven's scouts find those without magical parents—witches who might not even know they have powers. Many of the witches with non-magical parents grow up seeming odd or delinquent in the human world. When the scouts find them, they promise the human parents they'll take them to a prestigious college preparatory academy for the summer. They also promise a place of safety and acceptance. Many parents of these children are relieved that there's a place for their...unusual children." She looked at me, her eyes softening. "I think you know the outside world mistreats people with magical abilities."

My grandmother had told me countless stories about the outside world and their hatred of those of us with magic. It'd been the fuel for childhood nightmares.

I nodded, looking to my lap. "Yes, ma'am."

My fingers fidgeted as I kept my eyes down, feeling everyone's stares on the crown of my head. I waited for someone to say something—anything to interrupt the silence in the trailer. The refrigerator hummed, and the radio had been turned down for dinner. But those sounds did nothing to break up the loud silence here in the trailer.

Slowly, I lifted my head, my eyes bouncing around the

table before I realized that Luke and Emily were staring at their mother, who was staring at me, studying me.

The moment our eyes met, I swallowed a gasp, not wanting to show how intimidated I was by her. It felt like she was looking beyond my eyes—reading my thoughts, my memories. Staring into my soul.

We held eye contact for what felt like hours...but probably lasted only minutes.

When she looked away, I wilted in my chair as if I'd been released, as if she'd been holding me in an upright, locked position while she'd studied me. My upper arms hit the side of the table, my eyes still watching her...waiting for her to do or say something.

Annabel looked over at Emily, gazing at her for a moment before looking at Luke, taking the same amount of time to stare at him.

Nodding slightly, she turned to look back at me. "We'll do our best to tell you everything you need to know about the Coven and the Academy in the coming year."

"Does this mean she's staying?" Luke asked.

"Yes," Annabel said. "She's staying until the next freshening."

CHAPTER SEVEN

Dafni

THE VELKANS, WHOSE LAST NAME I LEARNED FROM THE hand-painted sign hanging outside the front door of the trailer, weren't wealthy, but they were rich in love for one another. Annabel had claimed they were under the protection of the Coven, but the protection they provided didn't seem to extend to anything further than the necessities. They only had *just* enough food, and having an extra person in the house had them taking what little food they had and stretching it further.

Luke came home every day with bags of food and supplies in his arms. I found out he worked at the Coven, in maintenance, and often brought home leftover food from the kitchens there. He'd open the door to the trailer, kiss his mother on the cheek, and tug affectionately on the two braids Emily kept her hair in. He'd nod to me in acknowledgment before heading to change and shower.

The steady buzzing sound in the trailer came from the electrical wires strung on wooden posts, much like the ones at my grandmother's cottage. The wires looked like waves as the posts got smaller and smaller the farther they were from the trailer. There was a point in the distance where the line of posts ended and the wires took a nosedive into the dirt. The Velkans warned me against exploring that far from the trailer. Their electricity came from the Coven, and they didn't want me getting too close.

I'd promised I'd stay away.

And Annabel kept true to her word. She'd let me stay with her family, in turn letting me regain the strength I'd lost in the woods. I'd been a lot weaker than I'd thought, and it took me a week to recover enough strength to use my magic.

I'd adapted to their routines quickly, finding the Velkans kind and welcoming. They made it easy to become a part of their well-oiled machine. I did chores and daily tasks beside Annabel and Emily, coming to enjoy their company. They seemed pleased that I knew how to clean, cook, and garden—all skills I'd learned back at the cottage.

The garden was their lifeline—without it, everyone in the house would only be able to eat what little food came from the Coven, and that wasn't enough to sustain anyone. They focused on growing hearty root vegetables and produce that could be canned, used when the cold winter months came.

I saw Luke at night when we all ate dinner together as a family. He didn't talk much about his work, instead teasing Emily and offering to do the dishes if he could pick the movie that night—though most often, he'd fold and let his sister pick.

A small black television with a video-cassette player sat on the counter nearest the kitchen table. After the dishes were done, we'd sit in our chairs and enjoy a movie together. I'd heard of movies and television before, seen them in the packhouse, but my grandmother had never had one in the cottage. Being in my kitten form at the packhouse, I'd never been able to sit and watch a movie without being interrupted by someone picking me up or insisting on smooshing their face into mine, peppering my nose with kisses. Every night with the Velkans, my eyes were glued to the screen, following the storyline, my attention rapt.

Here it almost felt like my grandmother's cottage, the way they followed the same routine each day—some form of cleaning, cooking, or gardening always needed to be done. But it was also different. Every night we ate dinner and then laughed together watching a movie. It was a comfort I hadn't known I needed.

Emily hadn't lied when she'd claimed Annabel was a wonderful cook. The way she melded flavors and textures...I couldn't stop eating. It took me weeks, but I regained the weight I'd lost in the woods. I felt stronger than I ever had before. Between the food I was eating and the new freedom I had, I felt lighter than I ever had before.

Still, there was a weight, deep in my stomach, pulling me down. Keeping me grounded in reality. That pressure of being who I was—being part of the Sarracenia lineage—ultimately made me feel heavy.

The summer grew hot, and I spent my days in the garden, helping the family weed and water. We rotated pumpkins and watermelon, harvested tomatoes before the bugs bore holes through their skin, and snapped ears of corn from their stalks.

The garden reminded me of my grandmother's. It was similar in size, but they spent more than twice the amount of time tending to it. They didn't use magic to encourage the plants to grow. Instead they put work into the plants, encouraging them to produce so they could eat. The Velkans worked for what they wanted.

My back ached from bending over to pull weeds. I'd try to help Emily trim the purple flowery bushes she called lobelia around the trailer, but Annabel had shooed me away, assigning me to the weeds sprouting up from around the rows and rows of onions. I'd accidentally pulled an onion bulb from the ground when I first started working in the garden, and the look of disappointment on Annabel's face made me never want to do that again. I took my time, making sure to only pull the weeds, but that meant more time leaning over the dirt.

The Velkans' garden was larger than Elise's had been, which made sense. This family depended on the garden for produce, whereas Elise grew some vegetables but focused more on medicinal plants.

Elise. It'd been weeks since I'd left her standing there with snowflakes sprinkling down on her from the sky. I wanted her and Kleio to know that I was okay...that I'd made it somewhere safe. I stood, leaning back as my hands cradled my lower spine.

"Annabel?" I called out. She was a few rows down, using a shovel to dig out some weeds that'd rooted deep.

She looked up from her work, beads of sweat along her hairline.

"Is there any way I could send someone a letter?" I asked.

Annabel looked down at where she'd been weeding. "Depends. How far has it got to go?"

I did quick calculations in my head. "About three hours or so away."

Her facial features relaxed. "I'm sure we could manage that. Luke can drop it off at the post office on his way to work."

She hadn't thought I was sending a letter to the Coven... had she? I would never put their family at risk like that.

"Annabel?" I called out again.

She looked up once more.

"What if I don't know exactly where to send it?" I asked.

She pushed a lock of hair out of her eyes. "There's a phone book that Luke got at the chamber of commerce in town a month ago. It's in the cabinet under the TV. Do you know the name of the person you want to send it to?"

I nodded. I'd bet the packhouse wouldn't be listed, but I knew Elise's last name was Wilson. Her dad's name was Roger —he'd be listed. If I addressed it to him, her parents would be sure she got it.

"I'll have it ready by the morning," I said.

That night, it rained, and I couldn't help but think of how good that would be for our garden. *Our garden.* I'd gotten so comfortable here that I was beginning to feel a part of their family.

I wrote the letter to Elise and Kleio, explaining that I was safe without disclosing my location. I tucked the paper into the envelope Annabel had given me. Maybe someday we'd see each other again.

———

October

In the fall, I used my magic to blow the leaves that had gotten stuck beneath the trailer up into the air, the different colors blowing together into a tornado that I flicked into the woods with my fingers.

There was harvesting and canning to complete, and Emily spent more time grumbling about the work than actually doing it.

"No one else has to work this hard for their food!" Emily complained, whining.

I held my breath, waiting for Annabel's reprimand.

"You're right," she replied, calmly—completely opposite to what I was expecting. "Most don't have to grow their own food, but those people have a car to get to a grocery store...a job that pays to buy food." She hoisted a basket of potatoes to her waist. "We don't have a car or extra money...but we have this." She looked out into the garden. "And we are thankful for what we have."

I watched Emily's bottom lip wobble at her mother's honesty. She crouched down in the garden, digging up potatoes and brushing the dirt off their skin before setting them in the grass behind her. The Velkans didn't have much, but they had more than I'd had at the cottage—they had *each other*, and that was something to be thankful for.

My muscles grew strong from the heavy baskets of produce I carried and the jars I brought down into the cellar next to the trailer. More often than not, I'd grab a book off the shelf in the kitchen, bringing it down with me. I'd take my time putting things away—a book in one hand and produce in the other. I could've lived in the cellar if the temperature hadn't been so cold. It was quiet and dark. The spider webs in the corners glistened with droplets of moisture. I'd spent as much time down there as I could until I thought the Velkans would miss me.

Down there, my thoughts were quiet, and my body was relaxed. I could spend some quiet time with books and my thoughts, reflect on the past weeks, months—the past years of my life. There was no one to judge me but the earth—and it never voiced its opinion.

The days grew shorter, and it became dark early. It was dark enough that instead of spending an hour or two after dinner outside, everyone stayed inside the trailer.

One night, instead of a movie, Luke brought out a deck of cards. They'd started off easy on me since I'd never played before. But as soon as I caught on to the game, they were ruthless and treated me like any other player. I found myself laughing out loud, wanting the night to never end.

I'd never been a part of anything like this—part of a family that worked together and relaxed together, who genuinely enjoyed one another. What would it have been like to grow up like this? *Having fun with my family?* Maybe then I wouldn't have grown up so sheltered and naive. I would've known what it was like to joke and let loose without the constant cloud of pressure my grandmother and mother had put on me to be perfect.

———

December

Winter arrived sooner than usual, and Annabel taught me how to make the purple concoction I'd seen her drinking every day. She used the trimmings Emily gathered from the lobelia bush outside, mashing the purple flowers in a bowl before adding them to the brew. It smelled terrible, and I wrinkled my nose as she directed me to stir the pot on the stove. As the brew cooked, the smell became almost familiar, reminding of the long days spent in the cottage with my grandmother.

"Good, Dafni, nice and slow—just like that." Annabel pulled two jars down from the cabinet above the stove, holding them with their labels facing me. "Remember what we add next?"

I glanced between the two jars. "Red rosinweed."

"Very good," she said, opening the jar and shaking in the

dried flowers. "Potions control emotions, and emotions control your power as a woman."

"Is that why you drink this?" I asked as I stirred in the red rosinweed, watching the dried petals disappear in the liquid. "To control your emotions?"

"In a way." Annabel leaned over, sprinkling in a few more petals. "It's part of the agreement I made with your mother to live here."

I stopped stirring, the liquid swirling around my wooden spoon. To make an agreement with my mother was akin to life in prison. She must've really wanted something from my mother to agree to anything with her.

"So long as I suppress my emotions with this drink, we can live here and Luke can work at the Coven."

"Why would you agree to anything with my mother?" I asked. My mother was a raging lunatic with an affinity for cruelty. Even since birth, I'd never agreed with my mother.

"I think you've already realized that I'm a witch." Annabel looked down at the concoction. "She deems me as a threat, and my children—"

"But Luke and Emily aren't witches," I interrupted, the statement also a question.

"No, no," Annabel said. "They aren't, but your mother protects all of us...so long as I drink this."

I took a moment to look at Annabel's face. Her skin was youthful and supple, her lips full. But her eyes—they looked as though they'd seen a hundred years.

"Luke and Emily's father is not a nice man," Annabel said. "I will gladly suppress my magic to protect my children."

I nodded, riding a small wave of jealousy. *What I wouldn't do for a mother who'd protect me.*

Annabel leaned over the pot, wafting the steam toward her face. She nodded once, turning off the stove. "This is done."

She took the pot and poured the purple liquid into a line of mason jars next to the stove on the counter. I went to work sealing the top of the jars with silver lids.

After Annabel put away the jars and washed the pot in the sink, she surprised me by setting the empty pot back on the stove. "Let me teach you another one."

I watched as she began pulling jars from the back of the cabinet, the lids covered with dust.

"This one you might appreciate." Annabel turned to face me, reaching out and cupping both of my cheeks in her hands. "This one creates unbridled rage."

"Rage?" I questioned.

Annabel arranged the jars in a line on the counter, turning the labels to face outward. "Rage is one of the most powerful emotions. I felt it coming from you when Luke brought you here." She motioned to the empty pot.

I picked it up and brought it over to the sink, filling it about halfway full.

"We'll make a diluted version today. I think in this moment you feel enough rage as it is."

"I don't feel rage," I said with my jaw clenched.

"If you're honest with yourself, I think you'll find that there's rage deep down inside of you...it's within all of us women. It tells you to do things and to say things that others might find unpleasant—but you know are right." Annabel grabbed onto a jar and pulled at the cork. Red flakes fell to the ground as the cork came free. "We'll start with a splash of honey-badger blood." She poured some of the blood into the pot, and we both watched as the red liquid clouded the water.

"Should we add some asafoetida?" I asked.

Annabel glanced up at me, a wrinkle forming between her brows. "How did you know to add that?"

I smiled. I looked over the ingredients she'd pulled and began plucking the jars I'd need.

She grabbed hold of the jar of crocodile teeth I had in my palm, her hand wrapping around mine. "Only a few of those. I don't have many left."

I nodded as I looked through the glass at the few pointed teeth inside.

With my ingredients lined up, I began adding them to the brew, following Annabel's direction. She communicated with me through clicks of her tongue when I'd added too much and a firm hand around my wrist when I needed to add a few more shakes.

"You're a natural," Annabel said as I stirred. "Who taught you?"

I remembered back to the cottage days. Grandmother next to the cauldron, talking about this and that, thinking I wasn't listening—but I always was. Her adages about different herbs and plants had stuck in my brain, and I remembered most of what she'd said.

"My grandmother," I said. "She was a talented potion maker."

Annabel stared at me for a moment, then nodded softly in agreement. "She must've been a talented woman, a strong woman to raise a witch like you."

The brew bubbled on the stove while Annabel and I watched in silence, letting the scent from the steam wash over our faces. I rarely thought of my grandmother. It was too painful. The way we'd parted—I didn't like to think about it. She'd raised me the best she could, alone in that cottage, without a partner or any help. It'd been just me and her as long as I could remember. The last time I'd brewed a potion was when I'd assisted my grandmother.

All this brewing reminded me of her. She'd always known

the right things to do, to say. She'd been the only one to stand up for me—when I'd been too small and my voice too quiet.

Annabel put her hand on my arm. Only then did I realize I was shaking.

"It's important to feel everything," she whispered. "Trust what your body is trying to tell you."

I let the rage potion simmer along with my insides.

PART 2

CHAPTER EIGHT

May
Gideon

Arcana loved to hear her own voice. It was a nice voice—don't get me wrong. It was just when I had to listen to her talk for hours without an interruption that it started to grate at my ear drums.

But I made myself sit...and listen...and maybe even learn.

I didn't subject myself to learning inside the same class-rooms the other witches at the Academy did—I couldn't. I wouldn't be able to pay attention to the instructor or the material. I'd tried before to attend class, just like every other witch here at the Academy, but it hadn't gone well.

There'd been pushing, screeching, and all-out fighting to sit in the chair next to me, behind me, and in front of me. The witches who had snagged spots near mine had spent the entirety of the class attempting to play footsie, pretending to fall into or onto me, and as soon as the instructor had dismissed class, they'd swarmed me, which ended in me running down the halls and locking the door to my dorm before they could catch up to me.

So instead, I was here, sitting on the dirt floor outside the classroom, my back against the brick wall as I listened to the instruction.

This was an air magic class where the witches were being instructed to shoot their air magic across the room, blowing an object off some sort of elevated surface. There was no table or object in this empty hallway, so I dug into the pocket of my green pants—the same color that every other witch here wore. It was like the Academy was begging life, something green, to enter this brown underground wasteland. They weren't succeeding.

I tossed a balled-up napkin from breakfast onto the floor in front of me. It rolled before hitting the brick wall, across from where I was sitting.

"Extend your arm, pointing your index and middle fingers from your dominant hand at your target..." Arcana directed.

I did as instructed, pointing my two fingers at the napkin two feet in front of me.

"Harness your magic, let it flow down your arm, grow in your fingers..."

My magic tingled down my arm, and I pinched my index and middle fingers together, trying to reserve my magic for the release command.

"And...release!" Arcana's words sent a shiver through my body, the magic flowing from my chest down my arm and into my fingertips. There was no stopping it, no altering its course. Flames shot out of my fingers, immediately burning the napkin. Black cinders floated a few feet into the air before falling onto the floor.

"Good, good!" Arcana shouted.

I breathed heavily, sitting in the dirt, in the hallway catching my breath.

I had fire magic, just as every male witch had. I wasn't particularly powerful, many of the witches here could best me with their powers even if I used my fire magic against them.

But here, at the Academy and the Coven, I was powerful because of my sex, how rare it was. And that made me a target.

I had a bullseye on my back, and every witch here was an arrow.

I tried not to show my face. I kept to the shadows, attending classes when I wanted to...from the hallway. My food was delivered nightly to my door or, if I was feeling particularly stir crazy, I'd sneak down to the kitchen after everyone else had gone to bed, the Coven witches who worked there preparing me a plate of whatever was left from dinner.

Mostly, I wandered the Academy at night, preferring loneliness to getting mauled by the witches down here. They were hungry...more so as I'd become older. This year had been the worst—and now that it was early summer, the Autumnal Equinox was approaching quickly. Just a few short months and I'd be forced to pick a partner.

A film coated my mouth as I thought about the next months.

I spit onto the floor, right in front of a shiny black boot.

I was so caught up in my thoughts that I'd missed hearing Arcana dismiss class *early*.

"Gideon?"

Ah, fuck.

"It's Gideon?"

"He's here?"

I pushed myself up onto my feet, walking as fast as I could

down the hallway lined with classrooms, back toward the main area of the Academy—the dome.

A stampede of heels clicked behind me, their breaths growing ragged the farther they followed me.

"Shh! Don't scare him away!"

They tried to be quiet, sneaky, as they followed me, like I didn't notice the noise their shoes and bodies made. My room was on the ground floor. I just needed to get there and lock the door.

The hallway was long, and soon witches began exiting classrooms on both sides as their classes dismissed, stopping for a moment, watching me speed walk by with slacked jaws before joining the growing mob behind me.

"Gideon!" someone yelled out.

Noise meant an increase in intensity. Everyone down here fed off one another. One yell turned into ten, which turned into fifty in a matter of seconds. Chaos was incoming.

That was what I got for trying to learn, trying to attend a class where I practiced my magic. Being the only male witch at the Academy might have seemed like a dream—the books I'd read had princes vying for princesses and knights going to battle for their partners—but here, the attention wasn't a dream, it was a literal nightmare.

The witches here didn't want to get to know me, they wanted me for my...maleness. It didn't matter if I'd sprouted five extra toes or another head—they wanted the clout, the prestige of being the partner of the newest male witch.

My walk turned into a run, which turned into a sprint. I was running down the hallway, bursting through the doors into the dome, the witches' hot breath on the back of my neck.

Their hands grabbed at my clothes, my jacket tugging back away from my shoulders, my arms being pulled backward as the sleeves rolled down my arms.

Once the jacket released my wrists, I was free for a moment. My feet dug into the dirt ground, pushing off as I tried to gain speed toward my room. I glanced behind me once, the faces of desperate witches surrounding me.

I put my key code into the door of my room, the accepting beep releasing its first decibel before I turned the handle, slipping through the door and closing it behind me. I flipped the latch—the extra one that didn't automatically lock every time the door closed.

My back against the door, I felt the witches' fists pound on the wood, my head bouncing up and down with the tremors.

That had been way too close. It'd be a while before they calmed down, before they left the door of the room they knew I was hiding in.

Still, soon, they'd leave. In my experience this stand-off usually lasted a day, and then they'd get hungry, sleepy, or bored.

This would all be over soon—both the witches pounding on my door and my time here at the Academy.

The Autumnal Equinox was quickly approaching.

Either I'd pick a partner or escape. My hope was on the latter.

CHAPTER NINE

Dafni

D*on't make me regret giving her to you to raise instead of putting her in the Academy where she belongs.* I sat straight up in bed, strands of my red hair stuck in the corner of my lips. Matilda still haunted me. Her voice still sent shivers down my spine and made sweat appear along the back of my neck.

The wet sweat instantly became cold against my skin, and I shivered again, this time from the cold. Wind blew the branches of the maple tree against my window. It was summer, but an unseasonable cold snap had blown in and cooled everything down over the last few days. It'd been a welcome relief to us in the trailer and to the plants in the garden. This year, I'd helped plant the garden in the spring. It'd been terrible to watch all of our hard work, the leaves of the plants we'd tended to as seedlings, turn yellow, burnt from the hot sun.

A shiver ran down my spine again as Matilda's voice echoed in my head. Like the chilly temperature outside, she was cold, still in the freezer, unable to reach me except in my nightmares.

My feet hit the floor as I rubbed my eyes. I'd snuck a peek into the freezer every time I was around when Annabel opened it to get a package of meat for dinner. I always saw the black pail sitting there, but I never saw the top, never saw the opaque ice that enclosed Matilda. It wouldn't hurt to check—just one time. I wanted to see for myself that she was frozen, still trapped, where she couldn't hurt me or anyone else. Just for my peace of mind. No one could blame me for looking. Checking.

I pulled down the nightdress I'd borrowed from Emily. This one was two sizes too small, riding up my thighs. I tested the door handle of my room tentatively.

The knob turned smoothly until the last part of the turn, when it stuck for a second, sending a loud *pop* throughout the trailer. I squeezed my eyes closed, waiting for Annabel to investigate or Luke to stomp through the house in search of the sound. No noises met my ears as I squeezed the turned door handle still in my palm. Slowly, as not to let the hinges squeak, I opened the door, letting the slightly cooler air from the kitchen wash over me. The refrigerator with the freezer above was ten steps away, if I took long strides. I'd walk over there quietly, check if my mother was still frozen solid, and quickly return to my room. A one-minute operation. I could do this.

Walking on the balls of my feet, I spread my toes to dampen the sound of my footsteps as I made my way across the kitchen. I counted my steps in my head, *seven...eight*, until I made it to the freezer. Gripping the handle tightly, I pulled, wincing at the sound the freezer door made when the suction broke. Billows of cold mist landed on my skin as a dim light from the back of the freezer shone on my face. Keeping one hand on the freezer door, I reached in, grabbing the top of the pail, tilting it toward me.

"The cat's still frozen." The voice startled me. I let go of the pail, letting it fall back into the freezer. I slammed the door shut before turning around, the back of my body plastered to the front of the refrigerator. The kitchen seemed darker now that I'd stared into the light of the freezer. A silhouette sat at the kitchen table I'd just walked by. How had I not seen that?

"You can check if you want, Dafni." The way he said my name made the nerves in my back tingle. He was right. There weren't any rules saying I couldn't.

It was my pail, after all.

I pulled my back off the refrigerator before I turned around and opened the freezer, letting the door swing open. I tilted the pail down again, this time running my hand along the hard opaque ice that encased my mother. I could see the blurry outline of her orange fur. As an extra precaution, I summoned my water magic, further freezing the ice, tiny crystals forming along the surface. Relief flooded my body, quelling my nerves. She was still contained.

I closed the freezer door slower than I'd opened it, wanting to take my time turning around.

"Come sit down with us, Dafni. We'd like to talk to you." That was Annabel's voice.

What were they both doing awake in the middle of the night?

I could never argue with Annabel. I walked over to the table, sitting in an empty chair.

"Luke heard some news at work today." She brushed light-red curls from her temple. "The freshening is happening sooner than we'd thought."

I stopped breathing.

"Luke found out this year is special—it's the year the male witch, Gideon, will choose a partner."

Luke nodded. "There will be evaluations this year. Each of the three elements will compete and present their top witch to Gideon, who will choose a partner from those three."

"Male witches are rare, Dafni, so this is a big deal for the Coven." Annabel reached out and grabbed hold of my hand. "Luke confirmed today that the scouts have picked up the human-born witches. They are in route and will arrive to the Academy soon."

I tried to swallow, but my mouth was suddenly dry.

"Since you don't have a parent to present you, joining the human-born witches is the safest way to get you into the Academy," Annabel said. "I don't think it's a good idea for you to be introduced as Dafni Sarracenia to the Academy, being who your mother is...where she is right now."

We all looked at the freezer.

"Joining the human-born witches would make your introduction more...anonymous." She wrapped her fingers around the handle of the purple potion in front of her. "You need time to acclimate and learn about the Academy and the Coven before you take your mother's place."

Luke nodded in agreement. He leaned his elbow on the table, pulling a piece of paper from his back pocket. Setting it on the table, he unfolded it. The paper was covered with what looked like a hand-drawn map.

"I'm not sure what your plan is," he said, "but I thought I'd map out the Academy for you."

I almost laughed out loud. I didn't know what my plan was either. In the year I'd spent with the Velkans I'd grown a whole year older and wiser. Annabel had taught me so much about potions, and I'd become adept at using my wind magic to manage the clouds. Still, I felt unprepared. I was entering the

Academy, about to live with more witches than I'd ever seen in my life, and I was planning to take over my mother's position—to be the Prime.

"Did I ever tell you about my time at the Academy?" Annabel asked.

I shook my head. I'd never thought about her attending the Academy, although it made sense that she had.

"It wasn't the best experience...witches aren't known for their kindness."

Don't I know it.

"More often than not, I'd get in trouble."

Luke scoffed. "*You* got in trouble?"

Annabel nodded. "Before I had children, I was quite the troublemaker."

He smiled, shaking his head.

"When I was angry"—Annabel looked at me—"usually because of your mother, I'd go off with a blunt metal object, whatever I could find, and etch spells into the bricks with my earth magic."

"*You* graffitied the Academy?" Luke asked, in even further disbelief.

"It was my little act of rebellion." Annabel laughed. "The spells never worked. I'm sure I wasn't powerful enough at the time." She sighed. "It seems silly now, but those little acts of rebellion are what helped me decompress. They are what helped me make it through my time at the Academy." She turned to me, her face suddenly more serious. "Those little moments of escape are what you're going to need to find if you want to make it through your time at the Academy. Maybe don't etch spells into the walls, but find your own little acts of rebellion."

I nodded as Luke pushed the map in front of me. He went over the floor plan of the Academy. It was underground and hidden among the rolling hills of the woods. Small houses scattered on the surface served as hidden entrances. They looked like normal, small cabins on the outside, but inside they were hollow, containing a trapdoor that was the entry to the Academy.

"Then there's the matter of your two powers," Annabel said. "They'll know who you are...or at least guess you're part of Matilda's lineage the moment they find out you possess two powers. It's best you choose one, probably your strongest to highlight, keeping your other magic hidden. At least until you become more confident inside the Academy."

I nodded. I didn't want to garner attention...at least not until I got my bearings inside this new world.

"Water," I said. "I'll claim to only have water magic."

Annabel nodded. "Now it's just a matter of getting you in with the human-born witches..."

Luke cleared his throat. "I've got a plan."

CHAPTER TEN

Dafni

Luke's plan was risky. That was what Annabel called it when he'd finished explaining.

"The human-born witches are arriving to the Academy tomorrow," Luke said.

"Tomorrow? Already?" She stumbled over her words. "I thought we'd have at least a full day or two to prepare..." She looked at me. "To say goodbye."

Luke ran his hand over his face. "The only information I get from the Academy is what I can overhear. Luckily, I heard about the human-born arrival as I was leaving today." He looked at the clock on the kitchen counter. "Well, yesterday."

"So, we have less than a day." Annabel took a sip of her potion. "The truck's arrival is happening today. Those girls are in the truck right now, probably scared out of their minds.

Those lying witches at the Coven promised their parents that they'd receive intensive college prep courses..." She looked down at her lap, the bottom lids of her eyes keeping the tears that welled up there from falling. "And the only thing they'll get at the Academy is forgotten."

Luke reached out, putting his hand over the top of hers. "There's nothing you can do right now, Mom. I know you're staying quiet to protect Emily and me."

It took a moment before Annabel gave a slight shake with her head. "Still...I should be doing something. Every year they trick more witches into coming, and what they go through down there..." Her hand tensed beneath Luke's.

"You can't do anything, Mom," he said. "I know you want to, but Emily is still so young. We can't give them any reason to lash out, to make our lives more difficult."

"I know." Annabel shook her head, looking down at where their hands still touched.

A wave of jealously, or maybe just longing, rushed through me. What would it have been like to have a mother like Annabel, a brother like Luke—someone to protect me?

"We're going to have to make this work somehow." Luke tapped his fingers on the tabletop. "If I'd overheard about the freshening earlier, we could've forged a registration...I could've slipped her information in with the rest of the human-born witch's paperwork."

"But that's no longer an option," Annabel said.

"*If*"—Luke talked louder, the words tumbling out of his mouth faster—"we can intercept the transport, Dafni can sneak in the back of the truck with them." He paused, looking over at me. "They'll have a set number of witches in the truck. The Academy hires outside contractors for transportation, and the Academy will be counting the girls as they arrive to make sure everyone's accounted for."

I nodded.

"You're going to have to push one of the witches out of the truck," Luke said.

My head snapped back. "I'm not going to push someone…"

"If you don't, there's going to be one too many witches when you get dropped at the Academy. There'll be questions."

Luke was right; there had to be one less witch in the truck so I could join. I looked down at my lap, at my small hands. I'd gained strength and muscle since I'd arrived, but I didn't know if I'd be able to push another witch my size.

"The girls will probably be so scared." Annabel looked down at her cup. "I know it's not in your nature to hurt, but you shouldn't have to push hard. She'll likely land on her feet."

"What will happen once they're out of the truck?" I asked, remembering my time spent alone in the woods, how it'd almost killed me—how it would've killed me if Luke hadn't found me.

"I'll be there," Luke said. "I'll grab her as soon as the truck pulls away and bring her into town. There, she can make some phone calls and hopefully be reunited with her family."

"Before the Coven's disremember potion takes full effect…" Annabel mumbled.

I tilted my head, looking at Annabel.

She sighed. "When the scouts pick up the witches, they administer a disremember potion to their families. It's slow acting—they don't forget their daughters all at once. The first couple of days they might forget where their daughter is for a moment before remembering, laughing the forgetfulness off. A week later, they'll be pausing as they walk by their daughter's room, trying to remember whose stuff is inside. Two weeks later, they'll be packing up their daughter's things, driving them to a donation center…and then they're just…forgotten."

That was terrible. No wonder Annabel had started tearing up as she talked about the girls in the back of the truck. She was probably imagining Emily being taken from her, then someone coming and taking all her memories of Emily away too.

Annabel waved her hand in front of her face, composing herself. "If we're quick enough, we can get the girl back to her family before any of that happens. The potion's effects are negated if the person who was supposed to be forgotten is around." She cleared her throat. "It's worth the risk to get you in, hopefully unnoticed."

They were right. This was the kindest way to lessen the number of the witches in the truck so I could join.

"Right. She'd be one of the new witches. They're just as inexperienced as she is."

I shot daggers with my eyes at Luke, and he tilted his head at me in apology.

"You're an inexperienced witch, Dafni," Annabel said, standing. "There's no way around it. You need more training."

I opened my mouth to argue. I was training outside with clouds and dew—at the stove, making potions with her.

She lowered her eyes as if she read my mind. "Actual training."

I sighed, leaning back in my seat.

"If you want to be Prime, you need to learn to act like a witch. Down in the Academy, they're cutthroat and vicious." Annabel paused, looking at me, her eyes softening. "You are none of those things."

I looked down at the off-white shirt I was wearing. It was simple—how my grandmother had raised me.

This was all happening quickly...much quicker than I thought it would. I thought I'd have time to prepare myself at least mentally for entering the Academy. I didn't know how to act like a witch, like my mother had. She'd cared for only herself and her position at the Coven. That wasn't who I wanted to be. I slumped back in my seat. I didn't want to turn out like her. Would I have to be like her, act like her, in the Academy? I didn't know if I could do that.

"You can do it, Dafni." Annabel returned to the table, her palms resting on the tabletop. I swore she could read my thoughts sometimes. "I've been watching you this past year... I've seen how much you've grown. We didn't think everything would happen so quickly, so soon, but maybe this is for the best. Sometimes the less time we have to think, the less we can overthink."

I raised my head to look at her.

"No matter what anyone says, this is your birthright." Her voice lowered. "Play the part. Play the game. Get what you came for."

I nodded. I could do this. Prime was mine. It'd always been mine. Yet my grandmother had raised me to be kind, virtuous—everything a witch wasn't. She'd known that one day, I'd be Prime, yet she'd taught me differently.

So different from my mother, who had been a mean and cruel Prime. But it had cost her. I looked down at my lap. I knew the cost. It was me. She'd forfeited a relationship with her daughter to be the Prime. And where was she now? Trapped in the freezer of an employee of her own Academy.

I wouldn't follow in her footsteps. I wouldn't make my mother's mistakes. I would have to make my own set of foot-steps—parallel to hers, but a different trail.

"Okay." It was the only thing I could say that wouldn't upset my stomach further.

———

Emily brought me the thread-worn green plaid dress I'd arrived in. After wearing the clothes the Velkans had provided me with for the past year, the material felt rough against my skin. The dress fit tighter around my body too—I'd grown stronger living here.

I stood in the kitchen wearing the dress and shoes I'd shown up in almost a year ago. The shoes' soles were thin, and the material above my toes threadlike. How had I walked for days in these?

Annabel fretted over every aspect of my appearance, wanting me to look the part of a human-born witch taken from her family and thrown into a truck.

"They pick up the girls in fancy black town cars to keep up appearances...to keep the parents believing their daughters are headed to a fancy college prep school." She smeared a bit of mud on my face, rubbing it into my skin. "Once they're far enough away, a cargo truck intercepts the town car, and the girls are thrown into the back of the truck after being injected with a tonic to suppress their magic. The ones who've already learned some about using their magic fight back for a bit before the injection takes effect." She nodded down to the mud still on her fingers.

"Why throw them in a truck together? Why suppress their magic?" I asked.

Annabel ran her muddy fingers through my hair until it looked like I'd rolled down a hill. "So they can't fight. So they feel helpless. The Coven wants complete submission from their witches, and this is the first step in getting it." She took a step back, placing her hands on my shoulders. "Just pretend you recently left your family. You don't know where you're going and you're completely disoriented." Annabel waited for my response before she tilted her head to the side. "Oh dear, you probably already know what that feels like."

She looked at the freezer before looking back at me. I was leaving my mother here, with the Velkans. I trusted them, but it still made me nervous to leave her. They didn't have water magic like me—they couldn't refreeze her with a flick of their fingers like I could. If Mother got a single paw loose from the ice, she could use her magic.

"She'll stay here, frozen," Annabel said. "You have my word."

I tucked my chin down in a nod.

"It's time to go. They'll be coming this way in the next thirty minutes," Luke said, walking into the kitchen. He'd spent all morning creating a diversion, something I hadn't been privy to.

I almost fell backward as Emily ran into me, squeezing my chest in a tight hug. She'd helped nurse me back to health. She was sweet and innocent. I hoped she stayed that way. I squeezed her back, careful not to get the dirt her mother had smeared on my skin onto her.

"I'll see you soon," I lied. It felt like the right thing to say, even though I knew it was probably untrue.

"Go, go." Annabel shooed Luke and me out of the trailer.

I left just as I had arrived, with nothing.

I turned around to see Annabel standing in the doorway of the trailer, Emily, standing next to her, watching me go.

"Oh, come here!" Annabel fluttered down the steps, coming toward me with her arms open wide. We embraced tightly; my face pressed into her chest. I breathed in deep committing her scent to memory. The trailer had become my home. All the meals shared, dishes washed, vegetables picked...

"Go, now!" Annabel said as she released me.

I looked back at Emily and the trailer, trying to commit that to memory too.

I closed my eyes and forced myself to turn around, to face my future before I got caught up in the past.

I followed Luke as he jogged away from the trailer and into

the woods. My previous time in these woods crept up on me, all those days walking without food, keeping my mother frozen in the pail. The memories sent shivers down my spine.

The woods were quiet, almost eerily so. There wasn't even a breeze. I looked above me, only seeing the green of the leaves and the brown of the branches. The trees had all twisted together, creating a complete canopy, void of any blue of the sky. I was thankful for the shade as we jogged.

The path Luke led me down was a narrow footpath full of branches that snagged my dress and rocks that I'd have a hard time maneuvering over if I were barefoot.

Sweat had already stained my underarms when we broke through the brush and into a small clearing. Luke took my forearm, pulling me across the clearing into the brush on the other side.

"Now we wait," he said. His breathing was calm, unlike my own ragged breaths.

We crouched in the brush facing the clearing that I now realized was a road. Narrow like the footpath we'd just taken, the road could fit a single car, like the one Elise and Everett and I had driven in.

Luke pointed to the road, slightly past where we currently crouched. A tree lay across the road, its trunk chopped cleanly by something sharp. "When the truck stops and the men get out to clear the tree, we move," he said. "I'll help you in the back with the other witches." He glanced up the road, looking for the truck. "Grab hold of the closest one and push her off the truck. Don't be afraid to push hard—you might only get one chance."

I nodded.

"You won't see me, but I'll grab her once the truck is gone. The other witches can't catch sight of me," he said. "They could see me around the Academy and then might start asking questions."

I nodded again, unable to form words. My mouth was dry.

The rumbling of an engine met my ears at the same time it met Luke's. I could tell by the way his body stiffened that he heard it coming. His hand met my cheek, turning my face toward his. "You can do this, Dafni. Help me. Help my family. Help yourself."

He let go of my face, not giving me anytime to reply before he turned toward the road as a white truck barreled down the road, its wheels bouncing along the rocks and gravel.

Luke grabbed my upper arm, his leg poised one in front of the other, ready to run. I mimicked his position, digging my shoes into the dirt below me. The tree Luke had brought down was big, but nothing that couldn't be moved by two strong men. We had limited time and too many unknown variables to account for. What if there were more than two men? Maybe they'd taken two trucks. Maybe the witch I pushed would fight me, maybe she'd scream and garner attention.

Negative thoughts abandoned, both of us faced the road, the engine noise growing louder as it got closer. There was no point in thinking of the what-ifs. We'd made the choice. We were here—I was ready to go. Beams of light hit the surrounding trees, illuminating the canopy of leaves we were under.

"Wait," Luke commanded.

My muscles twitched under his grasp, ready to contract at a moment's notice. The screech of the brakes squeezing the tires met my ears as the white truck barreled past us. Red lights met my eyes before the truck stopped just shy of the fallen tree. Expletives met my ears next. One word after another that I'd only heard come from my mother's mouth directed at my grandmother over my lack of "witchy-ness."

"Fucking tree in the fucking woods."

"Listening to those brats bitch for the last hour was enough; now this? I thought those injections were supposed to knock 'em out or at least subdue them... How much are we getting paid?"

"Not enough. Matilda better tip us extra this time."

"She booked us a year out. She likes us. She'll tip." The men left the truck, sliding out of their seats and walking toward the tree that had blocked their path.

Luke's grasp on my upper arm tightened. Our noses almost touched as we looked at one another. He tilted his chin in a nod before pushing off his legs, dragging me along behind him. The vehicle was a small cargo truck with a roll-up back door. Luke was right—the drivers were idiots and hadn't locked it. He easily squeezed the handle and pulled, the door rising as he slowly lifted it up. The back of the truck was dark, and it took a second for me to see the women huddled in the back. They trembled as a unit, contracting and expanding together in fear.

Luke looked over his shoulder at me. Our eyes met as they had many times before. This time his green eyes were wide with fright, different from the steady green ones I was used to.

"Push one out quick. I'll be there to make sure she's okay," he whispered before he gripped my waist, hoisting me into the truck.

I crouched, my feet meeting the bouncy floor beneath me. I had to be fast; the men would soon be done moving the log, and I didn't want to push someone out of a moving vehicle. The witch closest to the door was small, sitting with her arms wrapped around her bent legs. Taking Annabel's advice, I didn't give myself time to overthink. I grabbed hold of her upper arms, using the element of surprise and the extra strength provided by the adrenaline flowing through my body to gently push her out the back of the truck. She dropped feet first, and that, I hoped, would cause her to land on her feet.

"I'm sorry..." I whispered after her. She probably didn't hear me, but I hoped the sentiment reached her.

Against all my instincts, I didn't look out the back of the truck to see if she was okay. I had to trust that Luke would take care of her.

Reaching up, I pulled down the door, the woods slowly disappearing inch by inch until there was nothing left but a slice of daylight. A click of the handle let me know the door was closed.

The life I knew was over. I slowly turned and faced my future.

I couldn't see the girls—the human-born witches—but I could hear trembling before me. Their gulps for air and shudders against the metal frame of the truck made my insides quiver. The muscles in my legs gave out slowly, causing me to sink into the unsound wood flooring beneath me. I was in the dark. Alone. Well, not alone. I was with several other witches who breathed shallow and sharp enough that I could hear their gasps for air.

The truck rocked back and forth before the engine rumbled beneath my knees. They must've already cleared the tree. I hoped that Luke had grabbed the girl and was hidden deep within the brush by now. He'd return to Annabel and Emily and let them know that I'd made it, that I was on my way to the Academy. They'd help the girl reunite with her family.

The truck lurched forward, my body tumbling toward the group of witches along the back of the cargo box. One of them grabbed onto me, pulling me close, my body flush with theirs.

"What happened to that girl by the door?" A quiet wobbling voice met my ears. "I couldn't see."

A tremor ran through my body as my mind raced to think of an answer. "She panicked and fell," I lied.

"I wish I'd fallen out," the voice said, her body trembling against me.

I trembled along with her, my body acclimating to the rhythm of her fear.

CHAPTER ELEVEN

Dafni

THE WITCHES HUDDLED AROUND ME, ALL OF US HOLDING on to each other in support to keep us individually from being bounced around like rag dolls in the back of the truck. I wasn't sure how far we were from the Academy, how long we'd be back here, or if we had any more stops to make.

"They got you too?" a voice whispered. They were close enough to me that I could feel their breath on my cheek.

I nodded before I realized they couldn't see me in the dark. I cleared my throat. "Yeah, they got me."

"I got picked up in a black town car...I was just about to listen to my podcast when I got pulled out of the car and shoved in here," a voice said.

I looked around the ill-lighted truck trying, unsuccessfully, to see faces.

"They took all my things—my phone, my luggage," another voice said.

Annabel was right: The Coven had deceived the human-born witches.

"I feel so weak. They stuck me with something...and I can't feel my magic anymore..." a higher-pitched witch said.

Another girl whispered, "They stuck me with something too! I saw it—it was a purple liquid in a syringe."

Lobelia. It had to be the same purple concoction that Annabel sipped each day.

"My parents signed me up for an exclusive summer prep program, but this...isn't it," the girl next to me whispered. "I'm Brooke," she whispered again.

I nodded again before remembering that I needed to speak. "Dafni," I said aloud.

A chorus of "Hi's" filled the space.

The truck stayed quiet as we traveled, except for the witches' muffled sobs and yelps every time the truck's tires bounced over a rock.

The sound of the engine became softer, telling me we were moving slower. Getting closer to the Academy.

"Stop!" A muffled voice met my ears. The truck stopped. Several of the surrounding witches gasped, then paused, waiting.

It struck me when I realized what they were waiting for— their fate. They'd already succumbed to their outcome. Did they not have any fight? Were they just giving up?

Inhaling, I took in a deep breath. I'd remain strong even if no one else would. That was what a leader did.

The witches were packed in around me. From the sound of their whimpers and heavy breathing, there had to be more than six or seven. More witches than the two men who were managing the truck. Everyone around me had been lied to, brought here under false pretenses. If they used their fear and anger together as a group, they could overwhelm the men transporting us—fight and escape.

The door slid open, revealing two sweaty men with rounded bellies. The witches had gripped me throughout the ride like something that'd keep them afloat. However, when the door opened, I felt them pushing me forward, like an offering to our captors.

"We're here. Come out of the truck like good little girls, and we won't have to touch you again." The man's voice was coarse yet had a certain sliminess about it that told me he'd probably be happy to touch them again.

The witches next to me clenched my arms, holding me in front of them, trembling.

"I'll give you until the count of three to get over here, or I'm going to have to send my associate in to pull you out one by one."

The man standing next to him curled his fingers toward his palm before extending them, a smirk on his lips.

"One."

The witch behind me gasped, pushing me forward again, toward the men.

"Two."

A witch somewhere in the mass of bodies behind me cried out.

The fear of the witches behind me was contagious. I could feel it seep into my skin.

The hands around my arms tightened, the fingernails digging into my skin. These witches feared the unknown, what lay ahead of them. I already knew where I was going. I'd gotten on the truck willing to come here, to enter the Academy. There was no use in delaying the inevitable. I stood slowly, the girl behind me loosening the grip she had on my arm.

"There we go. Nice and easy." The man reached out his hands, flicking his fingers toward his palms, motioning me to keep walking toward him. The steps I took were short and tentative. I wanted to avoid him all together. I could get down from the truck myself. I didn't need his greasy hands on my body. The wood floor beneath my feet bowed, and I bent my knees to regain my balance. Behind me, the girls were rising to their feet, following my lead.

"Oh, what good girls you are. Aren't they, Steve?" The man nudged his associate, who looked disappointed he didn't get to pull the girls out of the truck with his hands.

My shoes reached the edge of the truck. The man's breath warmed my ankles as he looked up at me.

"You're filthy, aren't you?" His hands wrapped around each of my calves, holding me in place. "I'm going to help you off the truck, and then I want you to stand along the side of the truck with Steve."

I got one look at his bloodshot eyes and tried to keep my gaze anywhere but on his face.

"You got that, girl?" His grasp tightened around my legs. I looked down at him with my eyes closed, and nodded before looking away. "Come here, then."

He let go and motioned for me to lean over the edge of the truck and into his hands that grabbed me under the arms, lifting me down to the ground. As soon as my shoes touched the dirt, he pushed me toward Steve, who stood along the side of the truck. I tripped over my feet to the truck and lined up against it as he'd asked. I didn't want to give them any excuse to touch me again.

One by one, witches were lifted down and pushed toward Steve. We stood there waiting, our backs against the dirty truck. I looked down at the growing line of girls as they came around to join the line. They stood there shivering, even though it was a warm day.

The man came around from the back of the truck, pointing and counting us. "Nobody moves," he said. A tremble fluttered through the group. He disappeared around the back of the truck, the sliding door slamming closed.

We were somewhere in the middle of the woods. The trees towered over the truck, the top branches waving in the breeze that now blew along the canopy. Even though it was daytime, the light was dim enough beneath the trees that the crickets were confused, still chirping as though it was night. There were no signs, and the closest thing I could see to a road marker was a tree where a buck had rubbed his antlers and removed its bark. Down toward the ground where we stood, the air was stagnant, and I could smell the sweat coming off the girl next to me.

Stomping over to where I stood, nearest the truck cab, the man who seemed to be in charge wrapped his hand around my upper arm, squeezing it, pulling me close. "Steve, take up the back. You"—he shook me by my arm—"will lead the way."

I yanked my arm back toward me, out of his grasp.

"Oh, she's a wild one." I heard low chuckles from Steve at the back of the line. "I gotta keep an even closer eye on you."

A gasp left my lips as he grabbed me again, this time pulling my back against his chest, pushing me forward with his body.

We traveled in a line, some girls crying as we walked. The man breathed hot air against my neck. I increased my pace, trying to put some distance between our bodies. He matched me, guiding me toward a small tan house with a single door and a small square window. I almost didn't see the house, as it was covered with green leafy vines. It wasn't made of gingerbread and candy, but its size and sloping roof made it look like the witch's house from the story *Hansel and Gretel*.

Fitting.

He knocked four times on the door. After a moment, the handle turned and a woman with gray curls piled on top of her head stuck her hooked nose out the door.

"I've got eleven here for you, ma'am."

The door opened a little wider as she looked down the line of girls. Her face was blemished, spotted with raised flesh-colored bumps and marked with red sores that looked painful. "Very well. Send them in one by one."

The door shut, the woman disappearing inside the house.

"This is where we say our goodbyes," the man said. He opened the door and pushed me in.

Someone must have covered the single window on the inside, because the house was dark. I stumbled through the threshold, off balance from the man's strong push. A hand on my back adjusted my momentum slightly to the right before it left my back and my feet lost contact with the floor beneath them. I fell, my limbs flailing around me as I reached for anything that would stop me from barreling toward the ground. I found nothing but fast-moving air as my body twisted around.

Thump. My back hit something firm. My lungs contracted, wanting air that my body couldn't inhale. Flickers of black danced in my vision.

"Move out of the way, or you'll get crushed." A hand with long fingernails wrapped around my ankles and dragged me off the mat I'd landed on, pulling me through the dirt on the floor to the side of the room.

Thump. A moan followed.

A face soon appeared alongside my own—another witch, her body dragged over by the same woman with long fingernails. The girl breathed quickly, her eyes darting back and forth. We both laid there for a moment before we heard another thump.

I turned my head in time to watch another body fall from the ceiling. This time, a girl with long brown hair landed on her stomach. She didn't move until the woman grabbed her wrists and dragged her alongside both girls that'd already taken the fall.

Thump after thump, eight more bodies hit the mat and got dragged into a line along the dirt wall by the woman with long fingernails.

My body recovered enough that air could enter my lungs, and the black spots retreated from my vision. I lifted my head and sat up against the dirt wall, taking in the underground room we were in. It looked like a hole that'd been dug deep into the ground. The floors and walls were all pressed dirt that would crumble away if the woman with the fingernails drug her finger along it. An arched metal door with a complicated looking locking mechanism was the only thing in the room that wasn't dirt besides the thin mat we'd all landed on.

Our ragged breaths were the only noise that filled the space before the light from the trapdoor above us flickered for a moment before disappearing completely, the door slamming closed, leaving us in darkness. Gasps from the girls and some choked cries replaced our heavy breathing.

A warm, gritty hand found mine, weaving its fingers between my own and giving a slight squeeze. "It's me, Brooke."

I squeezed back. She pushed herself into a seated position, leaning back next to me against the crumbling dirt wall behind us.

"Let me see if I can..." Brooke brushed her fingers across my face, faltering around until she found the dirt wall next to my ear, her knuckles brushing against my skin. "I think whatever they gave us is starting to wear off..."

Pieces of dried dirt fell, tumbling down my neck and bouncing off my shoulder onto the ground where I sat. I pulled myself forward, the hand that held mine squeezing tightly.

"Here," she whispered, touching our held hands with what felt like...water. She rubbed the liquid over the outside of our hands, cleaning them, ridding them of the grime that scratched against our skin. Although the rest of my body was covered in dirt, that small part of my body felt clean, somewhat normal in a place that was anything but. I squeezed her hand clasped in mine as a thank-you.

I heard a loud *click* before the dim light of a single bulb mounted on the wall near the metal door illuminated. It wasn't a lot of light but enough that I could see Brooke's eyes next to me. They were wide, her hand gripping mine tighter with every breath she took. A breeze blew my dirty hair away from my face. Everyone looked up at the ceiling at the same time. A pair of black heeled boots slowly descended from the ceiling, floating gracefully down to the ground. The woman with the curly gray hair who'd "welcomed" us into the house before pushing us through the trapdoor used air magic to lower herself the distance that we'd all fallen.

I should've used my air magic to catch my fall, I thought. No. I was supposed to have one kind of magic—water. *Get it right, Dafni.*

The girls, except the one who'd fallen last, sat against the wall with their knees drawn up, just as I did. I looked like the other girls in muddy clothes. Their bodies were just as dirty as mine was, leaves and dirt tangled in their hair. Like Annabel had predicted, it looked like some of them had put up a fight getting into the truck.

The woman with the gray curls toed the girl who'd fallen last. She was still lying on her back, her chest rising and falling unevenly. Gray Curls shook her head before looking down the line at us. All the girls kept their chins down, staring at the ground in front of their tucked knees. Her eyes met mine, probably because I was the only one looking at her. She narrowed them, studying me before looking away.

"May I be the first to congratulate you." Gray Curls walked down the line of girls, her heels sending the dust up and around her shoes. "You're finally here, at the Academy, where you belong."

Someone sitting along the wall sniffled, their lips holding back a cry.

"The sedatives administered to get you here safely"—I had to fight to keep my eyes from rolling—"should be leaving your systems shortly."

"This wasn't what the brochure promised!"

Everyone lifted their heads to find the source of the outburst. Gray Curls's head snapped around, finding the girl who'd just spoken out of turn. She pivoted, walking two steps back the way she came, towering over the girl.

"You're lucky to be here. Witches need to be molded, trained."

The girl flinched as Gray Curls spoke, spit flying from her mouth, landing on the top of the girl's head.

"Your parents are human. They'll never understand you... and soon they'll forget all about you." She swiveled her head, looking back at the entire room. "Should you try to run..." She looked around, admiring the solid dirt walls and the closed trapdoor at the ceiling. "Should you somehow escape and make your way home, you'll find your parents will no longer recognize you. They've been administered a disremember potion. You no longer have a home, parents, or a family."

The girl who had spoken out tucked herself into an even tighter ball.

"Now all you have is the Coven." Gray Curls backed away and continued her march down the line. "You'll learn from your elders while you're here, and if you're fortunate enough... talented enough...you could become the chosen."

She raised her hand above her head, pointing to the metal framing around the arched door. The words *Become the Chosen* were written in strings of twisted metal, blending into the door. "That's what every witch wants, and what you'll have a chance to become here at the Academy."

Another witch yelled out, asking, "Where are the clothes we packed—our things?"

"*Silence!*" Gray Curls screeched. "You're lucky to be here! I can tell your human parents didn't teach you magic *or* manners—thankfully, the Academy will instill both."

The room was silent once again. Gray Curls smoothed the hair on the side of her head before continuing. "Now, this is a special year. Years like this only come once a generation and only when we have a male witch come of age. You all are lucky to be here, but all of you will also be at a disadvantage. There are other young human-born witches who have been here at the Academy for several years and witches born from magical parents who have been training and waiting for this moment since they were born. They'll be better prepared than you and ready for the evaluations that begin in a few weeks."

I looked over at Brooke, who stared at Gray Curls with her mouth open.

"Even more of a reason you should be listening to my every word—following the instruction your elders are giving you. If you want a chance at becoming the chosen, it will take fortitude, power, and the aptitude to know when to listen." Her eyelids partially closed as her glaring eyes made their way around the room, scanning our faces.

"So...we're not going to be taking college prep classes?" one of the witches asked.

"Enough!" Gray Curls snapped.

A collective gasp echoed across the room.

"When you walk through the door, there will be no more whining, no more complaining. You're here to train at the Academy and serve the Coven. You'll be nothing but grateful you're here. This is an opportunity to become the chosen. You don't know how lucky you are."

Gray Curls turned to the witch with long fingernails, who stood on the opposite side of the rounded room with her arms crossed, her claws tapping her arm in a steady rhythm. "Are we ready?"

Fingernails nodded once before walking toward the metal door and entering a combination of numbers into the keypad, her nails clicking with every key strike. The door took a moment to disengage all the locks inside it. With a single black boot, she propped the door open, crossing her arms in front of her body again.

"Strip." Gray Curls gave the command casually.

I looked down the line of girls, who looked just as confused as I felt.

She sighed before looking back at Fingernails. "Every year I forget they're imbeciles when they arrive." Her boots clunked along the dirt floor before she stopped in front of the girl who had challenged her earlier. "Maybe if I show you, you'll understand."

Gray Curls spun the girl around by her shoulders, so her back was to her. Taking the collar of her pale yellow dress between her two hands, she tore it down her back, the thin fabric shredding easily. The girl covered her mouth with her hands, keeping her shriek muffled.

"Take off your dirty clothes," Gray Curls commanded, stepping back and waiting.

The surrounding girls started pulling their clothes off slowly.

"Speed it up! All of it off! I don't want any of the filth you brought with you to make its way into the Academy."

Everyone moved faster, stripping the clothing from their bodies, leaving puddles of worn clothing in front of them. I followed suit, letting the faded green dress fall to my feet, peeling the underwear off and letting it fall on top of the dress. I stood like the other girls, covering myself the best I could with my two hands.

When everyone had undressed, shaking, not from the cold but from being uncomfortable and scared, Gray Curls motioned to me to walk through the metal door.

"We've got showers and uniforms."

The promise of clothes had the rest of the girls walking toward the door, pressuring me to lead the way. The arched door was short enough that I had to duck my head to walk through it. Tiled floors and walls replaced the dirt floor we'd just exited, the cool tile numbing my feet. Every few steps, I walked over a small drain on the floor. When I met the tiled wall on the far side of the room, I stopped and turned around, watching the girls line up on the wall, their backs to the tile.

Fingernails walked into the narrow room, bending down to pick up a black hose attached to a spigot on the opposite wall. It was finally light enough to see her features. Like Gray Curls, her face was covered in a mix of sores and warts, her nose long and bulbous at the tip.

I braced myself as she twisted the knob and squeezed the nozzle. Jets of ice-cold water hit my skin. The girls screamed as the spray hit them, crouching over, trying to avoid the icy water. Did they not have hot water in the Coven? Even the Velkans' trailer had tepid water—something I'd become used to living there. This was just plain torture.

I glanced up at Fingernails, manning the hose, the smile on

her face told me she was enjoying spraying young witches with cold water.

They couldn't treat us like this, like we were nothing more than farm animals. Even the animals at my grandmother's cottage got bathed with water warmed by the sun. This was inhumane, completely unnecessary. Was this what it was going to be like here? The seasoned witches preying on those who were new and weaker?

Everyone around me huddled in a cluster, struggling to get to the middle of the group, to get protection from the jets of cold water.

Being left on the outside of the group, Fingernails aimed the hose at me, and I winced each time the stream of water hit my skin. I found myself cowering with the other witches, their fear infectious.

A jet of water hit me directly in my face. I coughed, spitting out the water that had gone up my nose. It was enough to snap me out of whatever feeling of fear I'd absorbed from the witches around me—this wasn't right. Annabel had wanted to do something to stop this, to end the torment the human-born witches at the Academy went through. She wasn't able to do anything because she needed to protect her children.

But me? I could do something. I wasn't about to stand here and let Fingernails torment us. The witches next to me shook, bracing themselves for the next cold spray. No one else was doing anything besides recoiling and trembling together, waiting for the cruelty to stop. Staying part of this group, cowering in fear beside them, wasn't who I wanted to be.

I was only one witch, but I could take up space with my magic.

CHAPTER TWELVE

Dafni

I EXTENDED MY INDEX AND MIDDLE FINGERS, KEEPING MY
hand low at my hip. I sent my magic toward the stream of
water, right where it exited the hose. Flicking my fingers up, I
directed the stream the same way.

Fingernails shrieked as the cold water sprayed up her nose.

I bit my tongue, hard enough that an iron taste coated my
mouth, trying not to give myself away by smiling.

"You're all a bunch of heathens!" Her screech ricocheted
off the tiled walls and into our ears. I bit my tongue harder, still
trying not to smile. She reached behind her, turning the knob
further to the left, the water pressure increasing. We all braced
ourselves against each another.

Fingernails was thorough, not stopping until everyone was
drenched, shivering together in a group trying to find warmth. I

huddled with the other girls, Brooke once again finding my hand.

"Ladies," Gray Curls said from the doorway we'd walked through to enter the shower room. She was still dry, probably having hid back in the dirt room away from the water. "We have towels and uniforms in the next room. Please dress quickly, and a senior student will lead you to your dormitories." Gray Curls's heeled boots clicked past our huddled mass as she walked the narrow room, using a key she pulled from her pocket to unlock the next door on the opposite side of the room as the one we'd entered. This door was also metal, although rusted. "We will give you tonight to acclimate. Come morning, you'll be training with the witches here in this room." She paused as we took time to look around at each other. "There are only a few weeks until the first evaluation."

Gray Curls opened the door, and warm light from the next room flowed into the shower room, a stark contrast to the bright fluorescent lights that reflected off the tile. It almost looked welcoming. Our huddled group walked together toward the next room, separating when we got to the doorway that only allowed one body at a time. A long wooden bench stood in the center of the room, with eleven bundles of clothing and white towels spaced out evenly along it. The sight of clothes and towels had the witches rushing, drying their icy bodies and covering them.

I dried my body, squeezing out my dripping hair with the fluffy towel. The uniform left for us had more pieces than I was used to. White underwear and a white bra. A green plaid skirt and a pressed white button-up shirt. There was even a dark-green sweater, the color of the woods in summer, with a patch sewn on the left side of the chest. I ran my fingertips over the patch, admiring the stitch work. It was intricate, the letters *BTC* stitched in gold thread. *Become the Chosen.* Their motto...

their creed. Annabel hadn't fully conveyed to me their devotion to becoming the chosen partner of the male witch. Underneath the bench stood a pair of pointed-toe ankle boots with a small heel that matched Gray Curls's.

I could already tell that the shirt was going to be too big, even before I pulled it over my head. The second I put it on, the shirt swallowed my body—the hem falling just above my knees. There was no way I was going to ask for a different size. Gray Curls wasn't going to go out of her way to make sure I had an appropriately sized shirt, and I didn't need to call any more attention to myself—I'd probably already pushed my luck with the water stunt I pulled with Fingernails. The green plaid skirt had a drawstring on the inside waistband, and after I tucked the bottom of my long shirt inside, I pulled it tight. I drew my sweater over the top of my shirt, hiding the way the baggy shirt hung on my body.

Most of the girls got dressed before me, many of them trying to tame their hair with their fingers. I'd only finished pulling my boots on my feet before a wooden door opened on the opposite side of the room from which we entered. A witch, maybe a few years older than me, stood there, taking in the eleven girls in the room. The marks on her face weren't as unsightly as the ones on Gray Curls or Fingernails, but the sores were there. Some of them looked to be oozing yellow pus. The tip of her nose looked disproportionate to the rest of her face, like just that small part of her nose was growing faster. She wore the same uniform as us, although she'd ditched her sweater and unbuttoned the top of her shirt, so the swell of her breasts was visible.

"What are you staring at?" Her sharp voice snapped me out of my daze.

I looked away as fast as I could. *Stop attracting attention, Dafni.*

The girl stopped glaring at me and looked around the chamber. "Let's go human-borns."

The witches followed her instructions, making a line in front of the wooden door where she stood.

"I'll take your names and magic type before you enter the Academy," Gray Curls said, walking over to where the senior witch waited, producing a pad of paper and a pen from the pocket of her dress. "State your first and last name clearly, along with your magic type." She looked down the line, and I thought for a moment she'd stopped to stare at me. "The choices are *earth*, *water*, or *air*—no funny business."

Brooke grabbed my hand again and pulled us to the back of the line. The witches moved slowly, Gray Curls often yelling, "Speak up!" at those whose voices trembled.

"Name?" Gray Curls stepped in front of Brooke and me before we could follow the rest of the group into the narrow tunnel that led ahead.

"Brooke Sukedi, earth magic."

"And you?" Gray Curls looked at me, waiting for my name.

"Dafni Sarr—" I snapped my lips shut before another syllable could escape. *That* name was dangerous here. That name would bring attention to who I was, who I came from.

Her pen stopped scratching on the paper, her eyes raised to investigate mine.

"Sarrenti." It spilled off my tongue, the ending sound worryingly similar to Brooke's.

Gray Curls stared at me for a moment before her eyes returned to her pad of paper, finishing scratching my fake last name onto the page.

"Water magic," I said.

"Go ahead." She tilted her head toward the tunnel.

Brooke and I had to let our hands fall apart to walk through the narrow twisting hallways the senior witch led us through.

The group sounded like a herd of hooved animals, our heels clicking along the wooden floor beneath us.

We wove through several twists and turns, walking in a single line. The senior witch walked quickly as we all tried to keep up while still taking in our surroundings. The dim lighting of the tunnel gradually became brighter the farther we walked, and before long, we saw the literal light at the end of the tunnel—a giant dome-shaped room buzzing with activity.

It wasn't until I'd completely exited the tunnel that I could see the scale of the room. It was nothing like I'd imagined in my head from Luke's penciled description. My mouth fell open as I looked up and around the space. All of this was hiding here...underground.

The dome resembled more of an arena, like the ones from my grandmother's bedtime stories involving Roman gladiators and Commodus, the mad emperor. But this wasn't Ancient Rome. This was the Coven—an arena run by my mother, who used the witches as her personal gladiators. The circular space was immense, with witches mingling, cackling, and staring at us. Several couches and tables with chairs made the space look like a casual social area.

Looking up, I saw two levels above us wrapping around the entire dome. Witches hung over the metal railings, gazing down at the goings-on below. They stared at us, no smiles on their faces. Spaced every few feet behind the railings were doors with numbers on them. These were the dorms. There looked to be two levels of rooms, along with the ones on the main floor.

We were below the dirt. That much was obvious from the way we'd fallen through the trapdoor onto the floor earlier. There was a pentagon-shaped window at the tip of the domed ceiling letting in some natural light, but the rest of the light came from the lanterns mounted to the walls around the space.

There were no flickering flames but light bulbs. They had electricity down here, I realized with surprise.

"These are the dormitories," the senior witch said. Her voice was monotone and rushed. She seemed bored with us already. "The classrooms are through there." She pointed to a set of wooden double doors a quarter of the way around the circle from us. "And so is the Coven. You can go into the classrooms but not the Coven grounds."

She turned and walked across the dome, the witches standing around moved out of her way. We followed, unsure of what we should be doing.

"This is where meals are served." She motioned to the silver metal accordion door that was closed atop a white counter. Her boots clicked as she took a step closer to our group. We froze. She took another step toward us. "Don't bother trying to be friends with any of us. We aren't like you. We were born from witches. Real witches with important bloodlines. You were born from weak humans."

I looked around at the witches standing around, all of them stopping to stare. They weren't like us. Our skin was clear and smooth, our noses in proportion to our faces. Their features were grotesque, noses all mishappen and skin marked and bumpy.

Her voice was a ragged whisper. "Your kind never lasts long." With a lift of her upper lip, she revealed her teeth dripping with green poison.

I retreated, backing up into Brooke. I closed my lips. Another reminder I didn't have poison.

"Pair up!" she shouted, startling us as she switched tones.

I looked behind me at Brooke, who instantly grabbed my hand. I didn't know what we were pairing up for, but she'd already been there for me once, pulling water from the soil to wash our hands. The eleven of us spread apart in pairs of two.

A smaller witch, with short ringlets that spiraled down to her chin, stood partnerless because of the odd number of girls.

"Go with them," the senior witch directed the spiraled hair girl, pointing to Brooke and me. Ringlets kept her eyes to the floor as she toed over to us, standing nearby. "Follow me to the dorms."

The senior witch brought us to a set of spiral stairs that led us up to the second story of the dome. My feet hurt from walking so far in heeled boots. I wasn't used to the confinement of this type of shoe. After the first set of stairs, she led us up another spiral staircase, which brought us up to the third story.

"Human-borns are on the third level." She led the way, her heels clicking on each of the metal treads.

The senior witch used the toe of her black boot to kick each dorm open before pushing a pair inside, letting the door slam behind them. *So much for a welcome home.* After the fourth door slammed shut, she turned to the three of us before opening the door to the next dorm. She glanced around the room before ushering us in. "I guess this'll have to do."

The door slammed behind us, leaving us in the dark room. There were no windows. I reached out for a wall, hoping to find a light. My fingers found a knob in the wall that I pushed up, fluorescent lighting illuminated the room. Ugh. I immediately bent over, covering my eyes.

The squeak of metal on metal made me open my eyes. Ringlets had climbed to the top bunk of the only set of bunk beds in the room. Save for a wardrobe pushed into the corner of the room and an open door with a small shower, toilet, and pedestal sink, it was the only sleeping space in the room. She sat on the bed, laying her claim, gazing down at Brooke and me, as if daring us to challenge her.

"Are you okay sharing a bed?" Brooke asked. It looked like I didn't have a choice. Suddenly, I missed the bed at Annabel's house and the privacy the room had provided me.

I took a breath before exhaling out my nose. This was temporary, part of the plan. The sooner I figured out the Academy and took my place as Prime, the sooner I'd be in much more comfortable accommodations.

"I mean, I can sleep on the floor..." Brooke looked at the dirt floor we were standing on and cringed.

"No, I'm fine sharing a bed," I said. "I've shared one with my grandmother my whole life."

Her shoulders dropped in what looked like relief.

"Thanks for helping me back there—that thing with the water," I said.

"It's no problem. I can pull water from the soil with my earth magic. It was nothing." Brooke looked around the windowless room. It was damp and smelled like the cottage before we aired it out each spring. "We've got to help each other out, right?" She made her way to the bottom bunk, sitting on the thin mattress. "We're all each other's got now."

I looked down at my feet. It was true—I didn't have anyone here at the Academy. "Yeah," I whispered.

"Did you see the way they look—their faces?" Brooke asked.

They looked like my mother had, their faces disfigured, and their skin broken. I nodded as Brooke shivered, closing her eyes and shaking her head.

Do all witches look like that? I wondered.

I only had Matilda and Grandmother as references. Through her visits over the years, my mother, Matilda, had begun to look different—her nose growing wider and her skin breaking out in different bumps. Grandmother hadn't ever looked that way. Her skin, although wrinkled, had stayed clear of blemishes. I tried to suppress a shiver, my hands coming up to my face, my fingers feeling the smooth skin of my cheeks and nose.

Brooke sighed, sitting on the bed, testing its bounce. "I'm a quiet sleeper. I don't move much."

"Me either," I said. My eyes glanced up to Ringlets, who was still sitting on the top bunk, staring at us. "What's your name?" I asked.

She looked around the room like I was asking someone else before she answered. "Petunia."

A muffled bell rang outside of our room. "Dinner?" Brooke asked.

Must be. I opened the door to our dorm, peeking my head out. A line of witches on the bottom floor of the dome had already formed a line at the counter with the accordion door.

"We'd better get in line," I said.

CHAPTER THIRTEEN

Dafni

"You were recruited just in time!" the instructor, who'd proudly introduced herself as Arcana, exclaimed, clapping her hands as she stood in front of the eleven of us "recruited" witches. She sat on a metal rusted desk in the front of the classroom. With bricked walls, dirt floors, and no windows, this was unlike any classroom I'd ever imagined being in.

We all sat on benches without desks in front of us. There were no books, no pencils or papers, but there were posters on the wall. Some depicted proper body form to have when using your magic. Others had warnings not to practice magic on others. *An Untrained Witch is a Dangerous Witch* was printed with red ink on the bottom of one.

This morning, the other witches at the Academy seemed to group up with the witches of their own magic, heading toward separate classrooms along the long hallway outside the dome where we ate meals and slept in our dorms. The eleven of us new witches were rounded up, regardless of our magic, brought into an empty classroom, and given Arcana to teach us. She was the only one who seemed excited to be here.

"We don't have much time—only weeks before the first evaluations. My lovely earth witches will be competing first for the chance to be chosen by young Gideon!" Arcana clapped again, looking at our faces.

Brooke, an earth witch, trembled next to me, her eyes on her lap. "I'm going to throw up," she whispered.

I took her hand and squeezed it just as she had squeezed mine in the truck.

"We've got a few weeks to figure everything out," I whispered back.

"I'm sure you've seen him around..." Arcana wiggled her eyebrows at the group. "He's so young and *handsome.*"

She looked like every other witch down here. Her nose had grown, its tip now a bulb, and her skin was mottled by growths and bumps.

"I have only a few weeks to get you ladies into fighting shape! We will work hard. We will harness your powers. Who knows, maybe one of you newcomers could win Gideon!" Her eyes twinkled at the prospect. "Let's start with all of you showing me what you know."

Arcana grabbed hold of the witch nearest her and pulled her up in front of the class.

The girl shook standing in front of everyone.

"What kind of magic are you?" she asked.

I strained to hear her response.

The witch spoke so quietly I couldn't hear anything before Arcana shouted, "Me too!" clapping her hands. "Oh, I have just the thing." She walked around the desk, opening and closing drawers until she found what she was looking for. Bringing the small clay pot around the desk, she held it up to show the witch its contents before setting the pot down on the desk. "Let's see some earth magic!"

Brooke squeezed my hand tightly. I knew as an earth magic, she was watching this closely. Now that everyone in the room knew earth witches would be the first to compete, the tension between us witches was palpable. It felt real. We weren't just the new group of human-born witches, we were being pitted against each other—forced to work against each other to win the affection of some supposedly *handsome* male witch.

The witch at the front of the room peered down into the pot, extending her index and middle fingers toward what was inside. I held my breath as the pot wobbled back and forth for a moment before the witch lowered both her hands to her thighs, bending over to catch her breath.

Arcana leaned over the top of the desk looking into the pot. The smile that had been plastered on her face since we'd arrived dropped.

"Oh, dear. I thought you'd at least sprout something small, maybe something with leaves." Arcana picked up the pot, shaking the contents. "You've separated the pebbles from the soil. I guess that's something..."

The witch who'd just performed looked as if she were about to burst into tears.

"Sit, sit!" Arcana ordered.

The witch ran back to her seat, her hands covering her face.

Arcana scanned the room. "Let's get an air magic up here."

All the air magic witches immediately looked to their laps, giving themselves away. Arcana grabbed hold of a witch and pulled her from the bench to the front of the classroom.

I immediately recognized her, her ringlets—Petunia. She stood next to Arcana, her knees straight and her arms at her side. She gazed above the heads of the other witches, staring at the wall in the back of the room. Her ringlets vibrated—she was shaking.

"What should we have you do...what should you do..." Arcana looked around the room. "Aha!" She walked around the desk, opening and closing drawers once again before she pulled out a single white taper candle in one hand and a book of matches in the other. She put the middle of the candle between her teeth, before she used both hands to strike a match against the box. Once the candle was lit, she shook the match flame out and dropped both the smoking match and box onto the dirt floor. Arcana took the lit candle from her lips and turned it upright, the tip of the flame pointed toward the ceiling. She walked past the two rows of benches to the back of the room, meeting Petunia's stare. Raising the candle up above her head, high into the air, she directed Petunia to blow out the flame.

Petunia slowly raised her arm, pointing two fingers at the candle. Her arm moved up and down as the nerves she was feeling traveled down her arm, interfering with her aim. The witches on the benches ducked down to avoid getting hit by her air magic. Brooke and I bent down together, holding hands, keeping an eye on Petunia. She closed one of her eyes and used her free hand to steady her arm. I felt the curls on the top of my head move as the wind from Petunia's fingers traveled toward the flame.

Arcana's entire hand moved backward as the flame went out. A smile instantly lit up her face. "Very good! Very good! We have something to work with!" She made her way back to the front of the room, patting Petunia on her back in congratulations.

At first, Petunia simply stared up behind us, where the lit candle had been. Then the shock on her face slowly morphed into something sharper, darker. Her shoulders straightened, and a small smirk appeared on her face.

"What's your name?" Arcana asked.

"Petunia Fox," she said loudly, this time looking at the witches on the benches in their eyes instead of staring at the back of the room.

"Good. I look forward to working with you, Petunia," Arcana said.

Petunia walked back to her seat, still smirking, with her chin tilted up in the air.

"Now we need a water magic..." Arcana clicked her tongue as she looked around the room. If there was any time I'd wished I didn't have red hair, it was now. It made me stick out. "You, there—with the red hair."

Of course.

I stood and walked to the front of the room, tucking my hands into the pockets of my sweater so no one could see how my fingers fidgeted.

"Name?" Arcana asked.

"Dafni Sarr—" I paused for a moment. *Get it right, Dafni.* "Sarrenti."

"Water magic?" she asked.

I nodded.

"I'm just so good at my job!" Arcana exclaimed as she once again went around the desk and dug through the drawers. Her lack of preparedness showed otherwise, but I kept my mouth sealed shut. Right now, I needed to lie low. Learn.

"Yes!" She pulled a clear glass from one of the drawers and walked over to the wall, her hand running along the brick until she found a spot where a brick had fallen. Pressing her fingers into the dirt, she raised the glass to the wall, smiling as she pulled moisture, in the form of water, into the glass. When the glass was half full, she returned to the desk setting the glass on top.

"Freeze it," she directed, pointing toward the glass of water.

I looked at the glass. This was easy. I'd been freezing liquids under the tutelage of my grandmother for years. She'd had me freeze water and then milk daily until I'd mastered the skill. I was apprehensive, not because I couldn't do it, but because I didn't know how much of my powers I should show, both to the other witches and to Arcana, who would surely report back to the other instructors.

I looked out into the crowd. Brooke locked eyes with me, nodding in encouragement.

Petunia's ringlets moved, and I turned to find her tilting her head with her beady eyes staring at me and a smirk on her face that I could tell wasn't meant for encouragement.

What was it with her? She'd been weird since we'd arrived. Weren't we all suffering together? I knew the Academy wanted us to compete for Gideon, but I didn't think there'd already be rivalries among us.

Girls—women—witches needed to stick together.

Petunia had been the only one to succeed so far. Part of me wanted to hold back, stay in the shadows. If I didn't make a splash, no one would consider who I was—my lineage. The other part of me wanted to best her, to show her what power I had, wipe that smug smile off her face.

I focused on the glass sitting atop the desk. My magic tingled down my arm and flowed to the tips of my fingers. I pointed my index and middle fingers at the glass, using my control of my magic to freeze the water just enough before I pulled back.

Immediately after, I tucked my fingers back into my pocket, rubbing my fingertips against the fabric, begging the magic that wanted to exit to retreat.

Arcana walked over, rubbing the pads of her fingers against the smooth outside of the glass. "No frost..." she murmured. "Incredible."

I looked back out at my classmates to see Brooke smiling at me, while Petunia, I couldn't help but notice, appeared to be seething.

Looking back at the glass, I began questioning myself. Had I done too much? Should I have frozen the water, made it expand so much that the glass shattered?

Arcana started clapping.

I looked up at the dirt ceiling, wishing it'd collapse and bury me.

"We have another powerful witch!" she crowed as she escorted me back to my seat.

Brooke grabbed my hand again, squeezing it hard. We met eyes, exchanging tight smiles.

"I screwed up," I whispered.

"You did great," she whispered back.

I felt someone's stare and turned to find Petunia sitting on the bench behind me, glaring at me.

Brooke followed my stare and physically grimaced before she patted the top of our clasped hands.

Whoosh. A breeze tickled my nose.

I stirred, my mind groggy from sleep.

Click. A sound...like a door closing came from somewhere in the room.

Opening my eyes, I looked up above me. The mattress didn't have a Petunia-shaped bulge. *Where is she?* I sat up. Brooke tensed next to me, the sheet pulled from her body as I sat. Tugging the sheet to cover her back up, I blinked my eyes, scanning the room.

It was too dark to see anything, and now it was quiet, the air still.

Maybe what I'd felt and heard had been a dream. Arcana had been working us hard for the past week. After she'd separated us into groups based on our magic, she'd begun drilling us. The water magics had to brew the same potion over and over again until everyone got it right. The wind magics sent objects flying across the room, Arcana demanding they fly with enough force that they dent the wall on impact. Our instructor was the most frustrated with the earth magics. Only in the last few days had she given up hope of them sprouting anything green.

Whoosh.

The breeze was back.

I squinted, begging my eyes to adjust. There was a shadow near the door of the room—a shadow the size of a body with its arm extended in front of it.

"Petunia?" I whispered.

There was a gasp. Then more silence. What was she doing?

"I know it's you, Petunia," I said.

She didn't say anything. She might've even been holding her breath.

"What are you doing up in the middle of the night?" I asked.

It was quiet, but I heard her voice. "You wouldn't understand."

"What do you mean?"

"Not everyone can be perfect like you."

I stilled for a moment. I was far from perfect.

"I'm not—"

"Just go to sleep, Dafni," Petunia spat, the bed shaking as

she climbed to the top bunk. The Petunia-sized mattress bulge returned and moved as she tossed and turned, trying to get comfortable. It seemed like she'd been practicing her magic, pushing the wardrobe door closed with the wind she was creating.

I settled back into bed, pulling the blanket up over my head. I was almost asleep before she started whispering.

"This is my chance. I'm a better witch, more powerful... soon they'll see it."

———

I tied my boots tight; it was the only way I could walk in the heel without rolling my ankle. Petunia had left early for breakfast, and Brooke was still walking around with sleep in her eyes, searching for her plaid skirt. I'd have to meet Brooke at class—I couldn't afford to be late, have that attention on me. So far, I'd been able to get by undetected, the other witches none the wiser about my lineage.

Walking through the dome, I passed by witches eating breakfast, pieces of their conversations floating around the open space. Everyone was talking about the upcoming evaluations with a certain level of...excitement. Was this something they really wanted to do? Compete for a man? It all seemed silly.

"I can't wait for the earth task."

"I've heard anything goes—you can do whatever you need to do to win."

"Oh, I'm finally going to be able to take out Merideth without getting in trouble."

After living here for over a week, I'd come to understand there was a certain level of boredom in the Academy. Witches were expected to attend class, eat, and sleep. There was little else besides gossip for entertainment.

"I wish Gideon was around more."

The mention of Gideon caught my attention.

"Yeah, where does he hide?"

Oomph!

"Ow!"

A witch lay on her stomach on the floor in front of me.

I took several steps back, rubbing my shoulder where I'd hit her while I'd been eavesdropping.

The witch lifted her head, turning around, her mouth open, teeth dripping with poison.

"I'm sorry!" I called out holding my palms up in front of me.

"You *heathen!*" she screeched, pushing herself into a seated position. The index finger of the hand she was holding in her lap was bent at an unnatural angle. "You made me fall! You broke my finger—the one my magic flows through!" The witch looked down at her hand, her face growing even paler than it already was. "I won't be able to compete...the evaluations... I'm an earth magic...the first to compete..."

"I'm sure there's something the Academy can do," I stammered. "A potion, or maybe a doctor could reset it..."

The witch stopped spiraling, tilted her head back and cackled. "Do you, little human-born, think the Academy or the Coven cares about us?" She took a step toward me, her poison still flowing from her gums.

Instinctively, I took a step back.

"They don't waste resources on us. There are no doctors here. Every resource at the Academy is used for instruction. We don't get anything unless it is for training—to make us more powerful."

"Then shouldn't they fix your finger? You can't train without it."

The witch laughed again, this time while staring at me. It

made it so much more uncomfortable. "It's cute that you still think they care about us. I'm just one witch in the entire Academy. I'm disposable—" She pointed her finger at my chest. "*Just.*" Her long nail pierced the fabric of my white button up shirt. "*Like.*" She pushed harder. "*You.*"

A collective gasp echoed around the dome, and everyone, including the witch with her fingernail imbedded in my skin, turned to look.

At him.

I could only see the back of his head from where he stood on the opposite side of the dome. His black hair was a messy—in a way that told me he'd styled it with his fingers.

Almost immediately, I lost sight of him as witches flocked from all parts of the Academy to see him. They all talked at once, calling out to him, pushing each other to get closer. The mob moved and shifted together—one side being pushed, the witches stepping back and then the same thing on the other side. It took me a moment to realize that it was *him* causing the mob to move. He was trying to get out—trapped, drowning in attention he didn't want.

Gideon was just like every witch here, only he was trapped in a way the other witches weren't. No wonder he hid.

CHAPTER FOURTEEN

Dafni

THERE WERE THREE OTHER WATER MAGICS IN OUR SMALL group of new witches. We had a work bench to ourselves, four cauldrons and burners sitting on top. It was our little potion station—with ingredients in glass bottles on the shelves beneath the counter.

To say things were going well...would be a lie. Arcana drilled the water magics, having us make the same potion over and over again until everyone got it right. If one witch messed up one step, we all had to start over.

Suffice it to say, we almost never got to the point of a finished potion. Everything had to be measured accurately, added correctly, and mixed the right way. How Arcana paid attention to everyone in the room so closely, especially when she was also monitoring air and earth magics, I'd never understand.

However, today was different. Today we were making a love potion—a simple one—and the four of us had yet to mess up. We'd taken our time measuring. We'd sprinkled in dried ingredients and poured liquid with accuracy. Our stirring speed had been steady. Not too fast and not too slow.

I'd assisted my grandmother many times making love potions for my mother to use at the Coven. I tried to match pace with everyone—tried not to go too fast, seem too knowledgeable, but I hadn't needed to pay as close of attention to my love potion as the other witches who watched every bubble break with bated breath.

Tucked between the cauldron in front of me and my stomach, I mixed a healing potion that didn't need to brew over a flame for the witch I'd pushed over. If the Academy wasn't going to help her, I knew I could.

It was a simple potion, one that my grandmother had quickly mixed up when I'd returned to the cottage one day with a skinned knee and once a broken pinkie toe. The potion helped with pain and promoted healing. It wasn't an instant fix, but it would help her body heal.

When Arcana wasn't paying attention to the water magics, I corked the tube and shook the liquid, mixing the potion together. I tucked the tube between my breasts, letting the curved bottom sit on the bottom of my bra. Readjusting my shirt, I continued stirring my love potion—no one any the wiser. Maybe if I gave the witch a healing potion, she'd forgive me for injuring her. I didn't need enemies here.

Petunia, on the other hand, didn't seem to care about making friends. In fact, it seemed like she *wanted* enemies. I'd watched as she'd used her air magic to blow her fellow air witch's items off course. She'd even pointed her air magic at the ground, blowing dirt into the eyes of the earth witches that were crouched down, begging the dirt for a plant to sprout.

Arcana stopped lecturing one of the earth witches who'd gotten dirt in her eyes as soon as she saw an older man with a white mustache standing in the doorway.

"Robinson," she said, her voice syrupy as she stepped close enough to him to smell what he'd had for breakfast. "To what do we owe the pleasure?"

The man looked around the room, taking his time to look at each of us. "I've come to see the new witches, see how their preparations are coming for the evaluations."

"Yes, yes." Arcana ushered him further into the room. "We are working hard." She paused looking at all of us staring at her. *"Do something!"* she shouted.

All of us looked down and began practicing our magic in full force.

"Very good," Robinson said.

I looked up to find him staring at Petunia. She had three rocks the size of her fist spinning around her. The other air magic witches backed away as to not get struck.

Petunia smiled, all her teeth showing as she flicked her fingers, making the rocks spin faster.

Robinson clapped his hands as his eyes circled in their sockets following the spinning stones. "She's a powerful one," I heard him say to Arcana.

The water magic witch next to me yelped before ducking below the workbench. I leaned back just in time to dodge one of Petunia's rocks that'd come flying toward us. The rock arced in the air, ending its journey in my love potion. I hadn't backed far enough away to avoid the splash that followed the end of its flight. The hot liquid covered the entire front of my shirt, my face dripping with the pink potion. I used my fingers to wipe my eyes, blinking several times until I could see.

"Dafni!" Arcana yelled from where she stood with Robinson.

I licked my lips before wiping my mouth with the clean back of my hand.

"You're a mess! Return to your dorm and change."

I locked eyes with Brooke, who grimaced, and then with Petunia, who gave an overexaggerated shrug, as if she had no idea what happened. Behind her, two other witches were barely on their feet, doubled over, hit by the other two rocks Petunia had been spinning.

"Water magics, start over!" I heard Arcana shout as I left the classroom.

CHAPTER FIFTEEN

Gideon

My back hurt. There was no way to reach this spot behind the electrical box without being a serious contortionist. It was dark in the closet, the only light coming from the flashlight I'd brought in to help me see. I'd left it lying on the dusty floor, the light directed at the brick wall where it connected to the floor with flaky mortar. I held a piece of white paper over the top of the brick in one hand, a piece of black chalk in the other. The chalk I held on its side, using the long, straight edge to rub against the paper. Slowly, white letters appeared surrounded by the black chalk. *If only I can hold this position long enough to get every letter.*

This was the third etched word I'd found around the Academy's brick walls. The first word, *alloco*, I'd found when I was a child in one of the Academy's bathroom stalls. I'd rubbed those letters onto a small piece of paper like I did this one—standing on the shaky lid of the tank to reach the etching.

My eyes blinked, trying to rid themselves of the dust that blew up into them from my exhaling so near to the dusty floor. I picked up the paper, seeing I had two more letters left to rub. *Only a little bit more.*

I collected these unreadable words and carried the papers they were rubbed onto in my pocket while searching for the next word. They seemed to be written in some sort of foreign language. Over the years, I'd learned to make sure I always had extra pieces of paper and black chalk in my pocket for rare occasions like this.

I'd found three words throughout my life here at the Academy. The first one at age ten, then at sixteen, and now at twenty. I never knew when I would find one—often going years between sightings. But when I found one of these foreign words, it was like discovering buried treasure.

I stood, stretching my back so my muscles didn't seize up from the way I had to bend over to reach the brick. This word was a lucky find. If I hadn't been in the closet looking for cleaning rags—I wasn't going to let one of the Coven's nosy witches come in and clean my room—I would've never stumbled across it.

Bending back over the electrical box, I moved the wires out of my way before trying to replace the paper, lining up the letters I'd already rubbed onto it so I could continue. As I maneuvered my body, my foot accidentally kicked the flashlight to the left. The light flashed against the metal electrical box that half my body was squeezed behind.

My eyes blinked again. This time because of what I saw in the reflection of the metal.

Dark rings under my eyes. Veins that looked like black ink that dripped from those rings down my cheeks. No amount of scrubbing, of scouring, could rid my skin of the horror that grew bigger and darker each year I lived here.

I wasn't attractive, but neither were the other witches. Everyone who'd spent time here at the Coven and the Academy were affected—the men with dark rings below their eyes. The female witches' skin produced sores and warts, and their noses grew bulbs at their tips. I'd watched year after year of human-born witches entering the Academy with unblemished skin and small button noses, only for them to become infected...inflicted with whatever was causing the horror on our faces. Even Robinson, who'd previously spent little time underground, grew darker around the eyes the longer he stayed here, and with Matilda absent, he'd been around a lot more.

There was something wrong, something diseased causing this deformation. Maybe it was the sunshine or the fresh air that kept their skin clear. It wouldn't surprise me. Down here was just as ugly and drab as our faces.

I had to get out.

I liked to tease myself, or maybe I liked to torture myself, making up stories that maybe...just maybe these words that I couldn't read meant *something*. That maybe they were clues or the answer to a riddle that'd point me toward the way out.

I couldn't stay here much longer.

I'd been here for twenty years—raised at the Academy since I'd been a baby. Because I'd been born male, the Coven hadn't trusted my witch parents to raise me. My parents had handed me over right after I'd been born. As far as I'd been told, they hadn't questioned it, hadn't fought to keep me. It was what Coven tradition demanded—that I was to be raised by the witches here, at the Academy, where there were enough eyes to watch me, to make sure I grew correctly and developed my fire magic.

My fire magic had come early, at thirteen. I'd been young,

and there'd been the occasional "accident." Like when I'd lit Matilda's closet on fire, watching all her black clothes go up in smoke. Or when I'd chased my instructors down the hall shooting flaming fireballs after I'd been disciplined for missing a lesson. Now I had my fire magic under control and could summon it almost instantly to the tip of my fingers. I mostly kept my magic under wraps so as to not draw the attention of the witches here at the Academy.

Other than the year I got my fire magic, every year had been monotonously the same. I watched the freshening each year—the new witches coming into the Academy. I skipped most of my lessons, attending only the ones I wanted to from the hallway. I searched for the mystery clues etched into the bricks around the Academy.

But this year wasn't going to be the same—and would be anything but monotonous. This year, everything would change. This year I'd be forced to choose a partner. Someone I'd be encouraged—pressured—to create powerful witches with. Male witches were rare, and the Coven couldn't miss the opportunity to create purebred witches to increase their population. It was much easier than scouting and bringing in human-born witches, as they liked to do each freshening.

After all these years, I was running out of time.

The freshening had happened early this year, and new clear-faced witches had already been introduced into the Academy. So far, I'd stayed away from them. There was always animosity between the new human-born witches and the seasoned witches—created from the jealousy of seeing the human-born witches with fresh, sun-kissed faces. The seasoned witches wanted to see the light extinguished from the newcomers' eyes so they'd be just as miserable and pale as everyone else here.

Also different this year, after the freshening would come

the evaluations. A tradition for every male witch who came of age. The female witches in the three elements—earth, air, and water—would each compete, each element offering their most powerful witch for my choosing.

Three.

That was the number of witches I had to choose from to be my partner. They'd be touted as the three most powerful witches in the Academy. Each of them equally qualified to be my partner.

Only the best for the male witches.

It made me queasy, that I had everyone vying for my attention. My whole life, the community, almost entirely female, had ostracized me for being male. From when I'd been school-aged and taunted for being a boy in a sea full of girls to when I'd been a teenager and ridiculed for being shorter than my female counterparts because I hadn't hit my growth spurt until sixteen. The attention wasn't something I'd enjoyed, and I'd tried to keep to myself all those years. None of the witches had paid me any mind, besides the occasional teasing, until the last few years...when talk of me coming of age and the evaluations had started.

Now I just tried to keep myself hidden. Out of the way. For the time being, no one made me do anything, and I had access to whatever I wanted down here—one of the few perks of being a male in the Academy. Which was why I was here in the closet when everyone else was preparing for evaluations.

With a final swipe of the chalk, I finished rubbing the last of the letters onto the paper: *P-E-R-D-E-R-E*. Another word I didn't know.

Sighing, I tried to get out from where I'd contorted myself along the electrical box.

Click.

I froze, my muscles straining to keep my body still. There

was a flash of light from the outside before the door slammed closed. Rapid breathing filled the space. I wasn't alone.

"Hello?" I called out, pulling myself into a standing position as quick as I could. My toe hit the flashlight on the floor, sending it rolling beneath what looked to be a part of the furnace. The flashlight flickered before turning off completely.

"Who's in here?" The voice was feminine. I could hear her breathing heavily, like she'd been running. "This isn't my dorm room..."

I tucked the paper into the pocket of the ridiculously scratchy jacket the Academy made us wear. "No, it's not."

There was a pause before I heard fabric rustle and felt the warmth of her breath against my neck. Her hand rested against my chest softly before her fingers curled, grabbing onto the muscle beneath my shirt.

"Have you been in here, waiting for me?"

I sucked in a shallow breath, inhaling a scent that was excessively sweet. "No—"

"Shh..." Her finger met my lips, stilling them before she dragged down, hooking the tip of her finger on the inside of my bottom lip. "Let's not move our lips like that." There was a pause before I felt the lapels of my jacket being pulled down, her body sliding higher up my chest. "Let's move them like this."

I didn't have time to dart my tongue out, to wet my lips before hers pressed against mine. It was sloppy and manic, like she might not have known what she was doing yet still couldn't get enough. I groaned as I felt the green plaid skirt that all the female witches wore brush against my pants, teasing me, tempting me to find out what was underneath. Recently, I hadn't dared to get involved with a witch, not with the evaluations coming up. It'd been a long time...two years since I'd touched someone intimately. It'd gotten too risky. The witches all competed for my attention, and if I gave one just a sliver of acknowledgment, they'd all demand the same.

But this...this felt different. She wasn't trying to reach for my belt—she wanted to be touched in the most basic of ways.

I unfurled my fingers, bringing my hands up to her chest, wrapping them around her neck beneath her chin.

Her neck was...wet.

Was it blood? Was she bleeding?

I pulled away. The woman groaned in protest, her neck pushing against my hand as she tried to get close again.

"Are you hurt?" I asked, bringing my other hand to feel the side of her head. Where was the wetness coming from?

She grabbed ahold of my wrist as my fingers got caught in a thick section of twists by her ear. "I need you...your lips on mine." Again, she attempted to get close.

I sighed. I wanted to kiss her again, to feel her lips on mine. Maybe this next time I could take control, suck her lip into my mouth...bite down.

No. Something wasn't right. That sickly-sweet scent coupled with her throwing herself at me in a dark room...who was this witch?

I kept her a good distance away from my face with the hand still wrapped around her neck. "By chance, are you a water element?" The water elements trained in potions, mostly. Love potions were a common beginner's potion. The sweet scent rolling off her skin reeked of one.

"Yes. Are you?"

I fumbled for the door handle behind her as she giggled, thinking that I might've been searching for something else. We both squinted as light from the outside hit our dilated eyes. It took me a moment to see her clearly.

She was flames, fire, as wild and free as the curly hair that framed her face and hung down her back in long waves. A face that was clear of the sores that plagued the witches that lived here. Instead, there were tiny orange spots over the bridge of her nose and along her cheeks. Like the sparks that spit above a roaring flame.

I blinked a couple of times. Had I absorbed some of the love potion through her lips?

I watched her face fall the moment she saw mine. The dark circles, the black veins traveling down my cheeks. My face was negating the love potion—or maybe it was just wearing off.

I didn't want her coming down from the love potion inside the closet. She'd be scared, coming back to consciousness in a dark room with a strange man. I felt the need to bring her somewhere comfortable. Somewhere safe.

"Come with me." I pulled back my hand, replacing her neck with her hand, gripping her boney palm tighter than I would ever dare to grip her neck. I pulled her out of the closet and down the hallway into the dome. I felt the stares of the other witches piercing like daggers in my back as we walked past.

My room was on the far side of the dome on the first floor. Quickly, I unlocked the door and pulled her in behind me. I let go of her hand, watching her stumble into my room as I latched the door. When I flipped on the light, I found that she'd already made her way across the room.

"Books? You have books?" She ran to the bookshelf, kneeling in front of the rows of spines.

Had she already forgotten about wanting to kiss me? I sighed. I couldn't compete with books.

I had two bookshelves in my room that stood next to each other. One for fiction and one for nonfiction. They took up a decent amount of space in the room, but they were worth it. Books were my only source of entertainment and how I learned about the world above ground. I'd spent countless hours here in my room reading my books—both fantasizing and studying what life was like beyond this place.

She picked out a fiction title, a book of fairy tales. Sitting back on her feet, she thumbed through the pages. I couldn't help but notice the smile on her lips, how the corners of her eyes crinkled.

"You read these?" she asked. I sensed a bit of tease in her voice. She continued flipping through the pages as she waited for my answer.

"I have to learn somehow," I said.

She stopped, closing the book with her thumb still stuck between the pages. "Learn what?"

"How to be someone's partner." I didn't show it and didn't verbalize it, but if the Coven was going to force me to choose a partner, if I couldn't find a way out of here, I didn't want to make that witch's life as miserable as mine. Even if I wasn't attracted to them physically, I could still be a good partner. I had no one to learn from, no relationships to emulate, so I studied up on partnerships and relationships by reading books.

"You're learning that from these books?" she asked, one side of her red hair falling lower on her shoulder than the other as she tilted her head.

"What else would teach me?"

Her eyes blinked rapidly before she shook her head back and forth, looking back down at the cover of the book. She was coming down from the potion. What would she remember? Would she remember kissing me? Part of me wanted her to.

"These are fairy tales," she said, still looking down at the book.

I nodded. Those were my favorite. They always had a happy ending.

"What if I also wanted to be someone's knight in shining armor?" I teased.

Her cheeks turned a light-pink color that I watched travel down the sides of her neck, dipping down beneath her collared white shirt.

"Don't you think it'd be nice to be a knight in shining armor for the partner I have to choose?"

She looked up sharply, her eyes wide and her mouth open. "*You're* Gideon?"

CHAPTER SIXTEEN

Dafni

My surroundings suddenly felt suffocating. It was dark, a lamp cast a soft glow of light around the space. There was a book in front of my nose—a book of fairy tales. *How did I get here?* I pulled down the book, looking around. I was in a room that wasn't mine. A large room. It had a big bed and a desk. There was even a rug on the floor. A tall man with black hair and black under his eyes stood staring at me.

Gideon.

He looked at me as though I was a wild animal he'd spotted in the woods. He was still, careful not to move for fear he might make me skittish. His pupils were only slightly darker than the rings around them—the whites of his eyes the only division between the black of his under eyes and the dark color of his irises. As I stared at them, I felt like I was falling into a bottomless pit. There was no end to their depths.

I blinked several times. What was I doing alone with *Gideon*? I stood from my knees quickly, stumbling backward until I hit a desk. I'd put some distance between us, but his gaze made it feel like my skin was burning like it had when he'd been touching me.

He touched me.

Memories from the closet flipped through my brain like the pages of a book. His lips. His hands. His mossy scent that filled the closet. The way I'd wanted *him* to touch me.

"What happened to me?" I groaned, pulling the book of fairy tales up in front of my face so I couldn't see him and he couldn't see me. Kissing strangers wasn't something I did. I'd never kissed someone before. I hadn't known what I was doing. The kiss had been sloppy...but I hadn't been able to stop myself.

"A love potion happened to you," he said from where he stood. "I'm guessing you swallowed some during class?"

More memories flashed behind my eyes. The potion drills. The pressure Arcana put on everyone to be the best, to win so that *Gideon* would pick them as his partner.

Potion after potion, we had to brew. The warm splash of my potion from Petunia's rock that covered my shirt, my cheeks, and my *lips*. Ugh, it was sweet on my tongue and had warmed my insides immediately.

Arcana had instructed me to return to my room and change. I'd stumbled down the hallway, my skin hot. Craving, needing someone's...anyone's touch. I'd needed hands on my body, someone's lips on my lips. Opening the first door I'd found. Finding *him*.

I looked down at my shirt—my wet white shirt that was almost see-through. *It was all real.* I'd found Gideon in the closet and had practically mauled him. That kiss—my first kiss —hadn't been how I imagined it, and now I was standing in front of the man whose lips had touched mine, a book covering my red face and my breasts showing through the thin bra and white shirt I was wearing.

The healing potion. I felt with my fingers between my breasts, immediately finding the tube still resting there. A small part of me relaxed an equally small amount.

I lowered the book to cover my wet shirt, my eyes connecting with his again.

"I'm not usually like that," I said.

Gideon took a step away from the door, closer to me. "Neither am I." He took another step toward me, his face now illuminated by the light of the lamp on his nightside table. The closer he got, the more his eyes resembled shadows. Black veins that traveled down his cheeks toward his chin highlighted the black of his under-eyes. I involuntarily tried to take a step back but found nowhere to escape.

"What happened to you?" I asked in a whisper. I'd never seen a face like his. How could something so unpleasant be so oddly beautiful? It looked like someone had swooped a paintbrush under his eyes, the excess paint dripping down his cheeks.

"This place happened to me," Gideon answered as he continued staring at me.

I turned around, dropping the book of fairy tales on his desk. A plume of papers flew, fluttering to the ground. He was quick to fall to his knees, gathering pieces of paper with something black smeared on their surface.

I watched him on his knees, picking up the papers. Was I being rude? Yes, I was probably being rude. This man hadn't kidnapped me or refused to feed me when I was hungry. He'd kindly pulled me off his lips after *I'd* kissed *him* and brought me back to his room so I wouldn't further embarrass myself.

I could be cordial. I could be nice.

Falling to my knees, I tried to help pick up the papers that'd fallen. Gideon snatched them away from me before my fingers could graze the page. Curiosity got the best of me.

"What are those?" I asked.

"Stupid things I collect," he replied as he pressed the papers just as close to his chest as I had the book. One paper was facing me, the white letters surrounded by some sort of black substance.

"You collect Latin words?" I asked.

Gideon looked down at the page I'd been reading and quickly flipped it over so I could only see the back—a blank white page. "Wait, they're Latin?" he asked.

"Yeah, I recognized the word *perdere* on that page you just flipped," I said. "It means *destroy*."

Gideon looked at me, tilting his head to the side, staring at me again with those dark eyes. "You can read Latin?" he asked.

"Yeah..." I walked over to him, a new air of confidence in my step. I knew something this experienced witch didn't.

He held out the papers to me, shaking them slightly as if he was debating letting me take them.

I pulled at the papers he still gripped in his hand.

"You can really read Latin?" he asked.

"Of course, I can." My grandmother had taught me to read Latin at the same time she'd taught me to read English. It'd been part of the training she'd given me for when I'd enter the Coven. "Can't all witches read Latin?"

The corner of Gideon's lip twitched. *I guess not.*

He let go of the papers, and I flipped them over. The first one was *perdere*, which meant *destroy*—I'd already read that one. The other two read *alloco*, which meant *let*, and *ille*, which roughly translated to *the*.

"*Destroy, let, the*... That doesn't make a whole lot of sense, Gideon."

"That's because it's a code."

"A code?"

Gideon ran his fingers through the hair on the top of his head. The strands strewn, poking out at all different angles after he brought his hand back down to his pocket.

"Another stupid thing. When I was young, I'd always pretend it was a secret code or language—that once I understood it, would unlock a door, any door, to the outside so I could escape this place."

I looked up from the papers, our eyes meeting. The way he was looking at me—his gaze—made the darkness around his eyes, the lines down his cheeks look like tunnels to his soul.

Dropping my gaze, I shook my head to clear it. I couldn't get lost. I couldn't lose my way. Getting mixed up with Gideon would be a terrible idea.

He tilted his head at me the same way I'd been continually tilting mine at him, trying to figure him out. "I don't know your name."

My name? No, he didn't need to know that. This was just a minor detour—an unfortunate detour that ended in me getting my first kiss...or taking my first kiss. The memory that I'd try to rid myself of for the rest of my life. "I have to go," I stammered, shoving the papers back at him.

He grabbed them, moving aside to let me through the door. "I hope you're not disappointed in how I look."

I froze right as my hand turned the knob.

"It would ruin the whole knight-in-shining-armor thing I'm working on."

I almost smiled as I opened the door. He wasn't disappointing to look at—he was fascinating to stare at. But there was no way I was going to tell him that.

CHAPTER SEVENTEEN

Dafni

Was I one of those lovesick girls from the fairy tales my grandmother used to tell me before I fell asleep? I still had that funny feeling in my stomach, even a week after meeting Gideon. Maybe I still had some of the love potion floating around in there. That was the only explanation for the way I was feeling.

Our lips had touched. He'd brought me back to his room so I could recover from the love potion in private. That was all. We'd both stared at each other, each of us trying to figure the other out. I'd probably stared the most. He was unlike anyone I'd ever laid eyes on...but that was it. There was nothing between us.

All week, I'd kept the healing potion I'd made tucked between my breasts in my bra, scanning faces every time I walked through the dome to class hoping to see the witch I'd hurt. Without the potion, she had to be in a lot of pain, her finger still bent at an awkward angle.

It wasn't until today that I saw her, standing nearby a group of witches, her uninjured hand wrapped around the injured one, holding it in front of her chest like it bothered her.

As I walked toward her, I plucked the tube from my shirt, wrapping my entire hand around the glass so no one could see it. She didn't notice me until I got close, taking a step back, alerting her friends to my presence. They all turned and looked at me, their lips curling up.

I began extending my arm, holding the tube in my hand. The witches all bent their knees, pointing their index and middle fingers at me.

"Wait!" I yelled, bringing the potion back to my chest and closing my eyes.

They were about to strike me with their magic.

I slowly opened my eyes to see the witches still standing in the offensive stance, waiting for me to make my next move.

"I have something for you," I said to the injured witch. Slowly, I spread my fingers, revealing the tube resting on my palm.

I tried to hold my hand steady as she walked toward me, her boots clicking on the ground with every step. With her uninjured hand, she picked up the potion, holding it at eye level while swirling its contents in the glass.

I saw her eyes as soon as she pulled the tube away. She was smiling with them instead of her lips. Her friends jumped out the way of the tube as she threw it against the brick wall, the glass shattering and the potion spattering.

"I don't need any help—especially not from a human-born," she spat.

"I'm sorry," I whispered. "I made that for you. It was supposed to help with pain, promote healing—"

I jumped to the side as poison from her mouth hit the dirt floor where I'd just been standing.

My head cocked back and to the side as I stared at her. I'd just tried to help her, to do the right thing, and she'd literally thrown my kindness away.

Why was I apologizing to her for doing the right thing? It'd always been so easy to apologize, to appease others. I'd been trained from a young age not to rock the boat—to just apologize so everyone, mainly my mother, would be happy. It'd always come at the cost of my own happiness. Apologize so everyone else felt better. It'd never made me feel any better. Especially when what I was apologizing for wasn't my fault.

"I take that back," I said, my voice not wavering. "I'm not sorry I made that for you. If you would've taken it, maybe you'd be able to compete in your precious evaluations."

This wasn't a Coven of witches, this was a jumble of anger and resentment—with everyone teetering on the edge of their tipping point. Today I'd tried to help someone, and that offer of help had pushed them past their breaking point. Maybe she'd been too proud to take help from a supposedly human-born witch.

Fine. Don't take my help. Suffer instead.

My kindness in here was being misread as weakness.

I walked past the group of witches, the heels of my boots crunching the broken glass on the ground. Their eyes heated the back of my neck as I headed to the class they'd just made me late for.

———

Petunia was at it again. Arcana had the air magics practicing levitating—the witches sending wind from their fingertips toward the hard ground, their bodies swaying back and forth as they went airborne. Plumes of dust flew up from the dirt after their bodies fell, having become unbalanced in the air.

I could hardly pay attention to my potion, instead having to watch and make sure one of the air witches didn't land on the work bench and cause another unfortunate love-potion incident. Though this time, we were being drilled on making an expelling potion, and if I got any of this in my mouth, I'd be on my hands and knees emptying the contents of my stomach onto the floor.

The earth magic witches were on the opposite side of the room to the air magic witches and were trying to coax water from the dirt between the bricks. Brooke, having already mastered the skill before she came here, stood with her back against the wall, watching the air magic witches. We locked eyes for a moment—both rolling them as Petunia pushed one of the levitating witches, causing her to lose her balance and topple to the ground.

"Witches!" Arcana said clapping her hands together. "Robinson will be here shortly to observe the progress you've made over the past weeks. Please remember to do your best to show him everything I've taught you!"

Around me the water magics stirred their potions with more vigor, and Brooke even turned back around, willing a trickle of water from the wall. Petunia used her air magic to push herself even higher in the classroom, well above our heads.

The door to the classroom opened, and Robinson entered, standing with his legs apart and his arms crossed in front of his chest. With one hand he smoothed his mustache. This was only the second time seeing him, but he already gave me the creeps.

Arcana fluttered over to him, doting on him as she'd done the last time we'd seen him. The witches in the room continued to work on their magic as both Arcana and Robinson scanned the room. He pointed over at where Petunia was floating, nearing the tall ceiling, whispering something to Arcana.

Just below Petunia, another air magic witch floated up, her head parallel to Petunia's boots. After a quick glance down, Petunia bent her knee before delivering a swift kick to the witch's head, sending her tumbling several feet down to the ground. She landed with a thud, a cracking sound echoing along the brick walls.

I couldn't help but wince and wish I'd kept that healing potion instead of giving it to that ungrateful witch earlier. I was too far along in my potion in today's class to be pulling ingredients to make another one without drawing attention.

Robinson's eyes never left Petunia as Arcana rushed over to the witch Petunia had kicked. Arcana clicked her tongue at the injured witch as she held her limp arm up in the air, the witch crying out in pain. It looked from here like it was broken. She helped the witch to her feet, guiding her to the side of the room and pushing her back down into a seated position against the wall.

The witch with the broken finger had been right. They weren't about to help injured or even sick witches down here. We were all disposable, contestants in their sick game of *evaluations*. This wasn't right.

Loud, slow clapping caught my attention as I turned away from the witch with the broken arm. Robinson stood clapping, his eyes locked on Petunia.

She smiled, floating up there in the air, her fingers still blowing wind to the ground to keep her afloat, looking down on all of us.

———

That night, I lay in bed next to Brooke. She'd taken a long time to fall asleep, shifting between crying and simply shaking at the realization that the earth magic's evaluation would be tomorrow.

She'd finally fallen asleep, her breathing still short and choppy at times as she recovered from hyperventilating. Brooke was a strong earth magic, but the witches here were vicious, as we'd seen with Petunia today. With their futures on the line, they were unpredictable and prone to violence. I empathized with Brooke—my whispers of *Everything will be all right* falling flat—as they should've. Tomorrow everything might not be all right. She could very well be hurt...or worse.

It was late once my eyes finally became heavy with sleep. Above me the mattress springs flexed and squeaked as Petunia shifted.

"I will win."

I sat up, holding the sheet over Brooke so she'd stay sleeping.

"I'm powerful—the most powerful witch in my class."

Petunia was talking...whispering. Was she talking in her sleep?

"He's mine. He will choose me. I will become the chosen."

A shiver ran down my spine.

If she was talking in her sleep...those were her subconscious thoughts. If she was awake this late, speaking those words aloud to a quiet, dark room...she was more disturbing than I'd previously thought.

I kicked one foot out of the bed, careful to get off the mattress without disturbing Brooke. Both Brooke's and Petunia's breaths stayed even as I crossed the floor—I had to assume both were sleeping.

I closed the door to the bathroom before I switched on the light. Using the toilet, I let myself relax on the seat.

Petunia had been sleep-talking. People said strange things when they slept. Her words weren't unexpected. Judging by the attitudes of the witches down here, I was sure almost every witch had thought the words that'd come from Petunia's mouth at some point. But the way she'd said them, so sure of herself, so determined, made me uneasy.

My bare toes dug into the dirt ground. There was no staying clean here. The only time we cleaned our feet was in the shower, and then after, it was either straight into our boots or keep our feet bare and deal with the dirt on the ground. I wasn't about to sleep in my leather boots, therefore my toes were already filthy all over again. Sighing, I looked up. There was hardly room between the toilet and the brick wall in front of me, and my eyes traveled from the dirt floor to where the brick wall began.

What's that, there?

I bent over, looking at the etching in the brick. It was light and uneven, but it was there.

A heart with the letters *G* and *P* inside.

Gideon and Petunia.

Gag.

My stomach felt like it had butterflies flopping around inside it. Petunia had never kissed Gideon; had she even spoken to him?

Is this jealousy?

No. I didn't get to feel like that. I was supposed to become Prime. Feelings of attraction...of jealousy didn't apply to me. They couldn't. I had too much to learn.

CHAPTER EIGHTEEN

Dafni

THAT LEARNING INCLUDED WATCHING THE EARTH evaluations. They were the first competitors, and my relief at water being the last competitor filled me with guilt. Brooke, an earth element, was first, and she'd been so nervous when I'd left the room this morning to join the audience.

The witches of the air and water elements filed into the giant oval-shaped cavern, taking seats, their knees pressed to their neighbor's on the creaky metal bleachers that were erected on one side of the space. A stage stood against the wall opposite the bleachers, leaving the middle of the floor empty. Sconces mounted to the walls lit the space, casting a circular glow around cavern.

"This will be fun," Petunia whispered, her thigh pressed against mine. To my surprise, she'd followed behind me all the way to the cavern, choosing the seat next to me. The tight ringlets she usually sported looked wind-blown and loose—probably from all the haphazard air magic practice she'd been doing, or maybe from the rolling and the sleep-talking. She tucked the sides behind her ears, but I still felt the tickles of her fly-aways against my cheeks.

"Fun?" I questioned.

"Yeah, I can't wait to see who wins...who my competition is."

I stared at her, unable to formulate a response. This wasn't *fun*, this was unsettling and uncomfortable. The Coven was making the female witches at the Academy compete in what most likely would be a ridiculous task, to prove who was the most powerful in each element. Then those three witches would line up, like slabs of meat at a butcher, and Gideon would choose one witch as his partner. Whomever he chose, the Coven would expect to be his partner in *all* ways.

It was what the Coven wanted, to create powerful witches, and if they got a spectacle out of it as well? All the better. I didn't blame them for wanting entertainment—life here was dull and the witches were all gossips.

A shiver traveled down my spine as the image of Gideon's eyes burst into my brain, those dark shadows that had threatened to pull me beneath the surface. Was this what he wanted? Did he want to choose his partner from a contest?

"Oh! There he is!" Petunia bounced in her seat, her arm extended as she pointed.

I followed her finger to the stage across the cavern. Gideon was sitting in one of two wing-backed armchairs, his legs parted, his arms relaxed on the armrests. His back slouched against the back of the chair, and his eyes stared directly at me.

"It's *him!*" she squeaked, her thigh now vibrating against mine. "He's looking right at me!"

I looked at Petunia's face before looking back at Gideon.

His eyes never wavered; his head never moved. He was staring at us, but I knew in my gut he wasn't staring at Petunia, he was staring at *me*. My body heated, starting in my core. I was hot. The confined space next to all these bodies wasn't helping.

I tried to look anywhere, at anything else—the other witches, the tall ceiling, the way my heeled boots had to sit on top of each other in the small space I had on the bleachers, but my eyes always found their way back to his.

Double doors we'd walked through minutes ago, between the stage and the bleachers, reopened, and the earth magic witches began filing into the cavern. They walked in a single-file line. It was easy to spot the human-born witches—their bodies trembled. My eyes honed in on Brooke, who was walking with shaking knees, her hands clasped tightly together in front of her. She hadn't had much time to practice her magic, especially as a human-born witch. Her opponents were witches raised in families that taught and encouraged magic. At least she'd had the forethought to tie her long hair up into a tight bun on top of her head. I made a note to do the same during the water evaluation.

"I hope Brooke will be okay—" I whispered.

"Shhh...I can't hear!" Petunia snapped, smacking my thigh with the back of her hand.

I looked back to the stage where Robinson now stood in front of the empty wing-backed chair. Next to him, Gideon was still sitting in the chair staring at me. Another shiver went down my spine, this one shook my entire body.

"Stop wiggling!" Petunia smacked me again with the back of her hand.

Robinson cleared his throat and smoothed his mustache with his index finger and thumb before he spoke, his voice echoing off the cavern walls. "It is known that male witches produce powerful heirs. That's why we're cherished and beloved by our community." He smiled, looking out over the crowd. "Today a male witch has come of age, and it is time for him to pick a partner, someone who will help him produce powerful witches that will continue to provide for our Coven."

The earth element witches stood in a tight group on the floor—the human-born witches huddled together in the back.

"Some of you grew up in our community, and others of you are new."

"I wish I'd never been born from humans..." Petunia said beneath her breath.

"Yet you are all witches of producing age," he continued. "You all have the chance to compete to be Gideon's partner."

I looked at Gideon, along with everyone else in the cavern. He was still watching me.

"Since our Prime, Matilda Sarracenia, is gone searching for new ways to better our Coven, I'm here to stand in her place."

I snorted. *Yes, she's been very busy in the Velkans' freezer.*

"And to run these evaluations, as our Coven's traditions command. I am Arthur Robinson. I'm sure many of you recognize me—I can feel your admiration from here on the stage." He held his arms out to the crowd as if he was collecting said imaginary admiration. "The three elements—earth, air, and water—will compete in that order. I will give each element a task that coincides with its magic," he explained. "At the end of the evaluations, the winner of each task will come forward. Gideon will choose one of those three witches to be his partner. Those three witches are the most powerful witches in each of their elements, any of them a complementary partner to Gideon's flame."

He motioned to Gideon to stand. "Show them, Gideon, show them your flame!"

Gideon either wasn't listening or was ignoring Robinson,

his body still, except for his fingers, which tapped one after another on the end of the armrest.

"Gideon," he said again. "Please stand and show everyone your flame."

I didn't know how Gideon sat, motionless, with hundreds of eyes on him. I could barely stay still in my seat with just the two of his eyes burning me up.

"*Gideon!*" Robinson barked.

The cavern stilled. The tension between the two men was about ready to create its own fire if he didn't.

Get up! I mouthed at him.

Gideon blinked, breaking eye contact with me before he stood slowly, using the armrests to push himself up off the chair. He looked unamused as he stood next to Robinson, pointing his index and middle fingers toward the ceiling. Flames shot out of his fingertips, the tops of the them almost licking the ceiling of the tall cavern.

Robinson clapped his hands, along with most of the witches on the bleachers. There were a few human-born witches sprinkled among the crowd, cowered down, their chests near their thighs. "Aren't male witches just amazing?"

It *was* impressive. I found myself sitting with my mouth open, following the flame up to the ceiling. I'd never met a male witch before coming here, much less seen their fire magic. It was eerily beautiful.

Gideon extinguished his flame with a flick of his fingers before falling back into his seat.

Our eyes met again, our stare quickly interrupted by Robinson, who clapped his hands twice. "Now, if the earth elements are ready, let's begin!"

None of the witches on the floor looked ready. The task remained unknown until Robinson presented it at the evaluation. They breathed heavily, their knees bent and hands in front of their bodies, set to take on whatever was thrown at them. The other witches and I sat on the bleachers and held our breath, waiting and watching, dreading the time it would be our turn on the floor.

"Earth elements, your task is to break through the dirt wall on the far side of the cavern."

Everyone turned to face the wall opposite the doors they'd walked through.

"You may use whatever earth magic you desire to do so. The first one through to the other side wins."

The room quieted.

"You may begin!"

The instructions were simple, but the task was anything but. The dirt wall wasn't wide enough for every earth element witch to have a spot along it. Witches ran and then clawed their way toward the dirt, some seeming to forget they had magic, using their hands to dig into the wall.

I tried to find Brooke among the mass of witches clawing and fighting. Her brown bun popped up briefly near the wall, and I found myself clapping my hands along with the rest of the crowd, trying to encourage her. The dirt around where Brooke was standing began to darken, drips of mud trailing down the wall. Like in the room we'd fallen into when we arrived, she was pulling water into the dirt. The surrounding witches took advantage of the softened soil and began clawing through, creating a divot in the wall.

I stood and began shouting at the witches who were taking advantage of her work. "Don't let them use you, Brooke! Push them! Get them away!"

Suddenly, the top of my foot throbbed. I yelped, falling into my seat.

"Sit down!" Petunia spat, her heeled boot on top of my foot. "I can't see him when you're standing."

I looked to where she was staring—at Gideon. He was looking at us, a smirk on his lips. Did he find this all entertaining? Maybe he did. We were all supposed to be fighting over him—competing for him. He was just sitting there and watching it happen. My stomach turned.

I looked back to where I'd last seen Brooke. Her brown bun wasn't visible, but there was a group of witches climbing over each other where she'd created the weak spot in the wall. They were digging, pushing. Some were already halfway through, just the bottom of their plaid skirts and black boots sticking out parallel to the floor.

Flames shot up from Robinson's fingers, the sound silencing the crowd and stilling the earth element witches that hadn't made it through the wall. "We have a winner!"

The double doors opened again, and everyone turned to find a witch covered in mud being led in by an earth element instructor. She walked with her head held high and a smile on her face. She couldn't have been human-born. The confidence she walked with and how quickly she'd completed the task told me she had magical parents—she'd been trained from an early age. Did any of the human-born witches even stand a chance?

As she walked, I could only see the whites of her eyes and teeth, the rest of her features concealed beneath the dirt. The instructor brought her onstage, her uniform now plastered to her body, trailing mud across the floor.

"The earth element's most powerful witch is Flora Hargrove!" Robinson attempted to grab her wrist to raise it above her head but pulled back just before he made contact, primly brushing his fingers against his clean pants.

I sat in the sea of standing witches, my eyes on my feet. This wasn't about who was the most powerful. This was about who could trick another, who could cheat their way to the top.

Brooke had had the idea, created the soft dirt with her magic, and another witch had taken advantage to win.

Brooke.

Standing again, I stood on my toes, trying to find her brown bun in the wave of earth element witches walking away from the wall.

I spotted her, close to the ground. Was she okay? I pushed past the witches on the bleachers below me, jumping from row to row until I reached the ground. My uniform became covered in mud as I brushed against the witches walking in the opposite direction.

"Brooke!" I called out.

"I'm here!" she called back. She sat on the ground, her hands wrapped around one of her legs.

I crouched down next to her, my hands on the trampled dirt around her.

"One of them grew vines, and they wrapped around my ankle." She pulled her hands away, revealing brown cords twisted tightly around the top of her boot.

"Those harpies..." I grabbed on to the vines and pulled, trying to rip them apart. They were too strong and wouldn't budge. "Can you lift your foot any higher?"

"Maybe." Brooke tried to lift her foot but immediately winced. "Dafni, I think I twisted it." There was a fear in her eyes that I couldn't help but mirror back. If she was seriously injured, the Academy wouldn't help her.

I pulled again on the vines, leaning back using my entire body weight. A heavy hand settled on my shoulder. I flinched, looking up and behind me.

"Dafni, let me try," Gideon said.

I froze at the way he said my name, at the way the *f* snapped between his teeth and bottom lip. He must've heard Brooke say it.

I let go of the vines, using my thumb and index fingers to pick up Gideon's hand by the cuff of his jacket and remove it from my shoulder. "I don't want help." Gripping the vines again, I dug in my heels and pulled. Brooke cried out, covering her mouth with a muddy hand. I immediately let go, apologizing to her.

"Stubborn witchling." Warmth flooded my back as two arms reached around my body and grabbed the vine alongside my hands. His fingers flexed around the vine, the veins on the top of his hands popping from his skin. I could smell him—he had a certain mossy scent that I instantly remembered from the closet. Stupid scents and their stupid abilities to bring unwanted memories back into my brain.

In a swift movement, Gideon snapped the vine with his hands, the effort causing his chest to slam forcefully into my back. I fell forward, my hands extending to catch myself before I landed on top of Brooke.

My hands never met the floor or Brooke, because something grabbed my chest, stopping the fall. Everyone froze, Brooke's eyes traveling from the hand on my chest to my face and back down.

"Sorry!" Gideon pulled back his hand, grazing against my nipple that'd become hard in the last few seconds. *Stupid thin shirt and equally thin Academy bra.*

Without his support, I fell forward, landing in a heap on top of Brooke.

"Oww..." she moaned.

I quickly pulled myself off her, turning to face Gideon with my hands and feet still in the dirt. "I said I didn't want help!" He didn't get to come in all *knight in shining armor* and save the day after he'd just sat back and let this happen to Brooke. "I don't want help from someone who sits on the side, knows what's going on, but does *nothing.*"

Gideon's mouth fell open.

"You're supposed to be *so* powerful—yet you just sat there, and you *smiled*." My teeth instinctively flashed at him, nonexistent poison dripping from them. "I don't trust someone who does nothing when they have the ability to do something. I don't trust you."

I left Gideon slack-jawed. *Good.*

Standing I turned around to help Brooke. Reaching my arms beneath hers, I tried to lift her up to standing. She dug her heels into the dirt but couldn't get her feet beneath her body with her injured ankle.

I sat her down, my hands on my thighs as I caught my breath.

"Try again," Brooke pleaded. "I'm going to put all my weight on my good foot."

I crouched down, sliding my arms beneath her armpits, using my legs to lift her. She was halfway to standing.

"Come on, Brooke," I said, pulling, my thighs burning.

"I'm trying. I can't put weight on this foot without—"

She fell back into me. I stepped back, trying to catch my balance. I ended up letting go of her, my arms waving at both my sides as I tried not to fall. Brooke landed in a heap in the dirt by my boots.

"I'm so sorry, Dafni! I can't stand." She looked up at me, her eyes wide. "Maybe I could crawl?"

I looked around the cavern. The witches had cleared out and retreated to their rooms. It was almost empty.

"No." I looked at the muddy floor. "Don't crawl."

There was only one other person in the cavern. One I didn't want to look at, much less ask a favor of. I looked down at Brooke and then back to the set of wooden doors that was the exit—it was far away. Even if I got her to the doors, we'd still have to get back to our room on the third floor. There were two sets of spiral stairs. I wouldn't be able to get her back by myself.

I turned to face Gideon, keeping my eyes closed. I didn't want to see his face. I breathed in through my nose and then out of my mouth. Unfortunately, this was the only way.

"It'd be really great if you could help me get her back to our room," I said.

There was silence.

I cracked open one of my eyes just to see Gideon's smirk. I quickly shut it.

"I'd be happy to save the day," he said. "Like a certain knight in—"

"Quit it," I snapped, popping both of my eyes open. I gave him the nastiest glare I could muster. He could help me, but he wasn't going to enjoy it.

Gideon grabbed ahold of Brooke's arm on the injured side, and I took the other. We easily lifted her into a standing position.

"I still don't trust you," I said as we led my friend out of the cavern.

He peered around the front of Brooke, catching my eyes. "Then I'll earn your trust."

CHAPTER NINETEEN

Dafni

I UNLOCKED THE DOOR TO MY DORM WITH ONE HAND, while supporting Brooke with the other. Gideon and I got her onto the bed, sitting her upright along the edge. I winced at the mud that had already trailed into our room and was now on the bed I shared with her.

Gideon backed away, glancing around the room, taking in what little we had to fill the small space.

"I know it's not like your giant room," I said as I bent down and began untying Brooke's boots for her.

"It's small," he said, continuing to look around.

I pulled off one of Brooke's boots. She sucked in a breath as cool air hit her injured ankle. The skin was red and broken in some places from the way the vine had squeezed her.

"You can go now," I said as I walked past Gideon toward the bathroom. Maybe there were bandages or something below the sink. Out of the corner of my eye, I saw Gideon crouch down near the bed, running his fingers along the wall.

I couldn't find a first-aid kit, of course, but we had a bar of soap in the bathroom, and I found an old cloth that we could use to wrap her foot.

"May I?" Gideon asked, motioning to the wall.

I walked over with my supplies, stopping to look at what he was asking. There, in the brick, was the lightest of etchings; one of the words he collected.

I shrugged, and Gideon pulled a white sheet of paper and piece of black chalk from his pocket. He crouched down next to the wall as I did the same next to Brooke. We were close, although facing opposite directions.

"You shouldn't be living in such a small room with two other people," he said as he rubbed the chalk back and forth against the paper. "You shouldn't have to share a bed with Brooke."

"And where else would I sleep?" I lathered the wet bar of soap in my hands.

"Is it going to hurt?" Brooke asked, eyeing the suds forming.

"We have to clean the wounds," I said.

Gideon cleared his throat. "You could sleep in my room."

I lost grip of the soap, juggling the bar between my hands for a moment before I regained control of it.

Sleep in his room? In his bed? My body heated. Why didn't that repulse me? It should've repulsed me. But I could still remember the way his chest felt beneath my hand in the closet. His chest had been hard but still soft enough that it would be comfortable, maybe just to rest my cheek on...

I shook my head. *Snap out of it.* "We hardly know each other. I'm not sleeping in your room."

Gideon paused for a moment before he continued rubbing the chalk on the paper. I grabbed hold of Brooke's injured ankle, where it dangled by the floor. I began cleaning her wounds, trying my best to ignore the way she sucked air through her teeth.

"Just so you know, I wasn't smiling at the witches fighting," Gideon said.

I held the soap too long in one spot, and Brooke pulled her ankle back toward the bed.

"I was smiling at you."

I continued cleaning her skin, biting my tongue between my teeth. What was this feeling? Like bubbles beneath my skin? Were there remnants of the love potion still releasing in my bloodstream? I couldn't control it. I didn't like it.

I stood, the bar of soap in my hand. Gideon stood right after I did, the chalked piece of paper in his hand. I could see Brooke out of the corner of my eye, looking back and forth between Gideon and me as we stared at each other. I tried not to blink.

He stood there with a steady, wide-open gaze, not showing the slightest sign of blinking either. Was it the black beneath his eyes that made him strangely good at staring contests? How were his eyes not dry yet?

My eyes closed, and I squeezed my lids together tightly, willing my eyes to hydrate themselves to a level where I could see clearly.

"*Gah!*" I yelled, my fists clenched at my sides. "Okay, you win again!" How could he stay so calm and collected all the time? It was like he was constantly at room temperature, no fluctuation. "Are you torturing me because I haven't said thank you yet? Is that why you're still here?" Storming over to the door, I gripped the handle. "Thank you, Gideon. Thank you so much for your help." I opened the door, wishing he'd leave along with the ache in my chest.

"You're cute when you try to intimidate me," he said.

"I'm not trying to—" I gave up and blinked several times, my vision fully returning.

Gideon ran his hand through the hair on the top of his head before taking a few steps toward the door.

Fantastic, he's leaving.

"Can you translate this?" He held up a piece of paper with the word *conventus* surrounded by black chalk.

I crossed my arms in front of my body, holding the door open with my foot.

"Please?" Gideon asked. The way he tilted his chin down toward his chest made his eyes even darker and look deeper. Could witches hypnotize someone? I should find out about that.

"It loosely means *assembly* or, in this case, probably *coven*," I said as quickly as possible.

He walked through the open door and into the hallway before turning around. "Thank you, Dafni. Thank you so much for your help."

I slammed the door closed, breaking myself of his hypnotizing stare.

"That was intense," Brooke said.

Turning around, I found her sitting on the bed, her red ankle the only part not covered in mud.

"I can't believe he knows your name...and now he knows mine."

"Yeah, well, I don't care what he knows, nor do I want his help." I crouched down in front of her again, this time grabbing the cloth I'd left on the bed before the whole Gideon stand-off. "I can't get used to relying on someone who wants to support the Academy and the games they play." I wrapped the worst of her broken skin with the cloth.

"When I looked at him, before the task began, he looked bored—definitely not amused," Brooke said. She moved her ankle in circles, testing the binding. "I've heard he doesn't hang around the other witches...human or witch-born."

"Who did you hear that from?"

"The witches in my element." Brooke stood, gingerly placing weight on her ankle, before sighing and sitting back down. "What was he doing just now by the wall?"

I looked back at the word *conventus* etched into a brick near the floor. I could barely see the letters. How had he found it so easily? "He collects words he finds etched into the brick around the Academy. It's one of his quirks, like smiling at inappropriate times and calling me cute."

Brooke laughed. "Speaking of other witches, Arcana actually taught us something today." She lowered herself onto the ground next to me and used her finger to write *planto arbor* into the dirt floor. Her lips moved, mumbling the words right before a tiny plant pushed itself through the dirt, its green leaves vibrant for just a moment before they wilted, turning brown, the stem buckling to the ground. She laughed again. "It's stupid —no one can make them stay alive, but it's fun to explore my powers."

"It's not stupid, that's amazing. I wonder what other things you can create with your earth magic."

The door to our room flew open before reverberating off the wall the knob hit as a silhouette of wind-blown ringlets filled the doorway. I stood, helping Brooke to her feet, our bodies immediately crouched in a defensive stance.

"He wasn't looking at me...he was looking at you!" Petunia screeched, launching herself toward me.

Brooke slid between us, wobbling on her good foot. "Petunia, take a breath," she said.

"I just saw him come from our room. You haven't competed yet—you don't get to hog his time!" Petunia spit as she spoke. I watched where it flew, worried it might've been mixed with some of her poison.

"He was helping me," Brooke said. "I hurt my ankle, and he was helping Dafni get me back to the room."

"Liar!" Petunia screeched. "You didn't win! He wouldn't be wasting his time helping you." She began walking back and forth, pacing like a caged animal. Our room wasn't large, so it only took her five steps to make it from one wall to the next.

"It's true! He was helping us," I said.

Petunia pointed her finger at me. "That doesn't explain why he was staring at you through the whole task!"

"He was?" Brooke asked. I widened my eyes at her. *Don't encourage her.* She cleared her throat. "Wait...Petunia, how could you even be able to tell who he was staring at? There were so many witches on the bleachers."

"I could just tell. And then he watched her run down the bleachers toward you. He followed her."

"I don't want his attention," I said with both of my palms raised and facing her.

"Dafni's telling the truth," Brooke argued. "You should've seen them in here just a bit ago. She was the one that kicked him out."

"She got some special time with him. She isn't playing fair," Petunia whined.

I cleared my throat, stepping out from behind Brooke. "I'm not playing at all. This isn't a game to me."

"Good. Less competition." She flicked her index and middle fingers at me, sending a gust of air at my center. I buckled, my head hitting the brick wall behind me.

CHAPTER TWENTY

Gideon

THE FIRST EVALUATION HAD BEEN A BLUR. I DIDN'T remember much of anything besides *her*. She stuck out in the crowd with her red hair in the sea of blondes and brunettes. Like a beacon, my eyes were drawn to her, and once they focused, they'd refused to let go.

Robinson had to prompt me several times on stage to show off my fire magic—the magic all male witches had. I'd been too busy staring, locked in on *her* to notice. The way her eyes had darted around. The way she'd yelled out encouragement to her friend who'd been competing and then dropped back down into her seat, biting her lip while everyone else had continued yelling and cheering. She wasn't like the other witches here. She didn't wish for blood, for someone to fall. Nor did she cower, too afraid to do anything but look beyond her own situation. I could tell she was watching everyone, holding her breath hoping everyone would be okay.

Who'd won? I had no idea. It didn't matter. They didn't matter.

I only cared about the sparks on her face, the way she spoke to me, like I wasn't some stud whose only purpose was to...ugh.

I didn't like to think about that.

I just liked to think about *her*.

She didn't trust me. It was understandable. I wouldn't trust me either. I'd been raised by the Coven, given everything, held accountable to nothing.

I only had to abide by one rule: I couldn't leave.

It'd been the same way my entire life. The nanny witches who'd raised me had never said no. They'd never raise their voice at me for fear I'd cry and they'd get punished.

It wasn't until I was older and wiser that I'd realized the only thing they'd say no to was me leaving. I'd tried for years to find an escape, each attempt busted by a witch who'd been tasked with watching me—one of my keepers.

The last couple of years I'd given up on escaping...on finding a way out. I'd fallen victim to my circumstance and had accepted it.

Until her. Until the sparks on her face had lit a fire within me. There was a way out—there had to be. A place outside of this hell where we could be free, together. Dafni was the ember to the kindling that would light the Academy and the Coven ablaze. I wanted to be the one holding her hand as she struck the match... Maybe she'd ask me to use my magic to light the flame. I'd gladly do it.

I was getting ahead of myself—just like my comment to her earlier, about moving into my room. The way she'd reacted had told me I was out of line...had taken it too far. She didn't see it yet. She didn't see what I saw.

I'd have to go slow. Taking down the Academy and the Coven would come later. Somehow I had to get to know her better so she could get to know me, know that I wasn't some stud...I wasn't someone who took the attention of all the witches at the Academy seriously.

It'd taken a couple witches two years ago to help me realize there was nothing real about them. They wanted my attention for clout, for power. They were blind to what the Coven and the Academy had done to them...made them minions of their so-called army. I couldn't even listen to them talk. All they spoke about was the future of the Coven, the evaluations, becoming the chosen. It'd become robotic at this point, the same words regurgitated over and over again. I no longer spoke to the witches here, instead spending time in my room or searching for more words etched into the brick around the Academy.

But I'd speak to Dafni...I'd speak to her all day. She didn't make me feel like I was good for *one thing*—she treated me like I was good for *nothing*. And that was...refreshing.

There was a challenge there, a motivation I hadn't felt before. She wasn't dazzled by my position here at the Academy like the other witches were.

I could have any witch here, willingly, except her.

Someone who didn't like me. How odd.

How odd that I really liked her. Liked her more than any witch I'd ever met, and that'd been a lot of witches. I'd heard the adage—that everyone wanted what they couldn't have, and maybe that was the case with Dafni, but something told me it wasn't. Dafni was special. It wasn't her red hair or the sparks across her nose. It was the way she carried herself, the way she wasn't intimidated by me or anyone else here. She was a strong, powerful witch. If no one else saw that, that was their own fault.

Dafni had cut me deep, given me so little hope of capturing her attention, I felt like I could do nothing else wrong. I'd do anything to have her look at me, to simply glance my way. With her, I was at rock bottom. There was nowhere to go but up.

I had to do something to connect with her...to show her that she was special, that she had my attention when no one else did.

"Come, let's have our weekly chat." *His* voice always gave me goose bumps—and not the good kind. Arthur Robinson was a scary witch. He had influence in the Coven, and he knew it. He used it to his advantage, never caring about those who got hurt because of it.

I followed him to his room, walking through the halls of the Academy and through the doors to the covenstead. The covenstead reminded me of an anthill I'd read about in a book about insects. Made of tunnels underground, the hallways twisted and weaved. Rooms for the witches of the Coven were designated with wooden doors at uneven intervals. We always had a long way to walk. Robinson's room was deep within the covenstead.

"Gideon." His voice always made my stomach flip, sending swells of stomach acid up my throat. I nodded at him as he stood there, holding the door to his room open. He used his room both as an office and a bedroom. The entire room was sterile, with white-paneled walls he must've had installed to hide the dirt and minimal furniture. He had a bed, big enough for just him—I'd heard rumors of how he took witches back to his room, only to kick them out fifteen minutes later. Not that anyone had ever complained. Attention from a male witch, even fifteen minutes of it, earned bragging rights among the Coven.

This was the only time I was allowed to exit the Academy and enter the covenstead. Once a week, just for this meeting with Robinson. At first, leaving the Academy that imprisoned me and seeing more of the witch world was exciting—but over the years, it became tiresome. We were still underground, in windowless hallways and rooms that held witches that cared only about their legacy, about growing the Coven. I knew I was about to listen to Robinson drone on and on, lecturing me about my place as a male witch in the Academy and eventually the Coven.

I always felt itchy during the meetings—like my skin was crawling. The feeling was getting worse the closer I got to the end of the evaluations. That itchiness and stress only amplified my urge to leave. I needed to get out, get up to the surface.

"I've chosen your partner," he said.

I choked on my spit. "What?"

"The human-born witch with air magic—Petunia Fox."

I opened my mouth to protest. Nothing came out. My hands were shaking. I needed to busy them with something, so he didn't notice. I picked up the papers on the table next to me and aimlessly paged through them.

"Now I know, I know...she's human-born. Not what you were expecting. But I've been watching her during her instruction time. She's powerful. She'll easily win the air magic task."

I stopped flipping through the papers. There was a timeline on one of them—a sort of calendar of events. It was the schedule listing the evaluation tasks.

"What about the water element witches?" I asked. What I really meant was, what about Dafni? I kept replaying the words I'd said to her—that I was going to earn her trust. I'd meant what I said, but I wasn't sure how I was going to do that. It was hard to trust anyone here. No one was consistent or showed any vulnerability. It was all survival and fighting for attention. I'd always kept to myself to avoid conflict. Earning Dafni's trust would take time. I had to be there. Show up. Prove to her that she could trust me.

"There's nothing profound to report from the water element witches." Robinson picked up a remote from his side table and flipped on one of the two televisions mounted on the wall. "It has to be Petunia."

"I'm not choosing Petunia."

He flipped through the channels of the closed-circuit cameras the Coven had positioned around the Academy. "You'll choose who I tell you to. I'm your elder."

I bit my tongue, instead, reading through the papers as quickly as possible.

"See there—she's right there." Robinson clicked more buttons on his remote, zooming in on Petunia coming out of her room. She looked disheveled, a scowl on her face.

Behind her, right before the door closed, I could see *her*. Dafni sat slumped against the wall of her room, her red hair covering the sparks on her face.

I dropped the papers on the table, stood, and pulled the door to his room open. Something was wrong with Dafni.

"Hey! Gideon! Where are you going?" I heard Robinson yell down the hall as I ran back to the Academy.

CHAPTER TWENTY-ONE

Dafni

"Just get in here!"

I moaned; the voice was too loud.

"You've been out there all night. I can see your feet under the door, you bonehead."

"Shhh." The sound left my lips, drool falling out of them.

"Be quiet! She's just waking up!"

"I'm awake," I squeaked, my eyelids peeling open slowly.

Brooke brushed the hair away from my face, tucking it behind my ears as I lifted my head. A large body filled the doorway, light pouring in behind their frame. I closed my eyes tight. The light was sending pulses of pain through my brain.

I closed my eyes, flashbacks of *before* flooding my brain.

Fingers squeezed my cheeks, my lips popping open.

"Don't touch her like that."

"Dafni, wake up."

My eyes opened, meeting the concrete ceiling. It amazed me how the concrete, riddled with cracks, could support all the dirt above it. My right eye squinted as a face slid in front of it. *Brooke.* My left eye squinted as a different face slid in front of it. *Gideon.*

Gideon.

I pushed myself up, pulling my elbows behind me. Both Brooke and Gideon backed away from my face, Brooke's warm hands pushed me back down into a horizontal position.

Ouch. My head hurt. My stomach hurt. My whole body *hurt.*

"Who did this to you?" I hadn't been able to turn my head toward Gideon's voice, but it was his. His usual purr sounded more like a growl, the vibrations must've licked his throat as he spoke.

I closed my eyes. *Petunia.*

"It was Petunia Fox." Brooke's voice met my ears loud and clear.

I mumbled at her not to name Petunia. I didn't need any more drama with any of the witches.

"I thought so," he said.

I heard the door to our room squeak open. "Get some ice for her head while you're out," Brooke yelled.

The door to the room slammed shut.

Soft fingers smoothed the curly hair away from my face. I opened my mouth, willing words from my throat. It'd been too much. My eyes closed.

Time passed before cold ice pressed against my head. That felt good. The sting retreated as the ice numbed the lump.

"You scared me." The purr of his voice made my arms relax by my sides. "That's good, kitten. You need to rest."

———

However long later, once again I slowly opened my eyes, taking in the shadows in the room. Someone had left the bathroom light on and the door cracked, letting in some light. A large silhouette took up most of the room, with wide shoulders and hair that stuck up straight from their head like they'd just run their fingers through it. *Gideon.*

My hands met my forehead, squeezing it as the memories from last night flooded my brain.

Kitten. *Why did he call me kitten?*

I wiggled my toes...my human toes. I was still in human form.

My body instantly relaxed.

Wait...did I accidentally transform? I'd been unconscious, not in control of my body. It was entirely possible I'd changed into the little orange kitten.

Does he now know I shift into a kitten because I don't have poison?

I tried to lift my head. It felt heavy, like a pail full of milk. I relaxed my neck, my head falling back onto a pillow.

"That's it..." It was his voice.

I wiggled my body against the spring-filled mattress I laid on.

I was back in my bed.

"Try to stay still...for just another day..." His voice was soothing—almost as soothing as the cool cloth he placed on my forehead.

I drifted off, the back of my head numb and my body tired.

———

"You must've hit your head hard. You've been out for two days." Brooke helped me sit up, and I battled a wave of dizziness from the sudden movement. "Whoa. Let me help you to the bathroom."

My feet hit the floor, my arm wrapped around Brooke's.

Gideon walked forward to help, but she shooed him back, leading me to the bathroom.

"Are you okay on your own? Or do you want me to come in?" Brooke asked.

I grabbed on the pedestal sink and gave myself a minute to get my balance. My head was still woozy, but I could manage using the toilet alone. I shook my head at her.

"I'll be right outside if you need me," she said.

I used the bathroom and began washing my hands in the sink. I looked up at the mirror and cringed as I saw my face for the first time since Petunia's attack. My eyes were still swollen from sleeping, and my hair needed to be brushed. I put a finger to my lips, gasping as the gash stung underneath the pad of my finger. I must've bit my lip when I hit my head.

I froze.

Right above my lip, just above the corner, something was there. It looked different from the pimples I'd gotten when I'd been younger. It was red and angry looking—it was a sore.

Was this really happening?

I got closer to the mirror, examining my skin for any more spots. Nothing. I came back to the spot above my lip. This was just the beginning. Soon, like every other witch here, I'd have a hooked nose and warts, making my skin bumpy.

This was not what I had imagined when I came here. In truth, I didn't know what I'd imagined. Maybe a path laid out in front of me? Some sort of guidance that I'd somehow accrue from an unknown source. What had I been thinking? It'd been all too easy to visualize myself taking over the Coven, gaining information, and eventually infiltrating my spot as Prime. Before I'd come here, I'd thought it'd be easy.

A tear trailed down my cheek. I quickly wiped it away, not wanting the salt to stain my skin.

All my thoughts about coming here had been nothing more than wishful thinking. I choked a sob down my throat and back into my chest. With a flick of my wrist and two pointed fingers, I used the air magic no one was supposed to know I had, to pause the surrounding air. I stopped it from vibrating so that the embarrassing sounds about to leave my body wouldn't leave the bathroom.

As soon as I felt the air hesitate, I let it out—a deep, guttural cry that hurt my ribs as my lungs clawed for more air. Was it even worth it? I could just disappear, live in the woods— although that hadn't gone great for me the first time. Maybe I could hide in the Velkans' trailer? But what kind of life would that be? In both scenarios, I'd be hiding. That was exactly what my mother would've wanted me to do if I wasn't supposed to be dead already.

Maybe I wasn't meant to be a leader. I'd been born into the role—that didn't mean I was the right witch for it. If my mother was in my place, she'd already have the Coven under her thumb.

I dared to look back at the mirror. Luckily, my face was already so red from sleeping that no one could tell I'd had a complete breakdown in the bathroom. I flicked my wrist again, the fans in the ceiling resuming their humming.

There was a single knock on the door. I opened it slowly, looking out into the room.

Gideon was leaning against the wall outside the bathroom, staring at the doorway.

"Have you been crying?" His hands grabbed my upper arms as his eyes scanned my face. "Why didn't I hear it?"

I looked down at my feet. Maybe my face was redder than I'd thought.

Gideon wrapped his arms around me, pulling my entire body against his. I held my muscles tight, my body tense as our chests touched each other's. Even though I was stiff, he didn't let go. I took a breath in through my nose, inhaling his mossy scent. I let it settle in my nose, breathing out of my mouth, my lungs collapsing along with the rest of my body. Gideon held me vertical as I leaned against him, my body a perfect fit in his arms. Here with my face buried in his chest and his arms wrapped around me, I felt safe and protected. It was quiet and dark—it finally felt like I had the ability to quiet my mind.

There was a knock on the door to our dorm, and Brooke rushed over to open it. "Oh...hi..." She leaned on the doorknob, with her mouth open wide as a man with blond shaggy hair ducked through the door, his eyes wide as he scanned the room, only stopping when his eyes landed on me.

"Are you okay?" Luke asked. "The kitchen staff said something about an incident a couple days ago, and I just found out you were a part of it."

"She's fine," Gideon said, ending our hug and pushing me around him until I was tucked behind his body. His hands never stopped touching me as they moved, finally stilling, each gripping one of my forearms. My nose brushed against the back of his shirt. I closed my eyes, allowing myself a small inhale of his mossy scent through my nose.

"Dafni?" Luke asked, taking a step toward us as Gideon pulled me even closer against his body.

"I'm fine, Luke," I said, peeking my head out from behind Gideon's arm. I was sure I didn't look all that *fine*. My hair was like a mane around my head, and I knew my face was still blotchy and red.

"You know him?" Gideon asked, turning his head, his eyes meeting mine.

"Yes, I know Lu—" I snapped my mouth shut, immediately

realizing my mistake. I was supposed have come from living with human parents, presumably from far away.

"Her grandparents are old acquaintances of my mom's," Luke bluffed. He'd said the lie with such confidence, even I believed him. I supposed it was plausible someone two generations removed from me had known his mother at some point.

Gideon grunted, believing him too.

"If it's okay, I'd like to see her—just to make sure she's okay." Luke moved, trying to peer around Gideon's frame.

"You just did," he growled.

"I only saw a part of her face...probably half of it. I know my mother would feel better if I saw with my own eyes that she was okay."

"She's fine—I promise," Brooke intervened.

"Still, I'd like to see her." Luke planted his feet and crossed his arms over his chest. He was tall, and his body honed from working manual labor around the Coven and helping his mother and sister around the trailer.

Gideon stood still for a moment, the two men staring at each other. I couldn't see Gideon's, but Luke's face was stoic. He wasn't going to leave without seeing if I was okay with his own eyes.

Gideon must've realized the same thing. It wasn't worth the fight. He shuffled me over to the closet, where he grabbed my green sweater off the hook and passed it to me where I still stood behind him.

"Thank you?" I questioned.

He kept his gaze averted, motioning with his head to the sweater.

I looked down, following his eyes. I was in my Academy-issued nightgown. Brooke must've changed me out of the muddy clothes I'd been wearing when Petunia had knocked me unconscious. The gown was thin, the darker hue of my nipples showing through the fabric. My face heated as I quickly shrugged on the sweater to cover myself.

Once the sweater was over my shoulders, Gideon turned around to face me, brushing my hands away so he could fasten the buttons. He went slowly, his knuckles brushing against my stomach and then my breasts as he pushed each opaque button through each hole.

I couldn't breathe as he buttoned my shirt painfully slow. His knuckles drifted across my skin, lingering as if his touch was intentional...like he'd wanted to feel that part of my body.

I liked it. I liked how his fingers felt on me, how my sensitive skin reacted to the heat of his. How there was a pulse between my legs that made me want to bring his fingers to touch me lower... How my torso tilted toward his as if it was begging him to slide his...

Luke cleared his throat from across the room.

Gideon turned, stepping to the side to reveal me. "Satisfied?" he asked, giving a lively flourish with his arms.

Luke glanced at me up and down, nodding.

"Great. You can go now," he said, crossing his arms, mimicking Luke.

Brooke hung onto the doorknob, staring at Luke. "Or he can stay. He probably wants a break from work..."

"No, he can go," Gideon snapped.

She opened the door for Luke, who took one more glance at me before walking through the doorway and down the hallway.

Brooke shut the door, leaning her back against it. "Quite the family friend you got there..."

"His mother's been kind to m—to my family," I corrected.

She pushed herself off the door and sighed. "Well, I'm glad you're finally vertical. I'm going to need someone to watch the air evaluation with tomorrow."

Tomorrow? Brooke had said I'd been out for two days. That

meant the air task was tomorrow and the water task would be a few days after that.

"You've been absent from your classes for the last two days," Gideon said, as if he was reprimanding me. "You need to practice, get the feel for your water magic again."

I sighed. "I don't even know what to practice—the water task could be anything."

"The witches from your group were complaining about all the potion drills Arcana's been putting them through last night at dinner," Brooke said. That sounded like Arcana. "Maybe you could start there?"

Gideon nodded. "Get dressed. I know just the place."

CHAPTER TWENTY-TWO

Dafni

I followed Gideon through the dome, entering the hallway of classrooms that made up the Academy. We walked past the classrooms the more experienced water element witches used to practice potions, the empty classrooms used for practicing air magic, and classrooms with potted plants—many of which looked half dead—that were probably for the earth magics. This was much deeper into the Academy than I'd ever been.

My heels clicked along the floor, two taps to every one of his. I couldn't help but stare at his shoulders. He wasn't more than six inches taller than me, but the way he held himself made him seem larger. With his shoulders back and his head facing forward, he walked with a confidence I couldn't emulate as I walked hunched over, staring at my feet so I wouldn't trip.

"Here."

I almost ran into where he'd stopped in the middle of the hallway with his hand extended toward me.

"You're having trouble keeping up."

Against my better judgment, I put my hand in his. He gripped it tightly and continued walking, this time pulling me along with him.

Gideon stopped in front of a door, letting go of my hand. The loss of warmth had me bringing my hand to my chest. He pressed numbers into a keypad, and the latch unlocking echoed down the hall. I looked around. There was no one here to catch us, or to tell us to go back to the dorms.

"Are you coming in...?" Gideon held the door open, standing inside the room waiting. I tilted my head toward the ground and walked into the room. He let the door shut behind us.

With the flick of a switch, Gideon turned on the lights. It wasn't a classroom but a room dedicated entirely to potion making. The hum of boiling liquid and the crackle of the flames the small cauldrons sat on top of filled the air. A wooden work bench with all sorts of tubes, cauldrons and fires took up most of the space. Books covered the walls, their spines reaching out to me. There were shelves lining the walls with all sizes of flasks and tubes containing different colored liquids and dry ingredients. Some were labeled, others weren't. This place looked nothing like the rooms I'd trained in. Real witches worked here.

"Are we supposed to be here?" I asked.

Gideon bent over to look at a flask with green bubbling liquid. "I can go wherever I want." He reached out to touch the flask.

"Don't," I snapped. "That's an expelling potion. It's skin sensitive. A drop of that will have you bent over with your last meal on the floor."

Gideon dragged his hand back. Maybe I should've let him touch it. He'd be too busy puking, and I wouldn't be thinking about kissing him again.

I rubbed my hands together. This was all too tempting, all these ingredients and supplies at my fingertips.

"Can I make something?" I asked.

Gideon smiled. "Of course, you can."

My brain whirled, potions and their ingredients running through my brain. "What should I make?"

"Maybe an antidote to the love potion that was spilled on you," Gideon said. "I can keep some in my pocket in case you decide you want to kiss me again."

My face heated.

We were both thinking about kissing each other.

"I can see the way you look at me," Gideon said.

I made the mistake of looking into his eyes. They captured me, and I couldn't look away.

He tilted his head as he stared. "You want to kiss me again, don't you?"

I looked down, too slowly, my eyes stopping too long at the space between his legs. I heard a chuckle from somewhere deep inside his body. Immediately, I turned to face the work bench. He didn't need to see how red my face could get.

"Fine, fine, I won't tease you anymore," Gideon said. "But you really should practice. Make that love potion antidote I just mentioned."

I could do that. My fingers tingled as I looked around the room. There were more ingredients here than my grandmother ever had at her cottage. I started a circle around the room, glancing at the different bottles and their contents. I recognized most of the materials, although I'd never seen them in such large quanities. It must've taken years to gather everything here.

I grabbed jars and bottles off the shelves as I went around the room, collecting what I needed for the potion. *Jack pine needles, thimble berries, oyster mushroom extract, deer's blood, and wild licorice root.* I also grabbed a jar of wild bee honey from the shelf. It didn't add anything to the potion except to help it taste less bitter.

Gideon watched from the middle of the room near the workbench, arms crossed in front of him, his body turning as he followed me around the room. I could feel his gaze on the back of my head. I pulled down the back of my skirt just a tad, suddenly aware of how it had ridden up as I walked.

My arms were full when I came to the workbench, and I dropped my ingredients on the tabletop. They clattered, some rolling to the edge, threatening to fall on the floor. I caught them, setting them upright. *Thanks for the help, Gideon.*

I set a clean cauldron on top of the burner, looking around for matches to light it with. In classes, the matches were in the drawer next to our workstation. There were no drawers here.

The whoosh of the flame catching had me turning back to the burner. Gideon was leaned over, his index and middle fingers pointing under the metal grates.

I took a step back. I'd only seen it once, when Gideon was made to perform at the last evaluation. Males were the only witches that had fire magic. I couldn't help but to be impressed.

With his other hand, he fiddled with the gas, twisting and turning it in such a way that I wondered if he'd ever taken a potions class. The burner suddenly lit, the flame reaching a foot into the air. He stood, backing away from the flame.

"Jeez, Gideon." I bent over the burner, taking the knob that controlled the flow of gas in my fingers, and turning it down. "Don't you know how to work these things?" He could've started a big fire. There were so many flammable things in the room.

"There isn't really instruction for my element," Gideon said, his arms once again crossed in front of his chest.

I stared at him for a moment. *No instruction?* He shrugged.

I returned my attention back to the cauldron that was growing hot. I popped the cork of the flask of deer blood and poured it into the cauldron. It hit the hot metal, sizzling for a moment. Next I added the thimble berries, grabbing a wooden spoon from the crock on the workbench. I smashed them into the blood, the berry juices mixing in. A tart smelling steam rose from the cauldron. Time for the mushroom extract and licorice root. I stirred them in, letting the liquid come to a boil before I sprinkled in the jack pine needles.

Glancing in the cauldron, I turned down the flame until the liquid was simmering but not boiling. It needed a few moments to cook. Only when the potion turned a pink color, the same shade that my cheeks continually were around Gideon, would it be ready. My grandmother had made this exact potion many times for my mother to bring back to the Coven. Witches training in potions never got it right on the first try. Bad love potions were part of the territory.

I turned around, looking around the room. There were so many new-to-me ingredients and texts. Gideon put his hands on his hips as he turned his head sideways, reading the labels of the jars on the shelves, his broad back pushing against the white button-up shirt he wore. My heart pattered in my chest. The fast beat had me gulping air.

What was happening to me? Every time he was near, I reacted that way. My heart rate increasing, my breathing going heavy, an odd tingle between my legs. I'd been raised by women, exposed to only women—until recently, when the unfortunate series of events found me here. It couldn't be that all men made me feel this way, could it? I had spent a year with Luke and hadn't felt this way. I'd spent a terrible string of days with Wilder and his roommates and had never felt like this. Was it because Gideon and I had kissed?

Gideon turned around, and so did I—as quickly as I could, so he didn't catch me staring. I could hear his footsteps coming up behind me. I could feel his body heat against my back.

"You know I get whatever I want at this Academy." His voice turned into a purr.

I turned around to the cauldron and peeked inside. The perfect shade of pink. I took the wooden spoon, giving it a quick stir before scooping some up. I turned slowly, careful not to spill. Gideon was within striking distance.

"And I want—"

I didn't think, just acted, as I pushed the spoon between his lips. His hands clenched as the liquid slid down his throat. He bent over, sputtering and coughing, letting out a litany of curse words, some I'd never heard before, between breaths.

"What the *fuck* was that?" he gasped.

"The love potion antidote," I said, still holding the spoon in my hand, watching him.

"It's supposed to taste like asshole?"

"If you're referring to an anus, then you'll have to let me know how you found out what *that* tastes like." I turned around and scooped another spoonful of the antidote from the cauldron. I eyed the bottle of honey I'd grabbed but forgotten to add. It probably did taste like *asshole*, whatever that tasted like. "You'd better try a couple more spoonfuls just to make sure it's right."

Gideon's face lost color, and he shook his head. "No way— that stuff's terrible."

I extended the spoon further. "You never know, you might just fall in love with me," I teased.

He leaned forward, wrapping his lips around the spoon, taking the liquid into his mouth.

Ouch. I didn't know what exactly hurt or why it hurt, but it did. No one wanted a frizzy redheaded weird witch like me. I turned back to the cauldron, ladling another spoonful. I let out a breath. Why did I want him to like me anyway? He made my body feel out of control. I wasn't here for silly love games or to meet my prince charming. I was here for power, for control, for Prime.

"Do you know how to make other potions?"

I spun around, the pink potion flinging from the wooden spoon still in my hand. "What else should I make, Gideon?" I knew I was lashing out, but my feelings were hurt. "A learning potion because you don't attend classes? A pleasure potion so you don't have to stare at me with those...eyes?"

"My eyes? What's wrong with my eyes?" Gideon asked, a smile growing on his lips.

He knows what I meant. I scowled before turning around and continued ladling the extra potion into small flasks.

"But seriously, Dafni." Gideon leaned against the workbench, the liquid sloshing around in the cauldron as his hip pressed against it. "If you can make potions, all different kinds of potions, you should practice."

I pushed the cork into the flask forcefully. I probably wouldn't be able to remove it again without some pliers. "And why would I need to do that?"

"Because I know something you don't."

"And what's that?"

"What the water task will be."

CHAPTER TWENTY-THREE

Gideon

"You do?" Dafni asked, her eyebrows furrowed above her nose. It was the freckles on her nose I loved to stare at. No one at the Academy had them. Everyone had been here, underground, away from the sun, for far too long. Dafni had them, though, proof that there was life above the surface, a sun that didn't shine from only the pentagon window at the top of the dome.

The rest of us down here in the dark were rotting, slowly deteriorating, becoming disfigured. I'd had the black mask around my eyes since I could remember, but the veins falling down my cheeks were new. Further proof that this place was killing us.

The only sunlight I ever saw was from that damn window at the top of the dome. That was what made Dafni's freckles so intriguing. She'd been to the surface, experienced life outside of the Academy. The rest of us couldn't say the same.

"I do," I said.

Dafni paused for a moment before continuing to ladle the excess potion into a second flask she'd found. I shouldn't have teased her like that, drank her love potion antidote. I didn't think it would do anything...not that she hadn't made it right, just that the way I felt wasn't going to be suppressed by a potion.

"What is it?" she asked, as though she wasn't interested in my answer. Like the answer wasn't what every water elemental witch wanted.

"It's rage," I whispered. "They want you to make a potion that creates one of the strongest emotions."

"And you don't think I can do it?" she asked.

"I'm not sure even the seasoned witches at the Coven can do it," I said.

She glared at me.

"You can do whatever you want here at the Academy, right?" Dafni talked down at her cauldron instead of turning to face me. She was mad. Irritated with me. Her cheeks flamed red, and she scooped the potion with such vigor that it caused me to take a step away for fear of being splashed.

I chewed on my tongue, remembering the words that'd left my mouth earlier. They were true. I could do whatever I wanted at the Academy. There were no rules except that I was forced to stay here.

"If you can do whatever you want, then why don't you just leave?" Dafni asked.

"And how do you think I can do that?" I asked.

"Find a door. Use your legs." Dafni turned back to the workbench, pulling a clean cauldron from the shelf below.

"It doesn't work like that. The Coven has scouts." I ran my

fingers through my hair. "They'd find me. I'd lose the freedom I have here."

Dafni paused. "You call this freedom?" She shook her head. "Before I came, I used to think that maybe I'd like it here. Maybe I'd want to stay a while. But now? Now I want to get out, to help everyone here escape."

My nonexistent rebuttal got caught in my throat. I hadn't expected her to say that. Did she truly want that? To help? If I had an ally in this...a partner that wanted the same things I did...

"What are you staring at, Gideon?" The sound of her voice stopped the thoughts racing through my brain. The cauldron clanked against the stove as she put it down.

Had she caught me staring? The real question was, staring at what? I'd been observing everything that was *Dafni*. The way her skirt moved back and forth, riding up her hips, showing off just a tiny bit of her ass as she walked. The way her white button-up shirt was thin, doing nothing to disguise what lay underneath. Her perked nipples had almost been the death of me in her room as I buttoned up her sweater.

But there was something else I was entirely captivated with that had nothing to do with how she looked. She was brave and pushed for what she wanted. Dafni wasn't afraid of standing up and speaking. She might've been timid when she'd first arrived, but I saw a fire in her that had nothing to do with the flaming color of her hair.

I watched her neck twitch before she grabbed hold of a flask and went over to the sink, filling it with filtered tap water. They filtered everything that came into the potion room. The Coven didn't mess around with impurities.

Dafni quickly glanced at me before turning off the faucet. After pouring the water into the cauldron, she again pulled open a nearby drawer, looking for matches. Maybe she was more flustered than she let on. Just like before, there weren't any matches. I stalked up behind her, noticing the goose bumps that appeared as I bent over her shoulder, making sure my breath hit her neck.

"Let me help, kitten," I whispered. I put a hand on her lower back, enjoying the shiver that traveled from her neck down to my hand. Summoning my fire magic, I pointed my index and middle fingers to the burner, adjusting the gas knob so I didn't light her curls ablaze.

Dafni wiggled out of my hand, setting up another burner.

"Why do you need two burners, kitten?"

She grabbed another empty cauldron and set it onto an unlit burner. "You said I needed to practice, right?"

Color me amused. "You can do whatever you want, Dafni."

"Can I?" She pulled the drawer open again, this time not bothering to look for the matches. *Stubborn witchling.* Like I hadn't just lit her previous burner with my magic. She refused to ask for help.

"The fumes are going to your head," I whispered. Reaching around Dafni, I caged her in with both of my arms. She wiggled between them, her hair tickling my chin. I pointed my fingers at the burner, lighting the flame and adjusting the knob to a steady blaze.

She turned around to face me, the freckles on her face standing out against her pale skin. My eyes moved around her face, trying to connect the dots, like it would solve the puzzle that was *Dafni*.

Her hands met my chest, pushing me away from the bench. "I know my red hair and pale skin make me look different from everyone else here, but didn't anyone at the Academy teach you it's rude to stare?"

"I'm not staring, kitten. I'm admiring."

Dafni snorted. "Well, go admire some shelves and find me

wild carrot, red rosinweed, and a small jar of asafoetida." She spun around in a huff, her skirt lifting with the movement, teasing me again.

Water ran in the sink as Dafni began filling another pitcher. "You're admiring again..."

I turned to face the nearest shelf, pulling my eyes away from her. "Only admiring the shelves, kitten."

"Mm-hmm. Find me those ingredients, Gideon."

I dragged my finger along the rows of glass jars, glancing at the labels before they twirled under the press of my fingertip. *Wild Carrot.* I pulled the jar off the shelf. I'd never paid attention to how many jars were in this room. Shelves and shelves of ingredients. Dafni was weaving around the room, grabbing jars off of shelves without even reading the labels. She could do the job she'd given me in a third the time. But she didn't want me to stare at her. Like she didn't know that she was mesmerizing to look at. That all I wanted to do was sit on the stool and watch her work. I couldn't help but wonder if she had anyone else staring at her like I did.

White Rosinweed, I read. *Where the hell was the red kind?*

Dafni let her collection of jars fall from her arms and clatter on the table. She got to work, setting them up, labels facing her in a line along the workbench.

I turned around. "So, you know this guy, Luke, personally?"

Red Rosinweed. Finally. The glass jars clinked together as I held them in the crook of my arm.

"I don't pry into your personal life, Gideon, and you shouldn't be prying into mine."

Not the answer I wanted.

Dafni paused for a moment before corking a jar she'd just finished scooping out of. "I know him well enough to trust him."

That didn't make me feel any better. I turned around,

scouring the shelves for the last jar. "He saved my life," Dafni whispered so quietly, I almost missed it.

"Luke saved your life?"

She spun around, holding a dripping wooden spoon in her hand. She walked toward me, her eyes squinted and focused, like maybe she'd hit me on the side of the head with the spoon in her hands. Her freckles became more and more pronounced as she closed in. I had nowhere to go, my back to a shelf. Keeping the wooden spoon close to my ear, she reached around the other side of my head with her free hand, grabbing a small jar off the shelf behind me.

"Asafoetida," she said before turning around and walking back to the bench, setting the jar down with the others. I let a breath out of my nose before I walked over to the bench, setting the two jars I'd collected on the tabletop.

"What a good helper you are, Gideon. It must feel good to do something useful for once." Dafni's hands didn't stop moving as she spoke, now working two cauldrons, adding different ingredients to each.

Something didn't sit right with me about Luke. The way she said she trusted him instead of me. There was something deep inside me that yelled—no, screamed at me to stake my claim.

Pressing my chest into her back, I put my mouth next to her ear, keeping my voice low. "What else can I help you with, kitten? I love to be of use." I felt her breath catch for a moment, watched her mouth opening before closing again. *Good.* I was having the same effect on her she always had on me. "Maybe I could help you with this?" I put my hand over the top of hers as she stirred a cauldron, the warm steam from the liquid brushing our wrists. She had tiny freckles on her fingers too. How had I not noticed that before?

Dafni gripped the rounded handle of the spoon tighter,

trying to shrink away from my touch. Something about the way she gripped the handle made my cock stir in my pants. Images in my head of her freckled fingers wrapped around me, pumping me slowly...

"Should I help you with that?" I gestured to the glass jar I'd collected, the red rosinweed. She'd already uncorked it and set it next to the cauldron.

"Sprinkle some in that cauldron," Dafni said.

I picked up the jar, shaking it back and forth gently until a sprinkle of red powder floated down into the boiling cauldron nearest my hand.

"That's enough," she said, grabbing my wrist. Her breath caught after she realized she was touching me, wrapping her soft fingers around me. I pulled my pelvis away from her so she wouldn't feel my cock twitch in my pants.

Dafni let go of my wrist quickly, grabbing a clean wooden spoon and stirring the red rosinweed into the boiling water. I let go of the hand I'd been helping stir, letting her work. She was a wonder in the potion room.

Both of her hands were busy stirring separate cauldrons, the movements of her arms making her shoulders rotate, which made her ass circle round and round. I hadn't pulled myself far enough away to account for the way her hips would move when she stirred. We both stilled when I felt her ass press against the hard bulge in my pants.

"Kitten..." I groaned. The soft plush of her ass against the hardness in my pants made the tip of my cock weep, begging to be pushed through her cheeks, where I knew it would be warm and as wet as the potions she was stirring.

"Gideon, I..." Her legs squeezed together, moving back and forth as she flexed her feet in her boots, rubbing her skirt against me, making it ride up higher on her waist.

I slipped my hands beneath her skirt, placing them on her

hips. "Steady, kitten." Her hands stopped stirring the cauldrons in front of her. I hadn't felt her take a breath against my chest since she'd felt me hard behind her. "Breathe, Dafni." Using her name instead of the nickname I'd given her seemed to snap her out of whatever headspace she was in. She looked behind her shoulder at me, her green eyes wide, her mouth puckered open, her flushed rose lips making an O.

"What are you doing to me?" Dafni whispered, her eyes bouncing around my face.

"What do you mean, kitten?"

She looked down at my hands, hidden beneath her skirt. "I've never felt like this before."

"Like what?"

"Like I can't control my body. It's like my body's been taken over and my brain doesn't even have a say in what it does."

I bent over, bringing my face close to hers. I could feel her pants of hot breath against my cheek. "Doesn't it feel good?"

She thought for a moment before looking back up at me. "Yes."

"Then why don't you let me keep making you feel good?"

One cauldron overflowed, the liquid hissing as it hit the flames of the burner.

"Dang it!" Dafni turned back to the workbench, stirring the cauldrons vigorously to quell the bubbles. It did nothing to appease my cock, her rocking hips causing a groan to leave my lips. "I have to keep stirring these, Gideon."

Her hands were busy, her mind partially occupied.

"Let me help you, kitten."

CHAPTER TWENTY-FOUR

Dafni

Just keep stirring, Dafni. My brain was bouncing around, first to the potions bubbling in the cauldron. I needed to keep stirring so they wouldn't bubble over again. Then it bounced to Gideon's hands. How they gripped my hips, his fingers brushing back and forth ever so slightly. Subsequently to the hard bulge in his pants that he'd nudged between the cheeks that were not on my face.

I knew what *that* was, of course. Once Annabel had realized I'd never had the birds-and-the-bees talk, she'd sat me down and told me everything, my face as red as a tomato by the time she was done. But this was the first time I'd felt one pressed up against me. It felt bigger than I imagined it would—it only made the tingling between my legs stronger.

Him pressed against me and the pulsing between my legs made me move—my toes in my boots, my thighs rubbing against each other. If my hands hadn't been occupied, I would've slipped them beneath the waistband of my skirt.

"Gideon," I whispered, "someone could walk in."

His growl met my ear. "It *is* lunchtime."

I glanced up at the clock ticking on the wall above our heads. The *tick-tock* of the clock, the sound of the wooden spoons hitting the sides of the cauldrons, and our unsteady breaths filled the room. It was quiet but loud, my body and mind buzzing, waiting for his next move. He always had one, and they usually surprised me, although I tried to hide it. Gideon was so much more experienced than me. He'd lived at the Academy his whole life, had access to any witch he'd wanted. I, on the other hand, had grown up on a farm, where I'd killed frogs and lived on every word of the fairy tales my grandmother had spun at bedtime.

Gideon's hands traveled lower, down my hips, closer to my throbbing core. I held my breath, waiting, wanting him to keep going but still nervous about what he'd do.

"Can I keep helping you feel good?" His words tumbled through my ear, doing somersaults inside my brain.

Yes! Please do whatever you can to make me feel less like the boiling point I keep my cauldrons at.

"Mm-hmm," was all I could muster, my throat squeezing shut as I held back a more embarrassing sound from leaving my lips.

What was he going to do next? I knew what I wanted—his hands down my skirt, between my legs, his fingers helping rid my body of the tension that made me feel like I was about to burst.

"Keep stirring those cauldrons, kitten." Gideon's warm breath met my ear, right before his lips did, brushing against the outside. "Let me take care of you."

The moment I heard his words, his hands dipped low, where no one beside me had ever gone before.

I let out a breathy sigh when his fingers slipped beneath my skirt, pushing past the folds between my legs. His fingers slid easily through them, all the teasing already having made me wet, putting delicious pressure just where I needed it.

Gideon's fingers stopped moving once they reached the wettest part of me.

Why had he stopped?

His body slumped into mine, pushing me against the workbench. "Is this all for me?"

His fingers curled, scooping up the liquid I'd created with his fingers. I cringed as he removed his hand, bringing the wetness with him, holding it in front of my face. His fingers glistened with what he had retrieved from between my legs, the liquid pooling before sliding down between them, threatening to drip—right into my cauldron.

The hiss of my wetness hitting the side of the hot cauldron hit my ears at the same time Gideon's chuckle did.

"You think that's funny?" I spit out, more embarrassed than angry.

He was laughing at me, what my body had produced. It might've been my first time being touched by a man, but I knew that was normal. It had happened every time I'd touched myself before...

Gideon brought his fingers to his mouth, slipping them inside, his lips closing around them. His cheeks sunk in as he sucked them, his throat bobbing as he swallowed.

"Mmm...I'm full. Lunch can wait." Gideon's hand dived back under my skirt, finding my still-dripping core.

He liked it? I didn't have time to think before his fingers once again slipped between my folds and started moving. They didn't go anywhere, staying in the same spot, moving in a circular motion, massaging the most sensitive part of me.

Oh my. The way his thick fingers moved, the way he was pressing down, holding pressure against me, had my eyes rolling back and my head tipping back to where his shoulder met his neck.

My arms stopped stirring, my brain solely focused on the hand between my legs and the tingling it sent up my spine all the way to the tip of my nose.

The hand stopped moving. "Keep stirring, kitten." His voice was a command I had to follow. His hand continued moving the moment I continued stirring. My knees bent, my legs falling further apart, to aid his actions. His fingers put just enough pressure against me that I could feel them roll over my clit. Occasionally, he'd catch the nub between two of his fingers and roll it, sending pangs of pleasure throughout my entire body.

I began aiding his actions, moving my hips back and forth against his fingers, creating a feeling in my body that was beyond what I'd been able to create with my own hand.

I stirred the cauldrons in time to my hips moving against the pads of his fingers between my legs.

Up, around, and down.

Up, around, and down.

Up, around, and down.

The tingle between my legs started to feel like a twisting sensation in my pelvis, something that wound tighter and tighter with every rub of his fingers.

"Take what you need, kitten. You're doing so well," Gideon murmured into my ear, my hips only moving faster, my body pressing down harder on his hand after hearing his words. He was enjoying this as much as I was.

I let myself go, letting myself fall victim to the sounds of

Gideon's breath against my ear, his hardness pressed into my backside, and the press of his fingers between my legs.

It felt *good*.

It felt too good.

Felt so good I found myself letting go of the wooden spoons I'd been stirring the cauldrons with to grab on to Gideon's face that was nestled between my shoulder and neck. I clawed at his jaw as his fingers moved in circles vigorously between my legs.

Don't stop. Keep going. My back arched, Gideon's hardness leaving the warm nest it'd been nestled in, my head leaning against his shoulder as I yelled at the ceiling things I'd only heard in the hallways of the Academy. The words rolled off my tongue like I'd used them daily.

"That's it." Gideon's voice sounded muffled in my ear. "You feel like a fucking dream."

My own labored breaths that met my ears were the only sign that it was over. My vision was still dotted with black dots, my body limp, held up by Gideon's strong arms. *His muscular arms.* I'd fallen prey to him—again. My body stiffened at the thought.

"Easy," Gideon murmured, one arm wrapped around my waist, holding me up, the other hand moving between cauldrons stirring haphazardly.

Both cauldrons still bubbled evenly, neither had boiled over. The healing potion I was making looked ordinary, bright neon bubbles popping on the surface. The other, the rage potion, was being mixed under the careful watch of Gideon's hands, the green liquid steadily boiling. I breathed a sigh of relief. The potions were fine.

"I think I need to go lie down," I whispered. My body was jelly. What had Gideon done to me? He'd somehow drained all my energy, making me weak. This had to be some sort of latent power he possessed as a male witch. There was no other explanation for the way my knees buckled and my eyes fluttered closed. Gideon wrapped his arms around my body, and I melted against his warm chest. Why did he feel so good? He turned around toward the door that led out into the hallway.

"My potions!" I tried to yell. My voice came out of my throat hoarsely. Had I been screaming?

"They were just for practice," Gideon said.

I nodded the best I could, my chin hitting my chest as I forced my eyelids to open. What had he done to me that'd made me so tired?

His scent filled my nose as I let my cheek roll into his chest. "I'm going to bring you back to my room, kitten," he whispered before picking me up, cradling me in his arms. He walked toward the door, kicking it open with his foot, still holding me with both of his arms. Cool air from the hall rushed into the hot potion room.

I shook my head back and forth, trying to clear my head. "Can I grab a book?" There was so much information in the potion room I was prohibited from reading as an inexperienced witch.

"Which one, kitten?" Gideon purred, his stubble tickling my cheek.

I lifted my finger and pointed to one I'd eyed when I was gathering ingredients. It was a spell book, for beginners.

Gideon pulled the book from the shelf, handing it to me before wrapping his arm around me once again. I couldn't help but fold into him, curling myself around my new book in his arms. He was warm and safe for the time being. Like his fingers between my legs, it was something I'd never felt before.

CHAPTER TWENTY-FIVE

Gideon

MY FINGERS RUBBED TOGETHER, REMEMBERING THE feeling of *her*. The slippery velvet of the skin between her legs. The way she'd gasped my name as she'd clawed at my jaw, grabbing on to anything, trying to ground herself as I made her green eyes roll to the back of her skull.

When I'd carried her back to my dorm, her cheeks turned the sweetest shade of pink, her freckles shining golden against the hue of her skin. Her eyelashes fluttered against her cheeks as she'd tried to keep her eyes open. I'd worn her out.

She was in my room, lying next to me in my bed, sleeping off the exhaustion I'd caused her. Lying on my side, I watched her chest rise and fall with each of her breaths. She looked peaceful, the worry lines typically pinched between her eyebrows absent.

It was obvious she was inexperienced, the way she'd been

embarrassed when I dipped my fingers between her legs, bringing them to my lips wet with her arousal—the arousal she'd created just for me.

Her naivety had only intrigued me further. The witches at the Academy all talked, so they knew, or at least pretended to know, what happened during sex. Dafni didn't know what to do with me and didn't pretend like she did. She was mine to teach. I could help her explore her body, demonstrate the way I liked mine to be explored.

"How long have I..." Dafni looked adorable as she woke up from her long sleep next to me. Pieces of her hair stuck to her forehead. Her lips were dry, and her tongue darted out to lick them. She'd slept *hard* through the rest of the day and through the night. Part of me wondered if her body was still feeling the effects of her injuries.

"It's morning," I said, scooting in closer to her. I'd kept my distance while we'd slept, the bed the Academy provided me large enough to afford some unfortunate space between us.

"Urgghh," Dafni groaned, her arms raising above her head in a stretch before her hands reached down to smooth her hair. "I've missed three days of instruction now."

"And...?" I questioned.

"And I need to be there practicing with everyone else," Dafni said.

I rolled over, wrapping my arm around her waist. She stilled. "I already told you what the task was."

Dafni wiggled out of my grasp, crawling to the end of the bed. I lay back against the wall, admiring the view.

"You said it yourself—that rage was the hardest potion to make." Dafni's feet hit the floor, and she began searching for her skirt.

"I was teasing you about it being the hardest..."

"No, you were right. It *is* hard. I need practice."

"Okay, I'll let you go," I said.

She paced around the room, looking for her clothes. "Oh, you will?"

I smirked. She wouldn't find them. I'd dressed her in one of my undershirts last night. Her uniform was so far under my bed she'd have to get on all fours to find it. "Only because I want you to win."

Dafni paused, pulling the shirt down over her freckled thighs.

I looked at her until she met my eyes. "I want you to be mine."

Like a mouse in the kitchen, she squeaked, pulling the shirt further down her thighs before opening the door of my room and scurrying away.

I tucked my hands behind my head, leaning back into my pillow, waiting for the click of the door closing. She already was *mine*. I had the proof on my fingers. I brought them to my nose, smelling her scent. My dick twitched in my pants as I inhaled. The scent was still there—even hours later.

The door to my room blew open—had it closed?—a gust of wind hitting my face.

"*Gideon?*" The woman I recognized from the television screen in Robinson's room strolled into my bedroom, her heels stomping, sending dust into the air.

Petunia Fox.

I got out of bed quickly, throwing on the jacket that was hanging from the door of my wardrobe.

"Oh, I'm so sorry!" She slammed the door, mortar dust from the brick walls raining down. "I didn't know my air magic was so...powerful." Petunia stepped close enough that she reached the top of my head with her hand, running her fingers through the strands, smoothing it down.

I took a step back, out of her reach. "What are you doing here, Petunia?"

She rested her hand on her chest, right on top of her breasts, her eyes twinkling when she saw my eyes had followed her hand. "You remembered my name?"

Petunia took a step forward.

I took a step back.

"What else do you know about me?"

I stared at her, trying to keep my face as blank as possible.

"Did you know that I'll be competing for you today?" She flicked her fingers at my wardrobe, closing it with a burst of wind. "I'm planning on winning." Petunia took another step toward me, and when I tried to retreat, my back hit the brick wall. She pulled up the waist of her skirt, revealing more of her thigh. "Wouldn't you like that?"

Petunia didn't see me shaking my head because she was too busy looking around my room...probably visualizing herself living here with me.

"It'd be so much easier for me to win if you tell me what the task is."

"I don't know what the task is," I lied.

"I know you know." She snapped her head to me, her eyes squinting. "You have to know. You probably chose the tasks yourself to vet potential partners."

Slowly, I side-stepped along the wall, trying to put some distance between us.

In an instant, Petunia closed the distance I'd gained, her fingers wrapping around the lapels of my jacket, pulling my chest against hers. "Please?" she whispered, her lips brushing my ear.

My body tensed as her hands traveled up my chest, wrapping themselves around the back of my neck. Her touch didn't feel right—it felt harsh and exacting. She was touching me to get something from me. It felt so different from the way Dafni had touched me, her hands soft and her touch gentle when she'd wrapped her arms around me when I'd carried her back to my room.

I grabbed her wrists, removing her hands from my body, pushing them back toward her.

"I don't know what the task is," I said. "I'd like you to leave."

"You want me to leave?"

This time I took a step toward her, and Petunia instinctively backed away. "Yes, get out of my room."

"Dafni was just in here...you didn't kick her out," Petunia spat.

I refused to bait her further. Telling her I'd already chosen Dafni would only further enrage her.

Petunia continued backing away toward the door. "I guess I'll just have to impress you at the air task today...show you how powerful I am...prove to you that I'm better than Dafni." She opened the door. "Is that what you want? Do I need to prove myself to you?"

A growl escaped my lips.

"Fine. That's what I'll do," Petunia said as she exited my room, letting the door slam closed as she left.

CHAPTER TWENTY-SIX

Dafni

"Don't you look all bright-eyed and bushy-tailed this morning. You have a certain glow about you..."

Brooke was sitting on the bed when I scurried in, using both of my hands to keep Gideon's shirt pulled down over my thighs. The door closed behind me, and I let out a sigh of relief. I hadn't run into anyone on the way up here.

Brooke stood and walked around me, examining me from head to toe. "Are you wearing one of his shirts?"

I looked down at my body. Yes. Yes, I was. I vaguely remembered putting on one of his shirts to sleep in last night after he'd helped me strip out of my uniform. I'd been too tired to care what Gideon saw of me.

"Did you two...?"

"No!" My face heated as I turned away from Brooke's critical eye. "We didn't do...whatever you think we did."

"Then what did you do?" Brooke asked.

"We didn't do anything—"

"Liar."

"Fine!" I let myself fall back onto the mattress, covering my eyes with the crook of my elbow.

"Yes! Spill, Dafni." I felt Brooke's weight settle into the mattress next to me.

"He touched me."

"Where?"

I pulled my arm off my eyes, giving her the best glare I could muster. "Where do you think?"

Brooke's eyes bounced down between my legs before returning to my eyes. "Oh. Oh, my."

"Yeah, and it felt *good*." I tried to gauge her reaction, tried to read her face with my eyes. She kept her features neutral, her eyes trained on me. "And I let him know it felt good."

Brooke giggled. "That doesn't seem all that bad."

"Not until I have to see him again, see his face, knowing what we did yesterday."

She fell back, lying next to me on the mattress. "Maybe he'll want to do it again."

"Not anytime soon. I've got to get to class today, and then the air task is tonight."

"Promise we'll sit next to each other?" Brooke asked.

"Of course," I said. "We need to watch our *dear roommate* compete."

She rolled her eyes. "I'm sure Petunia will do whatever she can to win. She hasn't been back in our room since she attacked you. She must be spending all her time preparing."

We both cringed.

I pulled my extra uniform from the closet and went to the bathroom to change. I felt the loss of Gideon's scent as I removed his shirt and pulled on my uniform. The water elements' evaluation would be in a couple days. I needed to prepare as much as I could, so I wouldn't make a fool of myself in front of the entire Academy.

Without the distraction of Gideon's hands.

"I'll see you tonight," I called out to Brooke as I left our room in search of a cauldron.

Witches squished Brooke and me between them on the bleachers, our boots stacked on top of each other.

"There she is!" I whispered, nodding toward where Petunia walked in with the rest of the air elemental witches. Her ringlets were tight, and she held her nose high in the air. She scanned the crowd, narrowing in on where Brooke and I were sitting. The way she stared at us turned my stomach. She looked at us with such intensity, like she was challenging us—and we weren't even competing.

Some of the surrounding witches looked nervous, their eyes bouncing around the cavern. Other, more experienced witches stood tall, facing forward with their arms at their sides.

The cavern looked different from the last task. Instead of dirt, the ground was covered with several feet of sand. The witches walked gingerly through it, their heeled boots sinking.

"There he is..." Brooke bumped my shoulder before tilting her head toward the stage. Toward where Gideon was sitting.

He was sitting in the same wing-backed chair he'd been in during the last task—though this time he didn't look relaxed or bored. There were lines in his face from the way he flexed his jaw. He had his forearms resting on the armrests of the chair, his hands gripping the ends so tightly that his knuckles were white. The knuckles that had been between my legs. My cheeks instantly heated. And his eyes. They were staring at me.

I looked away as quickly as I could. His gaze was hungry, and I didn't need to feel the way his eyes consumed me.

Robinson took the stage, his voice booming throughout the cavern as he gave his welcome speech, explaining the rules and what was at stake. I let the sound of his voice wane, and instead of paying attention to him, I looked around the cavern, at the faces of the witches in the audience as well as the witches on the floor. They all had different colored hair and skin, were different heights and builds, but they all had the same expressions on their faces as he spoke. They pulled their brows down, focused their eyes as they glared at the stage, and closed, tucked, and tightened their lips.

I brought my hand to my own face, feeling the downward tilt of my eyebrows, the wrinkles between my brows. The way my neck tensed involuntarily every time Robinson's voice fluctuated.

Rage. I was feeling rage, and so was everyone else.

Everyone hated Robinson.

He had a definite *ick* about him—the way he stared at us, the way he saw the female witches as vessels instead of people. Robinson wasn't unlike my mother in that way—wanting the best and discarding anyone who was less than perfect.

From high up on the bleachers, Robinson looked small. He was a crumb surrounded by a colony of ants. It would only take one of us—one witch to nibble, and the rest would follow. We could swarm him.

"Look." Brooke tapped my leg before pointing over at Petunia. She was pushing the other witches aside, running to the side of the cavern.

"I missed it. What are they supposed to be doing?" I asked.

Brooke stood as everyone around us did, trying to get a better view. "They have to make it to the top." She pointed to the ceiling of the cavern. "First one to touch the top wins."

The witches on the sandy floor looked around, locking eyes with each other, as if they were daring each other to go first. Witches began pointing their fingers at the ground, gusts of air traveling down their fingers and into the sand. This created a plume of sand and only propelled the witch a of couple feet in the air before she fell back down.

"The sand—it's too soft to push off of," Brooke whispered.

Petunia, finding purchase on a large rock that hovered just above the sand, regained our attention. I could see the white teeth of her smile from across the cavern.

She was the only one smiling.

We watched as she kneeled on the rock, leaning over the side, sticking both of her hands into the sand. She stuck her tongue out between her teeth in concentration as she stared at her hidden hands. Only when we heard the screams of the witches on the floor did she look up, the smile back on her face.

The witches on the floor were sinking, being drawn beneath the sand by some invisible force. Sand blew up around them from where they tried to use their air magic, trying to raise themselves up to escape the pull of the sand.

"They're all sinking!" I yelled, looking around for a way off the bleachers. Maybe I could help them, make the sand wet so their air magic would have a more solid place to land.

Brooke grabbed hold of my arm, steadying me.

Once again, this task wasn't fair. The witches couldn't use their air magic in the sand and Petunia was up to something. I just knew it. I wanted to do something, anything besides just standing here. There was nowhere to go. I was trapped in the middle of the bleachers, surrounded by witches. My fingernails pushed through the skin on my palms. I'd have to push and climb over them to get to the floor.

"Look at the wall!" Brooke pointed at the wall of the cavern she had tried to make her way through several days ago. Sand bubbled up, breaking the surface. It looked like boiling water. "She's made an air current beneath the surface. The sand is moving so quickly below, it's created something like quicksand..."

We could do nothing but watch as the witches on the floor fought and clawed against the current, trying to keep their bodies from sinking.

The instant Petunia pulled her hands from the sand, the witches stopped sinking. Her steps were quick as she bounded across the now still sand, dodging the heads and shoulders of the witches trapped. She stopped at a group of ten witches who'd been clumped together, pushed next to one another by the quicksand, their hair and faces brushing against each other's on the surface.

Petunia looked back at the stage, checking to see if Robinson and Gideon were watching before she placed a foot on a witch's head, then, like balancing on lily pads, she stepped on the next head and the next until she was in the middle of the group. The witches winced, and their faces scrunched with the pain of holding her weight and the heel of her boot.

Pointing her index and middle fingers at the tops of the witches' heads, she blew a gust of wind down at them, the ten of them a solid surface to propel her upward. They cried out from the wind that whipped their hair and pushed them further into the sand. She floated up steadily, touching the ceiling before lowering herself back down onto the ground.

Robinson was standing on the stage, clapping, his mustache curved up, following the smile on his lips. "We have a winner!"

Petunia made her way to the stage, walking around the sunken witches, sand kicking up from the back of her boots. She didn't look at the crowd who were politely clapping or at Robinson, who was beaming at her through his beady eyes. Her gaze pointed directly at Gideon.

Climbing up on the stage, she walked toward where Gideon sat, bypassing Robinson, who was still smiling and clapping. She stopped, hands on her hips, in front of Gideon. With her back to the crowd, I could no longer see him. Petunia's ringlets bobbed as her head tilted, then shook back and forth. She took a step back, looking back into the crowd, scanning the witches until her eyes landed on me. I gasped as both she and Gideon stared at me.

"Oh shit," Brooke whispered.

"Let's congratulate the winner!" Robinson interrupted, grabbing Petunia's wrist from her hip and raising it above her head.

Everyone in the crowd mechanically clapped while Gideon and I continued staring at each other.

"I don't believe anything will be able to top that performance. Let's not wait around a few days for the water element's evaluations. Instead, we'll hold it tomorrow—then Gideon can choose his partner."

"Oh shit," Brooke said, louder this time.

Tomorrow. I'd be competing tomorrow.

I looked around at the witches Petunia had buried to further her scheme. I looked at the witches standing and clapping, that look of rage still on their faces. They needed me to help, needed me to encapsulate the anger they were feeling, mix it with my own and unleash it onto the Coven. There only needed to be a single spark for flames to erupt.

Was I ready? Probably? But I wasn't sure what I was ready for. I refused to compete for a man. He could choose whoever he wanted, tradition or not. Gideon would have to decide he was done with the Coven's customs and make that choice himself. If he couldn't do that, couldn't stand up for what was right, then he was better off choosing Petunia.

Tomorrow I wouldn't compete for him, I'd compete for the

Academy and the witches trapped here. I'd show them I was a powerful witch and a capable leader.

The witches began to file out of the bleachers as soon as Robinson lowered Petunia's arm. Brooke and I wove through the crowds and made our way toward the floor. The sand was as soft as it looked, and my boots sunk down in the grains.

I fell to my knees in front of one witch who was buried and began digging around her shoulders. "Help me, Brooke," I directed.

Brooke fell to her knees next to me, and we worked on digging out the witch's arms. As soon as she could bring her hands to the surface, we dug in our boots and pulled her from the sand. She lay on her back, catching her breath from the exertion. I waited until she sat up, and she nodded at me signaling she was okay before moving onto the next buried witch, digging in the sand to free her hands.

A cloud of sand bloomed to my right as knees covered in dark-green pants hit the ground and large hands began digging, helping free the witch I was digging up.

Gideon.

I looked at him and then back up at the stage where Petunia was still standing, alone, and glaring in my direction.

"You'll have to pick her tomorrow," I said as I looked away, digging into the sand.

Gideon pursed his lips, digging faster next to me.

"I don't want you," I lied. It was better this way. He could pick Petunia, and I'd worry about the Coven.

"You don't mean that."

We pulled another witch from the sand, helping her to her feet. I held on to her arm until she stopped wobbling and took tentative steps away from me.

"Just pick her." I brushed the loose sand from my hands and looked down at my clothes. They were dusty, with sand stuck between the pleats of my skirt. "Pick Petunia tomorrow. It'll be easier for you."

Gideon grabbed hold of my upper arms, turning me in the sand toward him. His eyes searched my face, bouncing from my lips to my nose and then to my eyes. "Can't you see? I'm not going to pick her tomorrow. I already chose you."

Our eyes stayed locked together as our chests panted against each other's. I wanted to trust him, to believe what he said. He made it seem so easy.

"I know this is new for you—it's new for me too—but I can tell you're feeling the same way I am. It's okay to be scared...to be nervous. Just don't hide what you're feeling because of it."

"Hey, over here!" Brooke called out.

I broke away from his stare to find her motioning toward where another cluster of witches was buried.

"Go get your prize," I muttered, nodding toward Petunia. I was so close to believing what he said—that he'd already chosen me, that he wanted me. I needed to give him a final push, the chance to choose someone else before I let him in. Maybe I was testing him. I probably was, but what was between us was new, and in this environment, trust had to be earned.

I turned my back to Gideon and began walking over to where Brooke had begun digging out another witch. The moment I fell to my knees next to her, helping her dig, the sand next to me moved. It was Gideon again. He took his time rolling up his sleeves before he dug into the sand next to me, offering a hand to the stuck witch as soon as we'd dug deep enough to free her. His muscles strained as he pulled her out, putting both hands on her shoulders to steady her until she regained her balance.

"Thank you," she whispered, her eyes staring at me. "We'd all still be stuck here if you hadn't started digging us out."

I nodded. "Of course." This was new—gratitude from the witches I tried to help.

Silently, we moved to the next witch, repeating the same steps until every witch had been freed.

No one else thanked me, but I wasn't after thanks—it was the right thing to do. I'd always imagined the Coven as a family, like Elise and Everett's pack. Everyone looked out for each other and helped one another. Maybe the witches here just needed an example of what being part of a family was like.

I looked around the sandy cavern one last time, making sure we'd gotten every single witch unburied. It was empty. I brushed the sand from my hands before hugging Brooke and thanking her for her help. She left the cavern, following the last of the air magic witches.

"Let's go back to my room," Gideon whispered. "I have a change of your clothes."

Looking down at my uniform, I could hardly tell that my plaid skirt was green. Everything was covered in sand and dust, and I'd begun to feel itchy.

He placed his hand on my lower back, pulling my body flush with his. "Let me prove that I already chose you, that I'd only choose you. There is no one else, Dafni."

I nodded.

His eyes widened.

This was me saying yes. This was me letting him in. He was right. It was time I let him in and not let the new feelings I had scare me away from something that might bring me joy.

He'd proven again and again that he wanted me...that he wanted to choose me. Gideon had never lied to me, and he'd done his best to protect me here at the Academy.

Maybe I could have both Gideon and the Coven? Did I dare get that greedy?

I let him take my hand and lead me from the cavern.
I was willing to take the chance.

CHAPTER TWENTY-SEVEN

Gideon

SHE'D ASKED TO SHOWER AFTER I DID. I WOULD'VE ASKED her to shower *with* me, but that might've pushed her too far too quickly. She'd finally let me in. Dafni didn't trust easily, and I wasn't about to ruin what trust we'd built between us by moving too fast.

I listened to the water flow off her body and hit the shower floor. I wanted to go in there, to help her, rub soap on her slippery body, rinse the sand from her curls. But I stayed back, sitting on my bed, the white undershirt I wore clinging to my still-damp skin—the briefs I'd put on to make Dafni more comfortable also sticking to my skin.

The muscles in my arms and back had felt tender beneath the flow of water from the shower head. I'd worked them today —maybe for the first time ever, digging and pulling witches from the sand. I never imagined that it would've felt good to work—to help the witches here. I hated to think of it now, but I would've never thought to help the witches if it hadn't been for Dafni.

It wasn't the way the Coven or the Academy worked. If a witch faltered or got hurt, it was because they were weak—unpowerful—not worth the Coven's time. Those ideas had been drilled into my head since I was young, and I'd never questioned anything I'd been taught. I'd kept to myself—maybe for self-preservation, or maybe because it'd seemed too daunting to challenge the Academy or the Coven. This was the most interaction I'd had with witches in years, and I wasn't proud to say that I was unaccustomed to helping.

I'd watched each buried witch's face relax in relief when we'd kneeled near them, like they'd been worried we'd skip them or decide it just wasn't worth our effort to save them.

Like me, that was what they'd been accustomed to, maybe even why they hadn't yelled for help after the evaluation was over.

My entire life I'd thought I was trapped down here...but those witches stuck in the sand had been literally trapped—and would've stayed trapped if it hadn't been for Dafni. She wasn't afraid to question the Academy and challenge the Coven's practices.

For the first time, I'd seen things down here differently—through Dafni's eyes. There'd been a determination in her that I'd never seen before. I'd watched the sweat form on her temples as she dug in the sand and pulled each witch out. She'd dug down deep, grasping for every witch who had been trapped, taking the time to make sure they were okay before she let them go. Only one of them had thanked her—but that hadn't mattered to Dafni. To her, every witch deserved her time and effort.

The shower turned off, and I heard the final splash of water hit the drain as she wrung out her hair. A freckled nose poked out from where the door opened, just far enough for her to look around the room before she exited the bathroom. Water droplets clung to the ends of her curls, and her skin glistened from scrubbing. She used both hands to hold up the towel she had wrapped around her chest. The bottom of the towel brushed the top of her knees—those cute little freckled circles in the middle of her legs. She stood there with them pressed together. All of me wondered what it'd look like to see her spread them apart.

"That's what you're wearing?" Dafni asked.

I looked down at the white shirt and black briefs I had on. "Should I get back into my uniform?"

"No...I mean..." Dafni bit her bottom lip still staring at me. She cleared her throat. "You said you have my uniform?"

"Sure do." I stood, walking to where I'd folded the clothes on my desk. I handed them to her, and she carefully continued holding up the towel with her elbows while she pulled the white button-up shirt from the pile. She held it up by the collar against her body, the bottom hem only reaching her hips.

"Can I borrow one of yours?"

I pulled at the shoulder of the shirt I was wearing. She nodded. I looked up and down her toweled body.

"Are you sure you want one? You could just drop the towel and hop under the covers."

"Gideon..." She sounded a mixture of annoyed and amused. I could work with that. My tongue brushed against my lips. Naked was preferred when it came to Dafni, but I couldn't wait to get a good look at her in one of my white see-through shirts. She'd run away so quickly the last time she'd had one on, I'd never got to appreciate it.

I tossed her a shirt from my closet, and she disappeared into the bathroom to change. When she emerged, my breath caught.

The simple white shirt hid almost nothing. In contrast to her pale skin, her darker nipples showed through the fabric. I watched as my gaze made them pinch into tight buds.

Dafni was in front of me, practically naked, and that wasn't the most attractive thing about her. She was powerful—not only with her magic, but with her fearlessness. Seeing her before me brought up all those feelings I'd felt while she'd been in the shower. Dafni listened to herself, believed in herself, unlike the rest of the witches who followed each other blindly. Everyone here grouped together and moved like a school of fish. She was an outlier, just like me.

The shirt fell to her shins but caught loosely on her hip, accentuating the curve of her waist. I couldn't think of anything else as I walked over to where she stood. All I could feel was the blood pulsing down to my cock. I needed to be closer, touching, smelling, inhaling Dafni.

"Gideon...I..."

Our bodies were close—another inch, and we'd be touching. Just a dip of my head and our lips would brush.

I slipped my hand along the back of her shoulders beneath her wet hair. Her green eyes shot up to mine. They were wide, her stare unblinking. I watched her face as I brought my hand up, wrapping my fingers along the back of her neck. Her lips parted and her eyes closed as her body shuddered beneath my palm.

"Dafni..." I whispered.

Her eyes popped open.

"Can I kiss you?"

I felt the vibration of the word *yes* through my fingers on the back of her neck and immediately slammed my lips onto hers. Our kiss reminded me of the first time our lips had touched in the closet. It'd been just as wild and uninhibited as this one.

Her hands tentatively creeped up my chest, pulling back for a moment when I moaned at the contact. She got braver as our lips continued to touch—her hands wrapping around the back of my neck, using the leverage to pull herself up against my body. I opened my lips, my tongue sweeping against her closed ones. Dafni pulled her face back, her arms still wrapped around my neck. She blinked at me several times, her eyes darting between mine and my lips.

"We should stop," she said.

"We can if you want," I replied.

Our breathing was rapid, our chests touching with each inhale. She let go of my neck slowly, her hands sliding down my shoulders and chest. Dafni pulled them back toward herself once they got low enough for her fingers to get caught on the waistband of my briefs. Her face turned that beautiful shade of red that matched her hair, and I held back a chuckle. *She's so cute when she's flustered.*

Dafni turned away and walked around me before climbing into my bed. I turned a little too late, only catching the back of her bare thighs for a moment before she slipped beneath the covers.

Climbing in next to her, I pulled the covers up over my stomach. I closed my eyes for a moment before I turned my head and looked over at Dafni. I stared at her. She had her eyes closed, though I could see her eyes moving beneath her lids. Her nostrils flared occasionally. The rest of her body didn't stay still either. I could feel her moving through the mattress we shared.

On the outside, Dafni might've appeared calm and collected as she lay beneath the covers with her arms straight at her sides on top of the blanket. But beneath the surface, I knew she was a wreck, her pulse wild, her thighs rubbing back and forth to try to quell the throb of blood flowing between them.

I knew what it felt like—the throbbing with each heartbeat as blood collected and pounded between your legs. My cock was hard and pulsing beneath the briefs I wore.

She was here in my bed, rubbing her legs together, shifting around on the mattress. I knew what the matter was—I knew why she couldn't sleep. And I knew how to fix it. If she gave me five—no, ten minutes, we'd both be sleeping like babies.

"Dafni?"

Her body stopped moving.

"I know you aren't sleeping."

She sighed, turning over to face me, her curly hair spilling over the pillow like a mane, then pressed her face into the pillow. "I can't sleep."

"You're wound up, kitten."

Dafni raised her head from the pillow, her curls framing her face. "Sorry—am I moving too much?"

"No, you're just not moving in the right part of the bed."

She squealed as I tugged on the bottom of the too large shirt she'd insisted on wearing to bed and brought her close to me, all of her curves sinking into my body. I pulled up Dafni's shirt, my hand snaking up her smooth torso and to the swell of the underside of her breast. I brushed my fingers against the soft skin, pressing my nose into her temple.

"You want this?" I whispered into her skin.

The pause felt like an eternity before she softly whispered, "Yes."

I brought my cupped hand along her sternum, letting gravity spill her breast into my awaiting hand. Her soft warmth hit my palm, and I waited a few seconds to appreciate the weight before I squeezed her soft yet firm breast.

Her nipple was piercing my skin, so pointed, I almost feigned an abrasion. "Ouch, kitten, you poked me."

"You're poking me right now," she said, wiggling her legs

together against the top of my thigh. The touch vibrated down my body, down to my hard cock, it swelling further, pressing deeper into her thigh. My fingers reached up, from beneath her shirt, trying to pull a button from the hole it was held in.

"Gideon...I think I'd be more comfortable with my clothes on," Dafni whispered.

My hand stilled, where it was trapped between her bare skin and my shirt. Good. She was telling me what she wanted. I kissed the side of her neck, just below her ear. Dafni giggled before I rolled her perked nipple between my fingers, eliciting a moan. She looked so beautiful, so tempting, lying there brimming with need.

"There are a lot of things I can do to you with your clothes on," I said.

Dafni reached down, palming my hardened cock in her hands. I hissed as she gripped me tightly. "Do you want to take your clothes off?" she asked.

I tried to grasp how she was feeling, follow the slight tremor in her voice. She was nervous but still eager—and by the way she palmed my cock, I'd have no trouble making a mess even with my briefs on.

"I can keep them on if it'd make you feel more comfortable," I whispered, leaning over, taking her lips again with mine.

I left the warmth of her breasts, my fingers tracing their way down her stomach and slipping lower. Her hand left my cock to grab onto my wrist, stalling the movement to the smooth skin she hid between her legs.

"Gideon...I've never..."

"Kitten." I removed my wrist from her hold, bringing my hand up to her face. In the dim light of my room, I could see the creases of worry on her forehead. I took my thumb and smoothed the skin, rubbing from between her eyes to her hairline, my fingers then tangling in her curls. "I'd never do anything to hurt you."

Her eyes closed for a moment, and I could feel her smooth exhale against my face. This was all new. Intimidating. She was nervous, and it was endearing.

My lips kissed along the bridge of her nose, following the line of freckles under her eye and along her cheekbone. Her body relaxed, once again melting into mine, her eyelashes fluttering against my eyebrows each time my lips met her skin.

I let my hand trace along her curves once more, bumping along her collarbone, feeling the swell of her breasts, my palm being poked by her hard nipple beneath her shirt. My hand dipped along the curve of her stomach, going lower, both of our breaths quickening in anticipation. The moment my fingers met her curls, her hand once again palmed my strained cock, and I plummeted down deep between her legs, my fingers sliding the moment they hit her wet folds.

"Kitten...are you trying to hide this from me?" My fingers were swimming, no drowning, flailing for the side so I could get the lay of the land.

"Gideon, I don't know how much teasing I can take." Dafni's breaths were quick as she panted against my neck. Her face had made its way there, her sweet lips brushing against my skin.

"I'm doing my best, kitten. You're so fucking wet."

"*Harder.*" She pushed herself into my hand, bouncing her hips up and down.

My cock twitched at her words. I was nothing but responsive for Dafni.

"So demanding," I whispered, nipping at her exposed ear near my mouth. My fingers moved quicker, my arm moving up and down at the shoulder as I rubbed.

Her hand moved in time with my own. The way her hand

clenched my cock harder over my briefs had me gasping for air. How did this feel so good? I was dry, everything was dry. But warm, everything was so warm, and she was so wet. The sound of my fingers sloshing through the sea between her legs made my balls tighten, warmth traveling up my cock.

"Kitten, I...I'm gonna..."

"Right there...don't stop...don't you stop, Gideon."

The way she said my name between gasps of air was my undoing. She panted as my briefs dampened beneath her palm, my cock twitching with every pulse of release. It seemed to only encourage her own undoing as she moaned my name over and over, creating a wave of warm liquid that coated my fingers even further.

When she stopped pulsing and her breathing came down to a somewhat normal rate, I removed my fingers from the flood between her legs. Her eyes were wide as she watched me push them between my lips, tasting her on my fingers.

"Gideon," Dafni whispered, "it's never been like that. I've never been so..." She pointed her index and middle fingers at the bathroom, a gust of air floating a hand towel through the air toward the bed. She caught the towel in her hand, tucking it between her legs.

I froze—my arm still caught beneath Dafni's body.

"Aren't you a... You have water magic..." The words tumbled from my lips as I freed my arm, pushing myself out of my bed and falling onto the floor.

"That—how you brought the towel over just now...that was air magic."

Dafni froze, her hand with the towel between her legs, her eyes wide, and her mouth open.

"You have two powers."

CHAPTER TWENTY-EIGHT

Dafni

"THAT MEANS, THAT MEANS, IT MEANS..." GIDEON WAS stuttering from down on the floor, looking up at me.

I'd *screwed* up. Big time. I was supposed to only have water magic. I brewed potions and made things boil over. My mind had melted so completely from my orgasm that, without thinking, I'd used my air magic to call the towel. *Stupid, stupid, stupid.*

I watched Gideon's face as his brain processed this information. His eyebrows scrunched together as his eyes bounced back and forth and up and down. "There's only one lineage that has two powers."

Gideon looked down at his briefs, the dark, wet stain on the front growing larger. He used his hand to try to cover the mess in his pants. "You're a Sarracenia."

I looked down, slowly pulling my hand out of the blanket, the wet towel still tucked between my legs.

"She's not here. And you're...her heir." Gideon crawled backward on the floor, away from me. I was Matilda's heir. The way he was looking at me told me everything I needed to know about how he felt about me. I was toxic, just like her. I was scalded by my lineage. Damaged.

"Don't worry, Gideon—I won't tell anyone what we did here together. Your secret is safe with me." I stood, pulling down his shirt to cover my legs.

"Yeah, you should go," Gideon, still on the floor, whispered, looking up at me like I was some sort of freak. "If Matilda found out what I did...she'd..." He shuddered, tucking himself further into a ball on the floor.

"You're scared, Gideon!" My voice left my throat before I sought it out. "You used me for your own gratification, and the moment you see something you don't like, you're just going to dispose of me? Ask me to leave?" He'd promised he wouldn't hurt me. "I'm not someone you can keep and mold to your liking, just to throw away when I do something that scares you."

I was no different from the Dafni that he met weeks ago, before he knew I had two powers. I hadn't suddenly grown a second head or a fifth limb. I was still Dafni, *kitten*. It was him that was different. Intimidated.

"I intimidate you, don't I?" I narrowed my eyes at his cowered form on the floor. "You can't handle me."

Gideon looked down at the fingers he'd just licked clean.

"Don't!" I shouted. "You'll never get to taste that again. You're nothing but a scared, sheltered boy who can't handle a witch that might be more powerful than you are."

I turned around, putting my back to his groveling form on the floor. I was Dafni Sarracenia. Let them grovel. They'd all be groveling soon. Matilda wasn't coming back.

———

Men are vile.

The only ones I'd met, besides Everett and Luke, had been disgusting, self-serving, and just overall horrible. How Matilda let one between her legs to conceive me was unfathomable.

Maybe it wasn't unfathomable. I'd been so close to letting Gideon go further, begging him to. That was my mistake. I shouldn't have let him get that close to me again. He'd pulled me in, hypnotized me. I'd begun to trust him—I'd let him touch the most intimate parts of me, including my heart. A major blunder on my part. Once he'd found out who I was... or who my mother was, he'd flinched. That tiny flinch brought my walls back up. Any trust built between us was broken.

"Ouch!" Brooke stood in the bed, hitting her head on the top bunk just as I was opening the door. She grabbed the blanket off the bed, pulling it up to cover her lower half. "You scared me, Dafni! I wasn't expecting anyone. Aren't you staying with Gideon? What happened?"

"I'm back. Men are vile."

"What?" Brooke squeaked. "But I thought you two were..."

"Yeah, it's not going to work out. We're...incompatible."

"That's unfortunate."

"Not really—I don't need any sort of distraction." I turned around so Brooke couldn't read the lie written all over my face. Gideon couldn't handle the real me. The one that was a Sarracenia, the future leader of the Coven.

"Is that why you're in here so late? Or now I should say, so early?" Brooke asked. "Tomorrow's your task. Actually, now it's today."

I pulled off Gideon's shirt, throwing it into the corner of the room. I needed the scent of him off me as soon as possible. The pressed nightgown I replaced it with felt scratchy and foreign against my skin—nothing like the soft fabric of his shirt.

"We're done," I said. "I don't want to talk about it."

"That's kind of rash, don't you think?" Brooke walked over to where I stood, bending her head down so her eyes met mine as they tried to stare at the floor. "Not all men are bad."

I watched her, keeping quiet, knowing she'd continue talking to fill the silence.

"Luke came back to check on you earlier. He hung out for a little while. He had his tool belt with him and fixed our wobbly top bunk." Brooke raised her eyebrows, trying to read my thoughts. "Not all night or anything like that." She giggled, tossing her brown hair behind her shoulder.

I smiled. Was that what I'd been like when I'd first met Gideon? Had I been smiling and giggling? It had been good between us—fun. We'd been building that trust. I'd been so close to letting him in all the way.

"Have you been up all night?" Brooke asked, interrupting my inner wallowing. "You must be exhausted."

"I'm fine," I said. Amazing what getting dumped and plotting a Coven takeover would do to your adrenaline.

Except there was no plot.

All this time at the Academy, and I still didn't know what I was doing or how I was going to take over. I had my last name, lineage, and two powers. And I knew the changes I wanted to make to better the Coven. It had to be enough. I'd have to adapt to whatever happened at the task. This was my time to prove to the witches in the Academy that not only was I powerful, I would use that power to lead.

"You should sleep." Brooke yawned, walking back to the bed. "I don't know where Petunia's been staying, but she hasn't been back in days. You can take her bed."

I looked up at the top bunk. A hair tie hit my chest before

falling to the floor by my feet. "You'd better braid your hair or something before you sleep. I don't know what went on with Gideon, but your hair seems to have taken the brunt of it."

I ran my fingers through my hair, my nails getting snagged on every tangled curl.

CHAPTER TWENTY-NINE

Gideon

THIS SUIT WAS TIGHT IN ALL THE WRONG PLACES. THE TIE squeezed my neck, making it hard to breathe—as if I wasn't already suffocating enough. This was the day I'd been dreading since Robinson began preparing me for it—the day I'd be forced to choose a partner. It was early, everyone else was still sleeping, but I couldn't stay in my room, not after what happened between Dafni and me.

Of all the witches at the Academy, of course I'd be attracted to a Sarracenia. It was natural selection or some of that Darwinian crap Robinson had made me read during our meetings. Dafni was the strongest witch at the Academy, and I was the youngest male. How had I not seen it? The way she knew so many potions even though she'd claimed to be human-born. That'd all been a lie. She'd obviously been trained her whole life to be Prime, a leader, the strongest witch in the Coven.

I'd found another word—a Latin word—on the wall in one of the mostly abandoned hallways I'd been casually pacing as I waited for the water task to begin. It was a short word, only three letters: *I-R-A*. Too bad I'd pushed Dafni away and she wasn't here to translate it for me.

Finding out she was Matilda's daughter had shocked me, and I hadn't reacted well. The Sarracenias' lineage was legendary and intimidating. Their family produced witches with at least two powers. I knew Matilda. She'd kept an eye on me growing up at the Academy. She'd been frightening, flexing her multiple powers, snuffing out lanterns with her air magic and making students' potions boil over with her water magic during class for her own amusement.

The worst was when she'd used her earth magic, causing a student's body parts to grow or a vine to come up from the earth, wrapping around their ankles, leaving them in tears and with red welts on their skin. She'd made sure everyone at the Academy knew who she was. That was how she kept her place as Prime—by threatening everyone with her powers.

Still, I couldn't get Dafni out of my head. The way she'd looked at me after I'd told her to leave. The sadness that'd come over her face, only to be replaced with anger.

I'd put on this terrible suit that the Coven was making me wear and come out here to pace, to work through my thoughts. Finding another word etched into the brick had only reminded me of her, brought back those feelings I'd had when she'd first read what was on my papers. I was in awe of Dafni. Her power, her naivety, her need to help others. I'd pushed her away. With every scratch of the chalk on the paper, I realized I needed to get her back.

"It's almost time." His voice interrupted the back-and-forth movement of my chalk.

I quickly rubbed on the last half of the *A* before shoving the paper and chalk into my pocket.

"Let's have a chat while it's still quiet, before the excitement of the upcoming evaluation begins."

Excitement? I could argue he might be the only one excited about today.

I followed Robinson down the hall outside the Academy and into the Coven. It was noticeably quieter in the Coven. It didn't have the same buzz of excitement as the Academy did.

Robinson held open the door to his room and followed me inside, latching the door behind him. "Have you given any thought to what we'd talked about?" He motioned to a chair with pilled gray fabric covering the seat.

"I've thought about it," I said.

"It's good, Gideon. It'll strengthen the bloodline to have new genes introduced. Maybe she'll give birth to another male witch."

I rubbed my palms on my black pants.

Robinson stood and began pacing in front of me, rubbing his chin with his hand. His word choice always felt wrong, too sanitary. Like we were talking about animals instead of witches, people. "Tonight you'll make Petunia the happiest witch in the Academy."

"And what if I didn't choose tonight?" I didn't know where I stood with Dafni, and there was no way I was picking Petunia.

Robinson's silence spoke volumes before he even opened his mouth. "You will choose, Gideon. You will choose Petunia Fox." He grabbed ahold of his remote, turning on the television. "Are you having cold feet?"

I shook my head. Not my feet. My heart. It'd only felt

warm when I'd been with Dafni. There wasn't another witch who'd make me feel that way—I was sure of it.

"Don't tell me another witch has caught your eye."

I stared at Robinson.

"If you don't pick Petunia, I'll make sure Matilda knows you didn't listen to me. She won't be happy with your defiance."

There it was again. The pressure, my life being planned for me—right in front of me. Expectations. The complete loss of control. Beads of sweat popped up along my hairline. I wiped them with my hand, pulling them into my hairline as I ran my fingers through my hair. I couldn't let Robinson see me sweat. He'd take advantage of my nerves, see them as a weakness he needed to correct.

Robinson used his thumb and index finger to smooth his mustache as he looked at me. "She'll find out who you pick."

Is Matilda back? A cold sweat broke out on my upper lip.

"She's not here yet, but Matilda will be here. We've been planning for this for years—since you were born."

Would Matilda know that less than a day ago I'd had my fingers between her daughter's legs? That her daughter had made me come through my briefs? Maybe that was some witch-craft she'd been taught. It had to have been. No other witch had made me stoop to that level. *Coming in my briefs. Get a grip, Gideon.*

"Here..." Robinson pointed the remote at the TV, his thumb pressing buttons, the screen illuminating with a familiar scene.

The outside of my room.

"I saw this a few days ago..." He pressed play, and a recording of Petunia leaving my room, a smile on her face, appeared on the screen. She'd stopped for a moment, wiping the back of her hand across her lips. It looked suspicious, her leaving my room, wiping her mouth—like we'd been kissing...or worse. "I'll gladly show *Dafni* this if you end up picking her to be your partner. I'm sure she won't last long beside you when she sees that you've been playing the field."

Something deep inside me snapped. I felt it break. The facade I'd tried to maintain, the way I'd been obedient all these years for the Coven.

"Keep her name out of your mouth!"

It felt like I was watching myself from the camera in the corner—watching myself hit the remote out of his hand, the device skittering across the floor, breaking into several pieces. The video paused, static lines running through the picture. The other TVs in the room continued to play recordings from around the Academy.

"Gideon!" Robinson bent down to gather the broken pieces of the remote. "We are supposed to be brothers! We're the two male witches—the only two. I'm showing you the way!"

"The disgusting, depraved, wrong way," I spat, spit flying from my mouth and landing with the broken pieces of the remote on the floor. There could be no more of this. No more of his secret recordings. They needed to be gone, disappear forever. Dafni could never see this. She'd never take me back— our trust had been broken by me just hours ago, and this video would be the final nail in the coffin.

I looked back up at one of the screens, narrowing my eyes as I saw *her*. The recording of her running back to her room after I'd kicked her out of mine. Those red curls caught my eye. I remembered the way they bounced, the way they'd curled just right around my finger the first time I'd felt them in my hands—that time we'd wound up in the closet together, with all the cords, brooms, and electrical boxes mounted to the wall.

"Gideon!" Robinson's voice was quiet—far away by the time I'd heard it, already outside his room and through the door that led back to the Academy. Back to *that* closet. The one I'd got entangled in with *her*.

I had to be quick before Robinson caught me on the camera and saw where I was going.

The door to the closet wasn't locked. *Idiots.* There were enough wires in here to take down the whole Academy. *Perfect.*

The amount of flashing lights and cords running in and out of the room made my fingers tingle. There were even boxes mounted to the wall that had stickers with *Memory* written on them. Those were my first victims. I grabbed on to them, tearing them from the wall, smashing them over my thigh before throwing them to the ground. When they hit the concrete, a deep chuckle rose from my chest. Fuck Robinson, fuck the Academy. It was therapeutic, the anger flowing through my arms from my chest, down through my fingers, releasing in the crash of metal and plastic on the floor.

They'd kept me here for so long. *For so long.* Keeping an eye on me—on all of us with the cameras they'd mounted. That was over. It was over. There'd be no more evidence—not of me or of Dafni or anyone.

The walls were empty, the electrical boxes gone. My muscles screamed at me as I looked at the mess of wires hanging and, in some places, knotted together. There was a thick black wire, one that was still plugged in to an outlet next to the floor.

That had to be the main power line. It had to be the electricity the Academy needed to sustain their operations. I grabbed on to the wire, the power that fortified the Coven buzzing beneath my hand. One yank, a pull, and everything would go dark. The evaluation would be ruined.

I yanked.

Sparks flew around my hand, singeing the hair on my wrist

and upper arm. I reveled in the sting, in the smell of burnt hair. It was the smell of freedom.

The silence was loud. I heard nothing for the longest time. Just the beat of my heart in my ears. I sat on the floor in the dark breathing and shaking, trying to catch my breath from all the adrenaline flowing through my veins.

I didn't know how long I sat there until I fully realized what I'd done. The opportunity I'd just created for myself. It was a dream. I was free.

CHAPTER THIRTY

Dafni

IT WAS TIME.

My uniform was pressed and clean, my hair was as tame as I could manage, tucked behind my ears and rolling down my back.

The lights hadn't turned on this morning when Brooke and I had woken up. Probably another intimidation tactic by the Academy. We'd found a few flashlights tucked deep in the drawers of the wardrobe, and they turned on after hitting them a few times on the brick wall, loosening the battery-acid corrosion inside.

She fretted about our room, popping in and out of the bathroom to look at herself in the mirror. There was a knock at the door, but I had no idea who could be coming to see us.

"It's for me!" Brooke rushed to the door. She smoothed her skirt and pinched her cheeks before opening the door.

Luke stood in the doorway, holding his own flashlight. "You guys okay?" he asked. "Something's going on with the power."

"We think it's the Coven trying to scare us, what with the evaluations nearly over," Brooke said.

He glanced up at the ceiling, a frown on his face. "That does sound like them." He looked down at Brooke. "Are you ready?"

"This—this—what is this?" I stuttered, glancing between Brooke and Luke. Seeing the two of them together had short-circuited my brain.

"I invited Luke to sit with me to watch the task," she said, looping her arm through Luke's. "I wasn't about to sit with Petunia."

A pang of jealousy echoed in my chest. It wasn't that Brooke was with Luke; it was that they had *each other*. It was what Gideon and I had once had.

I pushed that emotion away. That feeling wouldn't help me today.

"I know you and Gideon aren't getting along right now," Brooke said, "but don't let that distract you from the task. You're a powerful witch, Dafni. Show the Academy what you're made of."

I couldn't do anything but nod. It was time that I showed everyone what I could do. Even if Gideon didn't pick me—I could show them the power I had.

"We have to go," Brooke said, pulling Luke along with her. "Good luck! We'll be rooting for you!"

I paced our room like a caged animal—waiting for Arcana to come and collect each of us from our rooms.

This was my chance to differentiate myself from the rest of the witches here. I didn't have to be Gideon's choice—I could be the witches' choice. The Coven needed a new leader, and I could be that. Everyone here was a victim of my mother's tyranny, yet no one questioned her. She'd been here unchecked for years, and everyone was so far under her spell that they no longer questioned anything. It was time to create some doubt, some hesitation inside the Coven. The witches living here should be suspicious of everything. I could be the one to question the Coven's leadership.

Gideon had told me what the task would be. *Rage.* I could create it—I already felt it bubbling in my blood, and I'd felt it bubbling off the witches here at the Academy during the last task. They were waiting for that spark that would ignite a rebellion.

My pacing was interrupted by a fist pounding on the door. I opened it to find a line of witches standing behind the instructor who'd knocked. I joined the end of the line, walking by the water magics, each holding their own flashlight. Everyone walked down the two flights of stairs together, through the Academy to the cavern. It was silent, no one speaking as we walked into the unknown.

The cavern was loud when we entered. Lanterns with billowing flames lined the walls, illuminating the space. The sand had been removed, and the floors were once again dirt. On the far end of the cavern, near the wall Brooke had tried to climb through, were long tables with burners on top. There looked to be enough for each of us to have our own.

The witches on the bleachers were buzzing with excitement, their voices vibrating off the ceiling and walls. I scanned the rows, looking for Brooke. She raised her hand, waving back and forth as soon as we made eye contact. The line stopped moving, and I ran into the witch in front of me. She turned around and hissed. I took a small step back.

The line disintegrated as we huddled into a group facing the stage. Robinson was standing there, scowling down at me. *What did I do to him?*

I looked back toward the chair Gideon usually occupied. It was empty. *Where is he?*

Robinson droned on and on, standing on the stage in front of the witches of the Academy and the members of the Coven who'd shown up for the final task. They were getting restless, as was the crowd. The whispers between witches became louder than Robinson's voice on stage. My feet were getting sore from standing, the room becoming stuffy with so many bodies.

A gust of wind rushed through the cavern. There were no windows, nowhere for the wind to be coming from except...

The flames blew out. The cavern plunged into darkness.

A gasp echoed throughout the cavern, now suddenly quiet with the lack of light.

The witches quickly became a mess of whispers and wheezes and some screams. No one could see anything as we shifted back and forth, our balance thrown off from our lack of sight, bumping into witches and stepping on their boots. How long would they leave us in the dark? Robinson yelled from the stage, asking everyone to "wait just a moment."

It seemed the witches either weren't listening or didn't care because the panic continued to escalate. The group of witches on the floor acted like waves, falling into one another, taking down the witch next to them, one after another. I grabbed onto anything I could to make sure I didn't fall to the ground.

It was hard to know how much time had passed. The adrenaline pumping around us made time seem to pass both slower and faster at the same time. I tried counting at first but lost track every time someone bumped into me or cried out.

"Robinson, light them up." A familiar voice radiated through the arena, many of the witches gasping for a breath along with me when they'd heard it.

Heard her.

One by one, Robinson used his magic to relight the lanterns along the circular arena, returning the space to that spooky glow. Everyone righted themselves, adjusting their dresses and hair now that they could see. I'd somehow ended up in the back of the group, nearest to the bleachers and the door we'd entered.

"Welcome! I'm so glad to be back!" That voice. The one I'd heard in my dreams. The one that I'd dreaded hearing as a young girl at my grandmother's cottage.

She was here.

The witches on the bleachers were a mix of screams and cheers. I looked into the crowd, finding some of the witches standing, clapping, and yelling in support while others had sunk down in their seats, a look of fear on their faces.

"Dafni!" The loud, pointed yell behind me had me turning around, searching the crowd for the source. My eyes zeroed in on light-red hair—Annabel, standing at the cavern's entrance. What was she doing here?

She had Emily's hand in hers, both of their eyes wide. Emily stuck out like a sore thumb in the sea of green plaid in the room, standing there in her off-white, knee-length dress. I left the group and ran over to them.

"The freezer!" Annabel gulped in several shallow breaths. "The power went out at the trailer..." She took a few more breaths. "The electricity was out—it thawed!"

Annabel pointed a shaking finger to where Matilda was standing on the stage in front of me. "I took the pail out of the freezer for just a bit, early this morning. We had vegetables from the garden, and I was organizing them in the freezer. I didn't leave it out of the cold for too long." She grabbed ahold of my arms. "But I didn't know the electricity was out." Her eyes were quivered as she spoke. "I closed the door, and it never got cold. I should've realized that the lights weren't working, but I went right back outside to the garden." Her hand squeezed my arms again. "It's all my fault."

"It's not your fault." I rubbed Annabel's arms up and down, trying to soothe her. "I'm not afraid of her—not anymore."

"Sister!" *Her* voice rose from the chatter, everyone surrounding the stage turning around to look at who she was addressing. Everyone's eyes rested on Annabel. Although there was no spotlight, everyone's eyes felt like one, Annabel's eyes blinking as everyone stared.

Sister?

"I'm so glad you could join us!" Matilda stood on the stage. I finally got a good look at her. Dripping wet, her red hair pressed to the sides of her head, her curls flat.

Annabel shrank, although she tried to stand tall in front of Matilda.

"You're not supposed to be here." My mother clicked her tongue.

Annabel opened her mouth to speak, but Matilda interrupted her. "I see one of your sniveling offspring, but where is the other?" She scanned the crowd gathered around her.

A gasp waved through the crowd as everyone looked among themselves.

"I'm here." Luke's baritone voice vibrated through the crowd.

The witches moved, making way for him to come down from the bleachers, joining his mother and sister on the floor. Brooke followed him down, sticking close to his side.

I suddenly realized what this meant. If Annabel was my mother's sister...

I took a step back. She was my aunt. Luke and Emily were my cousins.

"I'll deal with you later, my dearest Dafni..." My mother's

voice rang in my ear as I backed away slowly. This was all too much.

"They're sweet, but do we need your cousins, really?" Matilda pointed her index and middle fingers toward Luke and Emily.

Emily's mouth quivered while Luke held his lips together tightly.

"You've gotten so close to them over the past year." Matilda turned back to face me. "You forgot about me. Dafni, *dear*, I heard everything."

"Don't do it, Matilda!" Annabel's voice was quiet, although her words resounded throughout the room.

Matilda turned, her face full of anger and spite. "You have broken our agreement, sister. You're not in your trailer, and neither are your children. You know how dangerous that is."

The witches surrounding Luke and Emily backed away slowly, leaving them out in the open, easy pickings for Matilda.

"I can't have them here, among the Coven. They're too much of a danger—"

"Matilda!" Annabel's voice was louder, her arms and fists shaking as she spoke. "They pose no danger to you or your Coven."

"They've been a danger since the day you conceived them with that dog, and they'll be a danger until they're dead in the ground."

"I'll take them back—right now." Annabel grabbed ahold of Luke and Emily and pulled them back through the crowd and toward the door. Emily's eyes met mine, full of fear and confusion, before they bobbled around the cavern. Brooke let go of Luke's hand she'd been holding, their fingers sweeping against each other's as he pulled away.

"Too late for that, sister. You didn't think there'd be consequences for keeping me trapped for the past year?"

A hushed murmur went through the crowd, bodies moving out of the way of Annabel as she dragged her children through the multitudes of witches.

"Maybe I should make your heart just as cold as my body has been." She was quick, the way she flicked her two fingers at Luke and Emily as they tripped through the crowd, following their mother.

But I was quicker.

Matilda had forgotten that I had known her my entire life, that her own mother had been the one to raise me. She didn't get to take away the people who had saved me after she'd left me in the woods to die. The people who'd fed me what little food they had and taken the time to nurse me back to health. The people who'd supported me on my mission to take the Coven away from her. She'd killed my grandmother, and there was no way she was going to take anyone else from me.

Something burned down my arm, starting in my chest, blazing its way from my shoulder, down my arm and through my fingers—through the two fingers pointed directly at my mother.

Rage.

It was anger bubbling up in my blood, forcing its way out of me. Flames shot out of my fingers, the crowd of witches diving out of the way. My throat felt raw as my voice box vibrated, a scream climbing up my throat and out of my mouth. She didn't get to take this from me—the family I'd found. That was mine.

The smell of burnt hair met my nose before the smoke cleared, and I took several steps back, turning my hand to look back at my fingers. They were uninjured. There was no black char, and the skin wasn't even red.

The cavern was silent. Not even the sound of breathing met my ears. Everyone froze in place, staring at me, their eyes wide and their mouths open even wider.

I'd just created fire magic. I wasn't supposed to be able to do that.

CHAPTER THIRTY-ONE

Dafni

MATILDA STOOD ON THE STAGE; HER EYES WERE JUST AS wide as everyone else's. The bottom of her dress was gone, her legs red with white blisters bubbling up from her skin. I needed to work on my aim.

"*No!*" Matilda's shriek blew all the lantern flames around the room sideways, dimming the room before the flames returned upright.

I looked back up at the stage, at my mother now on her hands and knees as she looked out at the crowd, her wet hair draped over her face. It was almost sad to see her like that, crumbled up in front of the witches that worshiped her. She'd been nothing but strong and dominating every other time I'd seen her. Intimidating my grandmother, intimidating and belittling me every chance she got.

Matilda turned her head, speaking to Robinson in words I couldn't hear.

He looked at the Velkans and Brooke, walking over to where they stood, backing them into the wall, near the entrance of the cavern, his index and middle fingers pointed at them. Emily clung to Annabel, who tucked her daughter behind her body, shielding her from Robinson. As soon as he had them trapped, he turned, guarding them with his back, nodding to Matilda.

"Enough!" Matilda screeched, quieting the cavern. She stood slowly, limping as she walked to the edge of the stage, her eyes glued to me. "There is nothing that will please me more than to see you fail tonight, daughter."

Mother turned, moving slowly toward the empty seat that'd been Gideon's for the last two evaluations. Out of the corner of my eye, I saw Robinson look behind at the Velkans before taking a step toward Matilda, conflicted about whether he should stand guard or help his Prime.

There was a flash of black hair and a white collared shirt.

Gideon.

I kept my eyes on the stage, my senses alert, as I watched him hand something to Luke...it looked like pieces of paper. Gideon disappeared just as soon as he'd appeared, leaving the cavern. Luke looked down at what Gideon had given him and passed it to his mother. Annabel looked down at her hands, moving slightly behind Luke so she could get a better look without Matilda or Robinson noticing.

I saw her look up, at me.

"Let's move on with tonight's competition," Matilda announced as soon as she'd settled herself in the chair. "It's an important night for the Academy and, in turn, the Coven. I'm sure my daughter won't try anything again...and put her beloved family at risk."

Robinson stood a little taller, puffing his chest out.

"Young Gideon, whom I'm sure will be here shortly, will be choosing a partner," Matilda continued. "Someone powerful. Someone who in turn will create powerful witches who will one day call the Academy home."

Bouncing ringlets caught the other side of my periphery. *Petunia.* She was sitting in the front row, a determined look on her face.

"Robinson, explain the task." Matilda slumped back in her seat. Having spent the last year frozen and being engulfed in flames seemed to have weakened her.

Robinson took a step forward, away from the Velkans, clearing his throat before he began. "You'll see there are work benches with burners set up." He motioned to the benches I'd seen when I'd walked in. "There are cauldrons beneath the tables and ingredients located in the baskets along the wall our earth elemental witches so *delicately* crawled through earlier this month."

I stood on my tiptoes, looking at the baskets overflowing with glass jars that I'd missed when I'd entered the cavern.

"You will have one hour to make a potion. One of the most challenging potions a witch can create."

The witches around me were silent, anticipating the naming of the potion. I already knew what it would be...so long as Gideon had told me the truth.

"Rage."

A collective gasp echoed throughout the cavern.

"Rage is one of the strongest emotions. It encompasses feelings of anger, irritation, and resentment. For a witch to create rage would signal their power, their ability to sway the strongest emotion we possess. Not all of you will be able to create rage." He looked directly at me. "In fact, I'm not sure any of you will." Robinson stood a little straighter. "You have one hour. Begin."

The witches began pushing, and I tripped over my own feet as the witches rushed toward the work benches. Finding an empty burner, I lifted the heavy cauldron up and onto the top, grunting as metal hit metal causing a screeching sound.

Ingredients.

The baskets of jars were noticeably picked over, the witches who'd rushed the benches having already picked their ingredients. Unfortunately for them, but fortunately for me, it seemed none of them knew what to choose to make the potion. I was able to find every ingredient I needed between two baskets. The jars of asafoetida, wild carrot, red rosinweed, a flask of honey-badger blood, and a bag of crocodile teeth filled my arms. I dumped them all onto the work bench, grabbing the jar of red rosinweed that almost rolled away.

The witches around me were already two steps ahead, their cauldrons bubbling and their wooden spoons stirring. I took the time to take a breath, inhaling through my nose and exhaling from my mouth.

I knew how to do this. I could do this.

I poured the honey-badger blood into the cauldron, lighting the burner with the matches provided. This time, I didn't have Gideon to light the burner for me. I paused. I could've used my newly discovered fire magic...but no. That was all too new. I'd probably end up setting the entire workbench on fire.

Popping open the corks, I added the rest of the ingredients, stirring the potion and adjusting the temperature. The potion started bubbling, and I leaned over, breathing in some of the fumes. I inhaled the scent of geosmin—that earthy just-rained smell. Good. That meant it was fermenting just how it needed to. Now it just needed time and occasional stirring.

I smoothed my shirt and continued stirring, wafting the scent of the potion to my nose to check its progress. When it turned a lime-green color, it would be ready. It took time and patience. The opposite of what rage felt like.

"Your face...did it always look like that?" I could hear her from way down the work bench. Matilda was walking, hunched over, along the line of cauldrons, taunting the witches just as she'd taunted me my entire life. "That really isn't going to work out. You should just give up."

Her voice got louder as she got closer. "You expect to win a male witch when you look like that?"

I could sense the tension, the irritation from the witches around me. Matilda was teasing them, mocking them. This wasn't how you ran a Coven, how you inspired witches. I continued stirring my cauldron. It was only a matter of seconds before she was in front of me.

Pop!

I threw my body over the top of my cauldron, screaming as my chest burned from the heat. The witch's cauldron next to mine had gotten too hot and exploded, sending drops of liquid up into the air. They rained down the back of my sweater, singeing the knit.

Too much honey-badger blood. It made for a volatile brew that often spit up. The poor witch next to me sunk to her knees wailing into her hands. It was too late to start over. Her chance at winning had ended.

I bit my lower lip as I talked myself out of comforting her. I had to win. Prove myself to the Academy and the Coven.

"*Dafni!*"

Everyone turned toward the yell that echoed throughout the cavern.

Gideon walked through the doorway into the cavern. He had flames shooting from his fingers, the tip of the flame singeing the floor. He looked at where I stood, glancing up and down, his nostrils flaring. With a flick of his wrist, the flames vanished, and he marched over to where I stood.

"Are you okay?" he asked. "I heard you scream."

I nodded as he looked at me up and down, seemingly checking if I was being truthful.

Matilda took a step back, slowly glancing back and forth between us, watching our interaction. "You and my daughter, huh, Gideon?"

He sneered at her, shuffling back and forth on his feet, his knees bent, ready for her attack.

Matilda looked back at me. "You've been busy, daughter. All the while, I've been held in a solid state—waiting for someone to mess up."

I opened my lips, drawing air into my lungs.

"It was only a matter of time."

She looked at Gideon, tilting her head to the side. "It was you, wasn't it? You cut the electricity."

He stood there, unmoving.

Matilda threw her head back, her cackle echoing in the cavern. "You set me free."

Gideon's eyes met mine. *No.* It couldn't have been him. Did he really want to hurt me that badly? Was he that scared of me that he had to release my mother? The look he gave me told me everything I needed to know. He'd done it. He'd cut the power and thawed my mother.

"It wasn't his fault," Annabel said from behind Matilda and Gideon. She approached the work bench slowly, palms raised in the air. Emily followed behind her, keeping close. "Like I told you, I took the pail outside and didn't realize the electricity was out."

Matilda laughed. "Typical Annabel. Always so careless. Don't tell me you've forgotten to take your magic-reducing potion as well?"

Annabel's eyes glared at her sister. "I stopped drinking it the moment Dafni left for the Academy."

Matilda's lips curled up, her teeth on display.

"I wanted to be ready, should she need me."

Matilda tucked her teeth away, her lips curling into a sinister smile. She turned toward Emily, her head peeking out from behind Annabel. "Did your mother ever tell you who your daddy is? The dog he was?"

Annabel looked at me with wide unblinking eyes before looking back at her sister. "Matilda—stop." She backed away, pulling Emily along with her.

"It's only a matter of time before you'll start sprouting fur. I wonder what color your hide will be?" Matilda twirled her hand around at the wrist, her fingers pointing out. The witches in the path of her fingers ducked down, gasping. "I guess it doesn't matter what color, does it? You'll be a dirty dog either way."

"It's ready!" I called out. This wasn't about Annabel or Emily. This was about me and my mother. Ending this once and for all.

Everyone turned to look at me, Matilda eyeing my cauldron. "If you made it, it'll never work. It'll be just as weak as you are."

I looked up from the potion, my eyes meeting *hers*. Her eyes never left me, her words making me feel like that little girl stuck on the roof, her criticisms taunting me.

However, this time, it was different. This time, I wasn't a little girl, stuck on the roof of my grandmother's cottage, afraid of my mother. She wasn't really my mother. She'd never acted motherly to me, helped me grow, nurtured me. I was nothing but an investment to her. One she'd always expected to cash in, to get her return on.

The funny thing was that returns were fickle. The investment someone made twenty years ago could be the right one, or it could be the very, very wrong one. My grandmother had told me *Never count your chickens before they hatch*, and Matilda had counted me before I'd hatched.

I hadn't really hatched until I'd left the cottage and was exposed to the world. Matilda had expected me to be obedient, serve her commands, be that naive witch I once was. I wasn't that witch anymore.

She'd taught me right from wrong years ago, really for my entire life. I knew from a young age she was completely wrong —the way she'd raised me, the way she'd treated my grandmother, the only woman who'd been kind to me when I was young.

Now I was here, in her world, overpowering her, and she didn't know what to do. Her eyes bounced from me to the surrounding witches. She was gauging their reactions, trying to mold her own to how they were feeling. She was a manipulator. I'd known it since I was young, but I couldn't put a word to it until now. Matilda tried to control everyone's feelings around her—including mine. It'd worked, her instilling fear when I'd been around her, the way she'd controlled my grandmother.

I looked down, breaking eye contact. My potion was ready. The green color was vibrant, and it smelled burnt. I spooned a bit of the liquid into my spoon, raising it to my lips. It was risky, but it was the only way I'd know it was correct.

"Dafni!" Luke's voice raised from the crowd, catching me off guard as he plowed through Robinson, running toward the work bench. The spoon dropped from my lips, hovering at my chin before he grabbed ahold of it, pulling it from my hand. "Let me try it first."

"Don't, Luke!" Annabel's voice rang out from across the cavern.

"Luke," I said, trying to pry the spoon from his fingers, "I don't know if I made it right. Don't—"

His hands ripped away from mine, taking the spoon and tipping the liquid to his lips. I watched the green liquid flow from the spoon into his mouth. I cringed as his throat bobbed, the liquid flowing down. The air stood still around me as I waited. I didn't breathe. My mind went blank, waiting. What if I'd made it wrong? Had I added too much of something? Too little? My lungs rebelled against the lack of air, and I exhaled, quickly inhaling, trying to rid my vision of the black stars that dotted it.

Was I hallucinating? Luke, or what I'd thought was Luke, grew in front of me, his figure morphing into something that wasn't *human*. His ears moved from the sides of his head to the top. His skin sprouted tan fur; his hands turned into paws with long nails. No, it couldn't be. The howl that met my ears all but confirmed it—as if his tan, furry body and snout hadn't.

Matilda shrieked, backing away toward the work bench and throwing gusts of air at the wolf Luke had become. It did nothing but ruffle his fur as he stalked toward her. She tried to pull from the earth around us. I looked above at the dirt ceiling, watching it tremble as Luke pawed toward her, bits of earth raining down on the witches.

"*No! No!*" Matilda was loud as she shrieked, backing up before the stage hit her upper back. "I should've never let you stay here, Annabel! You and your freakish offspring!"

"Stay away from my children!" Annabel said, dragging Emily along with her, toward Luke, unafraid.

The wolf form of Luke growled at my mother, his hackles raised.

"It'll only take a point of my fingers to ruin your son...and his sister." Matilda stood there drawing her arm up in front of her.

I looked back at Emily, her face in terror as tan fur sprouted from her arms and her ears pushed up toward the top of her head.

"One less Lycan to worry about."

There wasn't any more time. I couldn't second-guess myself. I needed to test the potion I'd made. I grabbed an extra spoon that lay between the two cauldrons on the work bench and quickly stirred my brew. It'd helped Luke transform into a wolf—the rage had turned him into his true form. The potion wasn't bad; it was potent.

I pulled the spoon from the bottom of the cauldron where the potion was the most potent. I put it to my lips, the liquid falling into my mouth and down my throat. I gagged at the taste —it was *awful*. I waited a moment, letting the spoon fall on top of the work bench. I almost immediately felt the rage...the fire magic boiled up in my chest, the feeling burning down my shoulder and into my arm.

Matilda walked closer to me. The evil in her eyes becoming more and more clear as she approached. "It doesn't seem to be working, daughter. You're not as powerful as you think you are." Her boots clicked together as she planted them into the dirt.

Don't make me regret giving her to you to raise instead of putting her in the Academy, where she belongs. I shook my head, trying to rid myself of the memory.

"Your grandmother might've raised you, but she clearly didn't teach you right." My mother's cackles rose from her chest and out her throat with slight gurgling sounds from the water left in her lungs from her time spent frozen in the pail. Her hand lifted toward me, the threat of water, air, or earth magic at the tip of her fingers.

I closed my eyes, waiting for whatever magic she chose to hit me with.

Air—I could be blown up or back several feet in the air, hitting the floor or wall behind me.

Water—Matilda could pull water from the kitchen, or even from the toilets, splashing me, shoving waves of liquid down my throat, drowning me.

Earth—there was enough dirt surrounding us that she could easily draw roots from the earth, wrapping them around my limbs, pulling me under, deep beneath the dirt.

I waited, anticipating her choice. It wouldn't be pretty, but I was ready.

"Use it, Dafni."

That voice froze my body, the sound of Matilda's gasp breaking my concentration. I opened my eyes...

Annabel was there, behind Matilda. She pointed her index and middle fingers at the cauldron, blending both air and water magic to raise a mist from the bubbling brew. "You can do it too, Dafni. Use your powers."

I glanced back and forth between the potion and Annabel. She nodded, her fingers still extended. I pointed my own index and middle fingers at the cauldron, willing the brew to vaporize into a mist. Together Annabel and I created a cyclone of mist— all coming from my cauldron.

"It's *rage*," Annabel whispered as she looked up at the green mist we'd made.

She tilted her head toward the rest of the witches standing along the work benches. I looked down the line, seeing witches scratching at their marred skin, others trying to cover their spitting cauldrons with their arms. Some just stood with sullen looks on their faces.

But they were all glaring at Matilda.

Annabel flicked her fingers, sending the mist down the line of water elemental witches standing alongside the workbench. I followed suit, watching the green mist float in the air, settling among the witches. They breathed in the mist, their demeanors immediately changing from apprehension to rage. Their eyes narrowed, their lips pulling back to show their teeth. Poison dripped from their canines, burning as it hit the dirt floor.

The potion was working.

A finger pushed through my lips and ran along the gums under my upper lip, the pointed nail clacking along my teeth. Her breath was rancid. I tried to keep my nose from scrunching. Not only was her face littered with bumps and sores, but her insides were also just as ugly.

Matilda looked down the line of witches and began slowly backing away. "The question is, did your grandmother ever want you to begin with? You're a witch without poison."

A collective gasp rumbled through the arena.

"I never wanted you."

"That's enough!" Annabel yelled.

She took the papers Gideon had handed her and flattened them against her thigh before she started reading.

"*Ira ille conventus perdere alloco.*" Annabel shook her head, rearranging the order of the papers.

Matilda threw her head back and laughed. "It's not enough to read the words, my idiot sister. Earth magic was always your weakness. Didn't anyone ever teach you that you have to mark the words into the ground before you recite them?"

Annabel took a breath before beginning again, the words in a different order this time. "*Alloco ira perdere ille conventus.*" Slowly, she raised her head and looked at me. Her eyes were wide with what the etched words meant.

Let rage destroy the Coven.

The flames flickered in the cavern.

Matilda whipped her head around toward Annabel. "No. It can't work. Those words...they were never written."

Dirt began tumbling down the walls.

Annabel's arm fell to her side as she looked around the cavern, displaying the words that had been rubbed onto the paper from an engraving on stone or brick. "It worked. My spells...they worked."

"Let me see those." Matilda stalked toward her sister ripping the papers from her hand. She flipped through the pages, dropping each to the ground after she'd read it.

The walls shook, dirt now raining from the ceiling.

The witches behind the work benches looked around the cavern and then at Matilda. Their home was falling apart around them.

I pushed another bout of mist from my potion into the air, letting it settle among the witches in the bleachers.

The cavern rumbled. I looked up at the ceiling, expecting an avalanche of dirt.

But this time, it wasn't the walls. It was the witches.

They came down from the bleachers, hands extended in front of them, teeth dripping with poison. The water magic witches climbed over the work benches, scalding themselves on their potions to get to Matilda.

She backed away, her hands held up, feigning innocence. "You can't do this! You don't want to do this! We've had such a nice life here!"

The walls vibrated again, more dirt falling.

"What can I do? Would you like supervised outside time?"

The witches continued to surround her.

"Stop this instant!" Robinson jumped in front of Matilda, pointing his fingers at the surrounding witches, jumping back and forth, not knowing who to point them at. There were too many.

"Just give me another ch—" Her voice became muffled

under the swarm of witches that attacked. They climbed over and under each other, each looking for a piece of her. The top half of Robinson's body popped out of the pile only to be dragged back in, the witches taking him down as well.

I stood there, watching, shaking, some of the rage left in my body. She was my mother, but this wasn't about me. There were witches here who had known her longer than me. Witches she'd tortured and trapped here their entire lives. Their rage was strong and needed to be released. I could give that release to them.

A large hand settled on my shoulder, followed by an arm resting against the back of my neck.

"You could've ended her yourself," Gideon said as we watched the swarm.

I nodded. I could have. "I wanted to give them this."

He pulled me closer against the side of his body. "I didn't know cutting the power would release your mother."

"How could you have?"

The cavern shook again. A few witches on the outside of the pile stopped attacking and looked up. The ceiling seemed lower somehow, the dirt falling in bigger clumps.

We'd have to leave—soon there wouldn't be a cavern...or even an underground Coven.

"They did it," I whispered. "Their rage destroyed the Coven."

"That and the potion," Gideon said, his lips brushing my ear. "You did it, Dafni. You created rage."

Slowly, the witches pulled themselves from the pile, smoothing their shirts and skirts as they stood. There was nothing left of my mother or Robinson. The witches' poison had disolved everything. They looked around the cavern, cowering every time the walls shook.

"And now I have to harness it," I said.

"You've been leading these witches since I met you. Rescuing Brooke, pulling the witches from the sand, standing up to your mother—they respect you." Gideon motioned to the witches as they nudged each other, nodding toward me and staring. "They'll follow you."

Their faces were marked with the sores and growths from their time here. They still looked a bit sullen and sad, but there was a glimmer of hope on their faces.

The entire cavern shook again. I grabbed on to Gideon's arm so I wouldn't lose my footing.

We had to get out.

Something wet nudged my thigh. I looked down to find Luke in his wolf form trying to get my attention.

"Do you know how to get out of here?" I asked.

He wagged his tail before turning around and trotting a few feet toward the door.

Dirt continued to rain from the ceiling, and the tremors were becoming more frequent.

"Come on," Annabel called out from beside Luke. She held Emily's hand, keeping her close. Emily reached out to Brooke, offering her other hand, and my friend smiled as she took it. My aunt glanced up at the ceiling. "It's time to go."

I turned to face the witches who now looked to me for direction. "Let's go, everyone." I motioned with my hands and began trailing the Velkans. Gideon walked behind me and almost bumped into me when I turned around just to see. Just to check.

Gideon was right—they were following me.

We made our way through the Academy. Gideon used his fire to melt the hinges off the kitchen door that locked from the inside, and we walked through the kitchen and up a steep set of stairs to the surface.

I closed my eyes as soon as the sunlight hit my face. Luke's wolf ran around the Velkans and Brooke, yipping and jumping.

Some of the witches cried out, the sun hitting their faces for the first time in years. They fell to their knees rubbing their eyes with their hands. I hadn't realized how dark the Academy had been. It was something I'd gotten used to along with everyone else.

It was a beautiful day, the sun was bright, but the rays not too strong. I closed my eyes, letting the light hit my face. It stung, having been without sunlight for so long. Holding my hand like a visor above my eyes, I looked out into the woods that surrounded us. The trees were a mix of yellow, orange, and red, signaling fall had arrived.

For the first time in weeks, I heard the birds chirp and the crickets rub their back legs together in a melody only the northern woods could create. It sounded like home. The smell of wind blowing off the trees, of bark and sap and just the crispness of fall reminded me of my time at my grandmother's cottage. When I'd been the happiest I'd ever been.

Gideon looked down from where he stood beside me, his eyes watering with the sunlight. It almost looked like he was crying.

He grabbed my hand and brought it to his lips. "Are we really out?"

"Yes, we are."

The black of Gideon's eyes looked darker under the natural light. I brought my thumb up beneath his left eye, running it along the black skin beneath them.

Maybe now that we were out, that color would disappear. What would he look like without it?

What did I look like in the sunlight? I looked down at my feet. This was also the first time Gideon was seeing me in the natural light.

His finger hooked beneath my chin, lifting my face up. "Your freckles are even brighter in the sun."

I wrapped my fingers around his wrist, pulling him closer to me.

"What are you going to do now that you're out?" I asked. Gideon had wanted to get out, to escape the Coven since I'd met him. My feelings for him couldn't get in the way of that. Now he had the whole world at his fingertips, he could go wherever he wanted.

Gideon leaned over, his lips brushing against my ear. "I'll be your shadow, following your sparks wherever they go," he whispered.

My breath caught as his thumb traced my bottom lip. He planted kisses along the side of my cheek, following my freckles to the tip of my nose. Gideon pulled back, looking down and searching my eyes for a reaction.

"What if I don't want a shadow?" I asked. "What if I want a partner?"

"A partner?"

I nodded.

"Who would you choose?" He swung his arm out over the open field. "You could choose anyone. You've proven you're the most powerful witch in the Coven."

I smiled. "I pick you, Gideon." I wrapped my arms around his waist, pulling him close. "Will you have me as your partner?"

"Oh, kitten," Gideon purred. "I chose you the moment you kissed me."

His lips crashed into mine, this kiss so much better than the first.

We pulled apart, before looking out onto the field. The witches who had acclimated to the sunlight stared at each other's faces, every blemish and unsightly bump glaringly visible. I brought my hand to my own face, feeling that bump I'd found days ago. There had to be something that would help—a cure.

There had to be some sort of healer.

Elise.

"I know a place we can go," I said.

CHAPTER THIRTY-TWO

Dafni

It had started off so promising. My feet had been light. They only got heavier as the adrenaline wore off. My mind became heavier, too, filled with flashbacks of the last time I'd been in these woods, on my way to the Coven.

A witch was hard to kill. Almost impossible. You needed poison. That, of course, I didn't have. But this time, I had something I hadn't come here with.

Friends.

This time, I wasn't alone.

I led the way, each of us taking turns pulling Emily along for the better part of an hour. Gideon held my hand as we walked, Luke's wet nose brushing against our calves as he passed us, scouting ahead before doubling back to report.

It was funny how things never seemed to go to plan, especially when you didn't have a plan to begin with. I'd been a fool to enter the Academy, expecting everything to just work out. It was only because of the friendships I'd made and the confidence I had in myself that I'd succeeded. This wasn't a fairy tale. I wasn't a princess who got her prince and the castle at the end of the story. Instead, I got a male witch and a coven full of homeless witches.

The air element witches kept a breeze on our backs, pushing us forward. The earth element witches cleared a path, willing the vines they grew with their magic to pull back the long grasses and young saplings. Water elements pulled ingredients from the woods for their potions as we walked, the pockets of their knit sweaters stretched to their limits.

Luke barked in the distance and then howled. We all froze for a moment before running toward him.

His tan wolf sat on his haunches, his nose to the sky next to a wall—a stone wall, the rocks uneven, the mortar holding them together jagged and patchy. My eyes followed the wall up, up to the top. A building, a house loomed behind the wall, standing higher than the wall, higher than the trees in the woods.

The packhouse.

I was back.

Although this time, I wasn't anyone's kitten.

Well, except maybe Gideon's.

EPILOGUE

Everett

"They want to see who?" Kleio rushed to keep up with my long footsteps as I made my way down the hall and to the top of the stairs. I had to see them with my own eyes. These *people*—I didn't know if you could even call them that. There was one of *us* with them. A tan shifter.

"The guard at the gates mind-linked me. They want to see my father," I said.

Kleio's breath got caught in her throat. She stopped following me, bending over, coughing over the spit she'd inhaled. I didn't have time for this. Still, I stopped and turned around, whacking Kleio on the back a couple of times to help clear her airway.

"Everett! You're doing it too hard!" She swatted my hand away as she stood up, her neck and chest red from choking.

Elise poked her head out of the room where the pack's pups

were playing. She'd taken a liking to spending time with the youngest members of our pack. Seeing her with the young ones stirred something deep within me. "What's going on?"

"Lyka, Kleio and I were—"

"What were you doing too hard?" Elise asked, eyeing Kleio's red neck and chest.

"Me." Kleio's lips raised playfully in my direction. Damn her.

Elise blinked, closing her eyes for a moment before the left corner of her lips raised ever so slightly. She was using her mind-link. They were teasing me. She'd gotten entirely too good at that.

"Everett!" Jack's voice bellowed from the room Kleio and he shared at the far end of the hallway. *"If you touched Kleio, I'm gonna kill you!"* He emerged from the room, his chest puffed out, and his eyes on me.

"So, Kleio can join me in hell the next time she chokes on her spit?" I asked.

Jack made it over to his mate in record time, eyeing her up and down before pulling her against his body possessively.

"I wouldn't go to hell!" Kleio sunk into his side as he wrapped his arm possessively around her waist, digging his fingers into her hip. "I'm a good girl—and good girls go...somewhere nice."

"That's not where she's going," I growled.

Elise's eyes widened right before I bent down and threw her body over my shoulder, her hands pounding at my back and her feet kicking my chest. Her and Kleio—the fucking duo that caused the most chaos in the packhouse. I should have never put Kleio in charge of Elise during the tournament. It had caused...this.

"Put her down, Everett! You can go all caveman on her later. Remember—*they're* here."

Shit. My lyka had a hold on me that made everything else disappear. I'd forgotten that *they*, whoever they were, were downstairs asking to see my father. The man who'd been dead since I'd killed him for trying to kill Elise. What could they want?

"Who's here?" Elise asked, her voice strained from the pressure my shoulder was putting on her stomach. I set her down on her feet, but not before I let every inch of her body slide down mine.

"People looking for my father," I said as I grabbed her hand, pulling her close to me. There weren't secrets between us anymore. We'd made an effort to be open with each other, no matter how hard it might be.

"Why would they be looking for your father? He's dead."

Kleio almost choked on her spit again as she laughed behind us. "Elise's so blunt—I love it."

"That's what I'm going to find out," I said as I tucked my mate behind me.

We were on the third floor, high above where the guards had the intruders corralled on the main floor, but I wasn't taking any chances. Kleio stood at my side as we reached the wooden railing and peered over the edge, down to the main floor, at a hodge-podge group that looked like they'd went unprepared for a hike and gotten lost for days in the woods. They were dirty—their skin and clothing brown with earth, everyone's hair plastered to their heads from a mix of oil, sweat, and dirt.

Elise popped her head around my side, peering over the railing. "Pumpkin! Is that you?" Everyone in the group turned around, looking between them.

Elise pulled her hand out of my grasp, running toward the stairs. A growl left my throat as I followed her. She was always running toward danger.

"I mean Dafni! Dafni? Is that you?"

The group parted, revealing the woman with green eyes. I followed Elise down the stairs, keeping my eyes on the group. *No one had better move a muscle in the wrong direction.* The closer I got, the more I could see that her hair wasn't the muddy brown that I'd seen from the third floor but a red color, almost orange, underneath all the filth. She walked forward toward Elise, reaching out to touch her extended hands.

I growled, the entire group paused before taking a step back. The whole group except the tan wolf, who growled right back. Fur sprouted from the back of my neck; claws extended from my fingertips. *Was that a challenge?*

"What are you doing here?" Elise kept her hands extended, even though Dafni pulled her hands back once she caught a glance in my direction. A brown-haired girl standing next to the wolf petted its hackles flat, trying to calm it.

"We're here for you...there are witches out there that need your help." Dafni glanced behind her at the door they'd just walked through.

"Witches?" Elise asked.

"I'd like to see the True Alpha." An older woman stepped forward a single step, separating herself from the small girl trembling at her side. The little girl looked pale, her face gaunt.

"Who are you? And why do you want to see the True Alpha?" I asked. If they didn't know he was dead, we'd pretend he was alive until we got the information we needed from them.

"Everyone here is in need of shelter."

"Who's everyone?"

"It doesn't matter who—"

"It does matter who. Who am I providing shelter to?" I didn't need an outside pack or Matilda to come knocking on my door, challenging my pack. It'd been a hard enough year as it was.

She shook her head, as if she was clearing it before she continued. "He said that if there was ever an emergency, the pack would take them in." She motioned to the little girl and the wolf standing behind her.

"Who did?" I asked.

"The True Alpha." She lifted her chin, maintaining eye contact with me. She was brave, I'd give her that. Not many would look me in the eye.

Kleio gasped behind me as the little girl collapsed onto the floor in a heap. The tan wolf lunged toward her, licking her face. The woman crouched down next to her limp form, placing the little girl's head in her lap.

"And why would he do that?" I asked.

"Because he's their father."

I took a step back. Their father? That would mean we shared a father...that they were my siblings.

Elise opened the door of the packhouse, revealing the sea of witches standing outside. I could tell, even from where I stood, that something was wrong. Their faces were disfigured, and they stood slouched, huddled in groups with their heads hanging and their eyes on their feet. Something had happened to the Coven.

"Elise!" I barked, stalking over to where she stood in the doorway. I grabbed hold of her, pulling her behind me.

"Don't be scared," the man with dark bags beneath his eyes said. "We aren't contagious. It's something with the dirt. The longer we're underground, the worse it gets."

"But we replaced the stone," I said, motioning to the green foliage around us. The woods had been healed. I'd seen it with my own eyes.

"Sometimes a pretty surface disguises the insides." Elise

stepped out from behind me. "The rot was deep beneath the soil. It will take time for the soil to recover."

Grabbing hold of Dafni's hands, Elise looked at her face, then ran one of her fingers over the bump above Dafni's lip.

"Can you help us?" Dafni asked.

Elise put her arm around the girl's shoulders as they looked out at the witches. "Of course, I will help."

My mate guided Dafni into the packhouse, the rest of the ragtag group following. I mind-linked Kostas to pull out the tents we'd used for the Deca Tournament and to set them up on the packhouse grounds. The witches would need shelter...and food. I mind-linked Bunny next, asking her to cook enough to feed—I looked out again, trying to count the witches standing just outside the door. Two, maybe three hundred?

"Are we really doing this?" Kostas mind-linked back to me.

I looked over at where Elise was examining the little girl, my half-sister, taking time to make sure she wasn't scared.

Elise was a healer—she'd already healed the woods on the surface, but healing the witches...maybe this was what we needed to do to finally rid the woods of the rot. I had faith in my mate, my lyka. She'd find a way to heal the witches, find a way to bridge the gap between us. The witches and shifters would be stronger working together instead of against each other.

I sent a silent thank-you into the unknown, thanking whatever divine intervention had brought Elise to my woods over a year ago.

She was my lyka, my luna, my mate—the savior of the North Woods.

THANK YOU

Did you enjoy *Magic in the Woods?*

If you did, please leave a quick review on Amazon. Reviews are crucial to independent authors like me. Your review also helps other readers find books they love!

Thank you,

Evi James

ALSO BY EVI JAMES

The North Woods Series
Entangled in the Woods
Shadows in the Woods

ACKNOWLEDGMENTS

If you're reading this, please clap.

I wrote this book over a year ago and then tore it up, set it on fire, and then rewrote it the summer of 2025.

It was hard. I pulled my hair out. But I did it.

I hope you enjoyed Dafni as much as I enjoyed writing her. There's something about a naive FMC finding her way in the world that I just love.

Thank you to Mandi, my editor. This story wouldn't be what it is without your guidance and input. I'm going to get sappy because it's the third book we've worked on together and I couldn't imagine anyone but you seeing my manuscripts before professional edits. I have so much confidence working with you and I know that after we've put the manuscript through the wringer, the book will be so much better. I can't wait for our next project. Thank you!

Anna—You're the first reader to tell me this story was "creepy" and I thank you for understanding my vision. Your edits and "wtf are you trying to say here" comments were invaluable. The story is so much better because of you.

Thank you to my readers! Thank you for taking a chance on my books. This series has been so fun to write and your excitement and enthusiasm for the characters and stories has completely changed my life. Thank you!

ABOUT THE AUTHOR

This is Evi's third novel.

Evi lives with her husband, two daughters, and a clingy cat in Minnesota.

Website: www.evijamesauthor.com

www.ingramcontent.com/pod-product-compliance
Lightning Source LLC
Chambersburg PA
CBHW032350310726
48973CB00007B/1944